HOPE IN PATIENCE

For Daniel and Matt, who kept me going when I didn't think I could, and for Mandy, Alissa, and Kristen, who taught me about being a mom.
I love you.

HOPE IN PATIENCE

Beth Fehlbaum

WestSide Books ®
Lodi, New Jersey

Published by WestSide Books
60 Industrial Road
Lodi, NJ 07644
973-458-0485
Fax: 973-458-5289

This is a work of fiction. All characters, places, and events
described are imaginary. Any resemblance to real people,
places and events is entirely coincidental.

"In Response to Executive Order 9066" (1982), copyright © by Dwight Okita. Used
with permission.

The name of Dennis Bambauer and paraphrasing of his video interview segment enti-
tled "Memories of Being Taken from Orphanage to Manzanar as a Child," November
6, 2002, copyright © Densho: The Japanese-American Legacy Project. Used with permission.

"It Goes Away" lyrics, from the CD *Love and Fear*, copyright © Tom Russell, 2006.
Used with permission.

Library of Congress Cataloging-in-Publication Data

Fehlbaum, Beth.
  Hope in Patience / Beth Fehlbaum. -- 1st ed.
    p. cm.
  Sequel to: Courage in Patience.
  Summary: After years of sexual abuse by her stepfather,
fifteen-year-old Ashley Asher starts a better life with her father and
stepmother in Patience, Texas, but despite psychotherapy and new
friends, she still suffers from Post Traumatic Stress Disorder.
  ISBN 978-1-934813-41-6
  [1. Interpersonal relations--Fiction. 2. Sexual abuse--Fiction. 3.
Family life--Texas--Fiction. 4. Post-traumatic stress disorder--Fiction.
5. High schools--Fiction. 6. Schools--Fiction. 7. Track and
field--Fiction. 8. Texas--Fiction.] I. Title.
  PZ7.F3317Hop 2010
  [Fic]--dc22

                                                        2010031118

International Standard Book Number: 978-1-934813-41-6
School ISBN: 978-1-934813-42-3
Cover design by David Lemanowicz
Interior design by David Lemanowicz

Printed in the United States of America
10 9 8 7 6 5 4 3 2 1

First Edition

HOPE IN PATIENCE

Hope is the opposite of Fear.
—A wise person

For those on the journey: *Steady on.*

~~~~~~

Mother don't come to my heart
Don't know what to do with you hide from your shadow
Hold up a mirror don't like what I see
Angle the mirror deflect what stings
Smash it into shards
Diamond-shaped pieces to
Slice My Skin.
Mother I'll have none of you please
Don't know what to do with the waves of rage
oh Jesus Christ I hate him so
He calls me "Kiddo" says, "Slap my hands."
Stands outside a door begs me to say, "I forgive you"
While I find pieces of myself are gone
Lost to blackness after he
Raped Me.
"Fine I forgive you don't do it again"

Ha! Forgiveness is
A cruel joke for
He'll just do it.
Again.
Thoughts like waterfalls
Slippery tumbling razor sharp edges
Too frightened to know the truth
Grasping at water with widespread fingers
Surprised when thirst remains
Therefore I decree I'll think of her never
After all
It seems to work
For her
"Stand tall! Live fearlessly!"
Dr. Matt says
But at this moment
I am short
And afraid
Of my
Rage.

Chapter 1

I wake up in a cold sweat most nights, and I think it's happening again.

I think he's in my bedroom, and I can feel him running his hands all over my body. He's rubbing my back, squeezing my butt, and trying to push his fingers down into where the tightly wrapped blanket makes a V, where my legs meet. He tries to roll me onto my back again and again, but I have my arms locked at my sides and my hands prayer-like across my breasts. My legs are pushed together and slippery from sweat, and I'm as stiff as a corpse. . . .

I grit my teeth and force myself out of the nightmare. I roll onto my back, unlock my hands, and open my eyes to prove that I am safe in my bedroom, just down the hall from my father and stepmother. The bathroom light stays on all night for my extra reassurance. I snake my hand from beneath the covers and rub the rough cedar paneling, then pull the comforter up to my chin, turn onto my side, and align my body with my dog Emma's. She paddles her feet, and I know she's chasing rabbits in her dreams.

The memories intrude again. I groan in frustration and pull Emma against me, hugging her hard. She lifts her head and, if a dog is capable of giving a dirty look, gives me one. She jumps down, circles once on the floor right next to the bed, and emits a weary sigh as she closes her eyes and tries to catch up with that elusive rabbit.

I slowly breathe in and out as I stare at the white ceiling fan spinning shadows, and once again, it's as if I am falling into that place—my old bedroom in Northside. . . .

My mother's asleep across the hall. My stepfather Charlie is standing over me in the night, and I'm frozen.

I close my eyes tight and hold my breath. My heart's racing, and I feel nothing. I think of nothing but being numb, and I *am* nothing—nothing but a shell encased in a cocoon of blankets. My head fills with a *whoosh*-ing sound, like when you put a seashell up to your ear. I hear his ragged breathing and the tiny groans he emits once in a while. *Why won't he leave me alone? Where is my mother?*

In the daytime, I always promise myself that when he comes in the night, I'll at least try to call for my mother. But when it's happening in the dark, I'm paralyzed with fear and cannot find my voice.

Many nights, I escape his touch by sleeping in my closet, hiding behind the clothes on the lower rod. The heat's unbearable, and I hold my breath so he won't hear me. I always think I hear his footsteps on the carpet in my bedroom, even when he isn't there. Every nerve in my body is on edge; I'm convinced he's going to open the closet door any second and turn on the light.

Sweat slides down my legs as I wrap my arms tight around my knees, trying to make myself as small as I can. I think I feel a draft; I'm not sure if it's the perspiration running down my face or if, instead, my worst fear has come true and he's discovered me. I loosen my grip on my knees enough to reach out and pull the clothes tighter around me, then check and double-check that my feet are still covered.

Pitch. Black. Darkness. I bend as close to the floor as I can and lay my head against the carpet. My eyes want to close, but I won't allow it. I use two fingers to part the curtain made by my winter coat and the pink, fuzzy robe that Nanny gave me for Christmas. I stare hard at the thin line of space between the door and the carpet, thinking that if I wish hard enough, I can pull the sun up and make it daylight so he will not come. I blink repeatedly, trying to focus my eyes on the pencil-thin gap, watching for any sign of morning.

When I think I see some light, I unwind my feet from the clothes and crawl from the back of the closet to the door. I don't stand up yet; I allow my fingers to walk up the door and quietly turn the doorknob. But this is difficult to do while trying to stay hunkered down in a crouch.

Tension. Spring-loaded tightness. What if I only *imagined* the sunlight under the door? Mom and Charlie say I can't tell my dreams from reality; what if they're right? What if I open the door and see him, his white underwear looking blue in the moonlight, standing at my bedside?

I close my eyes and bow my head. "Please, God," I whisper, hoping that Jesus or Allah or Jehovah or Somebody Up There is listening now—even though I know that He must not have been paying attention since I was nine years old, when Charlie started touching me and I started praying for help. I pause my shaking hand halfway up the door. Maybe I'll just go back behind the clothes. But what if I *am* right and it *is* morning, and it's time to get ready for school? I have a math test today, and I still need to study for it. I hold my breath, close my eyes, and twist the doorknob. The cool air of my bedroom hits my face.

I was right; the morning sun is real. He won't come in the light. It's early yet. I get ready for school as silently as I can. Then, fully dressed, I set my alarm to go off in thirty minutes. I crawl back into bed, burrow under the covers, and close my eyes. I feel my body relax for the first time since sunset the night before.

My clock radio clicks on, and a morning show host tells me that it's going to be a beautiful day.

I walk into the kitchen for breakfast. I say nothing to Charlie, just glance at him as I walk by.

"You're such a bitch in the morning," Charlie says, looking up from his breakfast. "No man is ever going to want to marry you."

"Wipe that go-to-hell look off your face," Mom tells me.

"There's no look," I say dully, but inside I feel like screaming. I wish I could crawl out of my skin and kill someone—me. It's an exercise in self-control not to grab a kitchen knife and stab myself in the neck. I want to die. I don't even know why I want to hurt myself so much, but I do. I feel like a ticking time bomb.

Mom slaps my cheek hard. "There. I wiped it off for you," she says.

"I didn't even know I had any kind of look on my face!"

"Bullshit!" Charlie says. He rises, throws his plate of food into the sink, and storms out of the kitchen.

"Way to go, Ashley Nicole," Mom says.

Just the start of another day in the Baker household. . . .

Thank God, I don't live there any more. I'm sure I would have killed myself by now. Even though Charlie broke my arm a couple of months ago, when he and my mom showed up here in Patience to take me home one night and I told him I wouldn't go, that visible scar of what he did to me is nothing compared to the ones nobody can see.

❧

My name is Ashley Nicole Asher. My parents got married young because they had to. They thought that making my first and last names sound so similar was cute. The *Nicole* in the middle inspired Charlie to meld my first and middle names into his nickname for me: Ash-Hole. What a guy.

I guess my mom and my father, David, didn't actually have to get married. My grandparents, Nanny and Papaw, weren't enthusiastic about their eighteen-year-old daughter marrying a nineteen-year-old fledgling mechanic, the son of a father he'd never known and a woman who changed husbands as often as she changed her underwear. My grandfather, a doctor, arranged for one of his friends to give my mom an abortion, but when my dad heard about that, he talked my mom into running off with him to get married.

They landed in the tiny East Texas town of Patience,

where my dad's older brother Frank had settled on fifty acres of land that's been in the Asher family for generations. Uncle Frank's still here; he and David own Asher Automotive, which operates out of a barn-like shop in the pasture up the hill from our house. Frank's a single dad to my cousin Stephen, who's eleven. They live on the other side of the acreage from us.

When I was three months old, my mom, who'd had enough of my dad's drinking and quick temper, took off for her hometown of LaSalle, a suburb of Dallas. My dad never went after her or tried to see me, and if Child Protective Services hadn't called him to come get me last May, I probably never would've gotten to know him. I wouldn't have found out that he's never touched a drop of alcohol since the day my mom took me and left or that he went through counseling to get his rage under control.

My mom remarried when I was eight years old. Things went pretty well at first, but a year after she married Charlie, he started getting creepy with me. It just got worse from there. It was like he thought the only reason I existed was to satisfy something in him—something I still don't understand. I'm learning, though, that trying to figure out why he did that stuff to me is pointless. I mean, did I ask for it? I was nine years old when it started, and sure, I grew boobs pretty early. But I was just a child, and Dr. Matt, my therapist, told me that what happened to me wasn't my fault. My mom said I flirted with Charlie, but I don't think little kids even understand flirting. See what I mean? It's crazy-making stuff.

For six years, Charlie became more and more aggressive. He went from watching me while I showered to touching me while I slept to what happened last May, when my mom went to pick up pizza. I tried to get her to take me with her, but she wouldn't. She told me I had to stay home and "play" with Charlie, who'd been squirting us with a water gun he'd found on one of his construction job sites.

I remember that he chased me; I know he tackled me. Then I blacked out. And when I came to, the lower half of my body was covered in blood. I still don't remember what happened while I was unconscious. Sometimes little pieces of it blip through my mind; it's as if I once had a box containing a million puzzle pieces and somebody threw the box in the air, making the pieces fly everywhere. Now I'm trying to catch those pieces and assemble the puzzle in midair. I told my mom what I did know for sure: that Charlie had been molesting me for years. And she didn't do a damn thing about it.

The next day at school, I was pretty much a mess, and when my best friend Lisa noticed how spaced out I was, she made me tell our theater teacher, Mrs. Chapman, what had happened. Mrs. C. called Child Protective Services and repeated what I had told her. Within a couple of hours, I was at the hospital and the rape exam showed that he did. Rape me, that is. The hospital called the police, and Charlie was arrested. Then CPS started trying to figure out what to do with me.

Before I knew it, my dad—who I couldn't have picked out of a lineup—showed up in the CPS offices to bring me to Patience, and I've been here ever since. I moved in with David and his wife, Beverly, and her son, Ben, who my dad adopted when Ben was two—he's twelve now. Our house is a log cabin that David, Bev, Ben, Frank, and Stephen built several years ago, and it's in the middle of a forest.

I didn't have a choice about moving here; it was either David or the emergency shelter. Nanny and Papaw were so pissed when CPS called them and said that Charlie did those nasty things to me that they threatened to sue the State of Texas. *They* sure weren't about to take me in.

When the police investigated to see whether I'd been raped, my mom told the police that I was a slut with a track record of sleeping with a ton of boys and that the rape kit found tears and bruising in my "region" because I liked it rough. Makes me sick to think about it—not only because my mom's the one who said it but because it's not at all true. I admit I'm not a virgin any more, but it's not like I *chose* to have a thirty-seven-year-old man tackle me and rape me in the front *and* in the back—they filled me in on this little detail at the hospital, too. I'd never even held hands with a boy, much less had sex with somebody I actually liked. And now, to be honest, the idea of having anybody touch me at all just creeps me out. I'm still working on not cringing when David puts his arm around me, even though I know he's not going to be like Charlie.

When I moved to Patience, even though nobody was coming in my room at night to mess with me any more, I still hid in my pine wardrobe (because I have no closet), whenever things freaked me out. Over the past few months, I've started to realize that no amount of hiding works, seeing as how the stuff inside my head is impossible to hide from. If I could manage to never sleep, then I'd be home free—maybe.

16

Another thing I found out is that I'm mentally ill. I figured this out because every week, I see Dr. Matt, who is a mental health professional. Besides that, when I google stuff like *post-traumatic stress disorder*, it pops up under the heading *Mental Illness*.

❧

Last Fourth of July, Charlie drunk-dialed me; he told me that I'd broken my mother's heart and that because of me, she'd never be the same person. I broke apart inside as the knowledge that she didn't care that he'd raped me clashed with my fear that what Charlie was saying was true. Following that phone call, I held a knife with its sharp point right between my breasts and begged David to let me die. "It's too hard!" I told him. "It hurts too much!"

Ben was there, too, and what I did terrified him.

It's embarrassing even to think about that now.

Dr. Matt told me that suicide is a despicable thing to do to people who love you. He told me that if I kept thinking up ways to die, he, my dad, and Bev would have to send me to a place where I couldn't hurt myself. That got my attention.

He helped me to start seeing that clawing my skin, and tearing out my hair and thinking about suicide were like extreme temper tantrums I was having in reaction to not getting what I needed from my mother.

I've always been book smart; I learned the terms for what was happening to me—*molestation, sexual abuse, incest*—by snooping through the books in the school counselor's waiting room when I was an office aide in seventh grade. So when Dr. Matt tells me I'm having "tantrums" because I'm angry at my mom, I get it on a book level. But really getting it—like the way I understand that it rains because water droplets in the clouds get too heavy and fall to the ground? No. I just can't wrap my mind around it. The way my mom is just hurts me so much, I can't even describe it. When I'm upset, all that book thinking goes right out the window, and Jesus, Allah, Jehovah, or Somebody Up There only knows what I'll do when that happens.

❦

Right after I moved to Patience, I enrolled in an English II summer school class that Bev taught. She used this cool book, *Ironman*, by Chris Crutcher, to teach us how to write in response to literature. To be clear, I didn't take English II in summer school because I'd failed it in Northside. No, I took it to get ahead—because, let's face it, I'm an ION: an Invisible Outsider Nerd.

The popular kids always peg me as being really smart, even though I'm not. But I love books and writing, and besides that, what else did I have to do with my time? Reading about somebody else's problems was a lot easier than dealing with the shit-storm of my own life. Still is. In Bev's class, we learned a lot about literature, writing, and ourselves. And though you'd never think we would all have that much in common, we bonded in a way that I'd never before experienced in a class. Besides learning how to write an expository essay, we discovered that all people are pretty much the same: they just want to be understood and accepted for who they are. Bev told us on the first day of summer school that studying *Ironman* was a quest for truth—and she meant it.

Ironman wasn't like any other novel I'd ever read in school. For one thing, the characters talked and acted like real teenagers. They swore sometimes, and they talked about having sex. The main character, Bo Brewster, had problems with anger. He kept calling his football coach an *asshole*. He fought with his dad, but he was close to his teacher, who it turns out was homosexual. I'd never before read a book that had a gay character. And Bo's girlfriend was sexually abused; I'd never before read a book with a character who went through that, either. Her home life sounded a lot like the one I'd just escaped, and it made me feel less alone, like less of a freak. Even though *Ironman* wasn't on our district's approved book list, Bev chose it because she knew it'd draw in the kids who were taking the class because they'd failed it. And I suspect she thought it might help me, too.

Mr. Walden, the principal of Patience High School, had given Bev creative license in that summer school class because she'd only found out at the last minute that she'd have to teach it. As long as we learned to respond to literature by writing an essay, Mr. Walden didn't really care how the class was taught. Bev was a longtime teacher in the district; her students always scored high on the state standardized test, and he trusted her judgment. That all changed when some people got upset about *Ironman* for the very same reasons that I loved it, and then things got uncomfortable for Mr. Walden.

❧

Right before the school year started, Bev and I were working in her classroom. We were hanging a border above the whiteboard when Mr. Walden's secretary, Marvella Brown, tapped on Bev's door. She stepped into the classroom, wafting the overwhelming scent of Chantilly. She cleared her throat, then said in a very loud, nasty-sounding voice, "Mrs. Asher, I just want to make sure you know that you're expected to use district-approved books in your class this year, not the sort of filth you taught in summer school." Marvella had a funny look on her face, and she kept jerking her head toward the hallway as she spoke.

Bev's eyes got huge, and her voice shook a little as she responded: "Well, Marvella, I'm glad you told me how you really feel. At least now I know where I stand with you."

Marvella put an index finger to her lips. "Ssh," she hissed, then tilted her head, listening.

We heard a *CRASH!* in the hallway, then Mr. Walden's voice: "Gabe! Why'd you leave that ladder right here in the middle of the hallway? Now look at this mess!"

"Uh, I'm sorry, Mr. Walden. I was just changin' the light bulbs. Are you okay? Did ya . . . did ya stub your toe or somethin'?" Gabe asked.

"No, I didn't stub my toe, I—just clean up this mess! I oughta dock you for those bulbs, you dumb son of a…" As he continued his hallway tirade, I moved to stand behind Bev. I started rolling the border strips, twisting them into spirals, unrolling them, then re-rolling them. After a while, it sounded as if Mr. Walden was leaving our wing. He was still yelling at Gabe, but his voice became fainter as he got farther away.

Realizing that the principal was out of earshot, Marvella turned back to us with her hand clapped over her mouth, stifling a giggle. She listened for a moment longer, then whispered, "Ashley, could you close the door?"

I peeked around Bev at Marvella.

"Go ahead, Ashley. It sounds like he's gone," Bev said.

I stepped into the hallway. Gabe had righted his ladder and was sweeping up the broken light bulbs.

"Is the coast clear?" Marvella whispered hoarsely.

"Gabe's in the hallway, but nobody else." I closed the door and slid into a desk in the row closest to Bev's. Nervous, I started tracing the boxy outline of a panther's head that someone had carved into the desk.

"Whew!" Marvella exhaled. She looked around for a place to sit that was big enough to hold her and finally hiked herself up onto the edge of Bev's desk, exhaling again. She plucked a tissue from the box on Bev's desk and dabbed her forehead. "I'm sorry, Bev. I didn't mean a word of that."

"Then, why—?" Bev asked, shaking her head, her eyebrows furrowed.

"Because that jackass was in the hall the entire time—" Marvella began.

"Marvella, you're going to have to let go of your anger with Gabe at some point," Bev said.

She was referring to Marvella's son, Gabe, a tenth-grade dropout and all-around disappointment who'd gotten tangled up with a white supremacist group for a while. Last Fourth of July, he and another man had nearly beat to death Jasper Freeman, a mentally disabled African American man who used to be a fixture on the streets of Patience. When Marvella found out about it, she nearly twisted Gabe's ear clean off. He was put on probation in exchange for agreeing to testify against the other man. Gabe's been keeping a low profile ever since, behaving himself and working as a custodian at the high school. I think he's even more afraid of his mother than a potential cellmate named Bubba, and maybe with good reason.

"Not *my* jackass, Bev," Marvella said. "The other one, our esteemed leader. He *made* me give you that speech. And he was in the hallway, listening, just to be sure."

"So you don't think the book I used in summer school was filth?"

"Heavens, no, Bev! But Walden's serious as a heart attack about you stickin' to the approved book list. And I just sent in an order for exit test workbooks. I think he's gonna expect you to do a lot of drill-and-kill this year."

"Drill-and-kill?" I asked. "What's that?"

"It's where you drill students so much on test prep, you kill their love of learning," Bev said. She walked around her desk, opened a top drawer, and tossed her stapler into it. She stood behind her desk, rolling her chair back and forth. "There's a lot more to learning than that damned test!"

"You're preachin' to the choir, Bev. But Walden's not thinkin' that way. He's just determined to keep *you* under control."

Bev sat down hard in her chair, ran her fingers through her hair, and said bitterly, "Oh, yes, I'm *such* a rebel. God, that guy's a—"

"Jackass?" Marvella and I said together.

Bev managed a tiny, rueful smile.

"Well, I found a way to keep him out of *my* hair." Marvella reached into the pocket of her tent-sized denim jumper and withdrew a BlackBerry. "He thinks he lost his favorite toy and he's spent the entire morning looking for it." She snorted, "Ha! He keeps saying, 'Dammit, Marvella! Where's my BlackBerry?' More like Crackberry if you ask me." Marvella was too gleeful at her own mischief to continue. And when she laughs, every inch of her jiggles.

Bev sighed as she got up and started back toward the whiteboard. "Marvella Brown, you are a trip. I'm lucky to have a friend like you."

"I do what I can," she said, heaving herself off Bev's desk and walking toward the door.

"Yeah," Bev said softly, looking lost in thought as she bit her lip. "We all do, don't we?"

❧

When I first came to Patience, I wasn't that nervous about starting at a new school, seeing as how Bev's a teacher there. By the time fall came, I already had friends from summer school, and having spent so much time there already, I knew the layout of the school. What I wasn't prepared for was being repeatedly asked, "How'd you break your arm?"

If I told people the truth, it would lead to even more questions. I felt awkward enough already, without having everybody and their brother knowing about what had happened to me. So instead I deflected them; I just answered their questions with more questions.

"How'd you break your arm?"

"Where's the bathroom?"

"How'd you break your arm?"

"I'm so lost. Where's the cafeteria?"

"How'd you break your arm?"

"Do you know where Coach Griffin's room is?"

It generally did the trick.

In spite of the questions, I was still glad to be back in the routine of school again. I nearly went crazy the week after my arm was broken. That happened on August 10, and school didn't start until the 28th. I had to lie still with my arm elevated for the first week; that wasn't a good thing because I kept thinking about my mom and it hurts so much to do that. And I wanted to start running with Bev again— she got me started on distance running this past July, and it really helps me relax and cope with all this shit—but I had to wait until X rays showed that my bones were fusing and healing.

After that was confirmed, I got the go-ahead from the doctor to start running again, arm in a cast and all. It was cool because I'd signed up for cross-country and practice started before school reopened. I was slow at first and my arm ached, but that didn't really matter because I'm a slow runner anyway and I was pretty much covered in pain, both inside and out. To me, the world seemed so full of darkness that I was always surprised when the sun came up every day.

There was one thing I looked forward to every day, though: seeing Joshua Brandt. He's sixteen, a junior, and he went to the state finals in cross-country last year. He's about four inches taller than me and has a killer set of dimples. He's lean, but his legs are very muscular. The thing I like most about him is that he seems like a really nice person. I don't think he knows I exist, though, and that may be a good thing because I don't know what I'd do if he ever asked me out.

I can imagine going out with a guy, and I like hearing other girls talk about what it's like to have guys pay attention to them. But actually being out with a boy and taking a chance on being touched? Jeez, it just wigs me out. My heart starts racing, and I end up with my shoulders slammed against my earlobes, with every muscle in my body wanting to go on lockdown. The words *Leave me alone! Leave me alone!* go scrolling through my mind at warp speed.

I wanted to hurry up and heal from what had happened to me—all of it. I wanted my arm to mend overnight so I could get the cast off and be able to forget it all: everything that happened that night when Charlie broke my arm—and what he did to me in the six years before that. I longed to be able to scratch the dry, itchy skin inside the cast in the same way that I ached for a new start, one where all my pain about my mom and my scaredy-cat nature would just disappear.

It's so bad that sometimes I wish the reason she isn't there for me is because she's dead, instead of the way it really is. Sometimes I wish that I *had* been with guys my own age before what happened with Charlie. Then at least it would mean that I'd been able to *choose* to be with somebody in a physical way, instead of being forced. If I could, I'd just cut off those parts of myself—but I wouldn't even know where to start with the blade.

∾

I finally got my wish to get rid of the cast when the second week in October rolled around. David and I were just walking out the door to leave for my doctor's appointment to remove it when the phone rang.

"This is David. Who? And who are you with?" David turned his back to me, then glanced back over his shoulder to see whether I was listening. "Ashley, could you excuse me just a sec?"

I walked out of the kitchen but stopped just beyond it in the hallway and listened.

"No, I am not interested in a meeting between the Bakers and Ashley. . . . Counseling? Yes, she sees a counselor, a psychologist. Why? No, she does not need to see your— No, I will not ask her to do that. She's fifteen years old, Mr. Sanger. She's still a child, although I know that didn't matter to your client. You're filing a motion to do what? Are you kidding me? Look, you need to speak to Alejandro Guzman, the Anderson County prosecutor. No, there's no way we'll consider asking him to drop the charges. All right, then, you do whatever you think you have to do, but—Right. I guess we'll see you in court."

I stepped into my bedroom doorway, then came out of it as if I hadn't been eavesdropping. "Who was that, David?"

David sat down heavily on one of the bar stools, and a horrible screech filled the room. He jumped up, and Loki, our habitually angry cat, shot out from beneath him, a gray streak of indignation.

"Damn cat," David sighed, shaking his head. "He comes out of hiding once in a blue moon, spits and hisses at me, then disappears again." David was looking at me, but he seemed to be staring right through me.

"David? Who was that on the phone?"

He didn't answer at first, but then he opened his arms to me. I moved closer to him, but I didn't enter his embrace. He reached out, put his hands on my shoulders, and pulled me closer. I crossed my arms over my breasts and looked at my feet. It's just a habit now; I picked it up to deflect Charlie.

After a few moments, he explained, "That was Charlie's lawyer, Ash. Charlie's insisting on havin' a trial. He's not going to plead out like we'd hoped. They're tryin' to get us to drop the charges."

I felt my body tighten up, my spine curving in. I stepped back from David. "So . . . I'm going to have to see him again?" My voice went higher than normal.

"Yeah, I guess so." He sighed and then asked, "Do you—you don't want to drop the charges against him, do you, Ashley?"

"If I do, does that mean I don't have to see him again?" I asked, surprised at how much I sounded like a little kid. I felt like I was about four years old.

"Well, yeah, I guess. But . . . is that the right thing to do?"

"I don't know, David. All I can think of right now is how much I don't want to see him again. I'm . . . scared. I'm scared of him." My throat was getting tight, and I held my breath.

"I know, sweetie, but—"

Whoosh . . . the noise whispered in my head. I hadn't heard that in a few weeks. I couldn't meet David's eyes, and it felt like my chin was Super Glued to my chest.

"Ash, look at me. Will you try to look at me, please?" I shook my head, and a tear ran down my cheek. David gently pulled me a little closer to him, then leaned down to try to get me to look at him. "Are you in there, Ashley?" He gave me a hopeful smile.

I forced myself to meet his gaze and tried to smile back, but I couldn't. Feeling my body relax a little, I allowed him to pull me closer in a hug and laid my head on his shoulder.

Barely above a whisper, David said, "Ashley, honey, I know you're afraid, but he won't be able to touch you any more, he—"

"It's not just that, David," I breathed into his shoulder, then inhaled his scent, a mixture of Right Guard deodorant and fabric softener. I exhaled a shuddery breath and wiped my cheeks and nose against his shirt, then laid my head on his shoulder again. He gathered up my legs and held me in his lap, rocking me back and forth like a little kid. It felt so good. It was like being covered in warmth and love. And it wasn't sick, like when Charlie made me sit in his lap and held me tight so he could touch me wherever he wanted.

"What is it, baby?" he said into my hair.

It took me a little while to be able to put it into words. "It hurt so much last time I saw my mom, David. She—she's really mad at me for . . . telling—"

David abruptly stopped rocking me, and his voice was angry when he spoke. "I need you to hear me when I tell you this, so please listen. Are you listening? Are you?" He held my arms and shook me a little. I took in a breath but didn't let it out. "Look at me!" he said.

I forced myself to look, and his eyes were like black coals.

"Ashley Nicole Asher, you are the best thing that ever happened to your mother. And if she can't see that, *fuck her*. You matter, honey. You matter to all of us who love you, and don't you ever forget that. If your mom is so selfish and fucked up that she can't see that you're the best thing in her life, then that's her loss. *Her* loss. Are you listening? Do you hear what I'm sayin' to you?"

"Let me go, David. Please," I said, trying to get my arms loose and sliding my legs out of his lap, my old "run like hell" instinct kicking in.

He abruptly let go. "Ashley, I'm sorry. I didn't mean to scare you—"

"Let's—let's just go, okay? We're going to be late," I said, going out the front door. "I'll be in the truck."

CHAPTER 2

Human Ecology is usually my favorite class, besides English III. The first six weeks of school, we learned how babies are made. I mean, I think we all know *how* babies are made. What we actually studied was how they grow from a couple of cells at conception into an infant. Ms. Manos is a cool teacher. Some kids say she's *crunchy*. I'm not totally sure what that means, but I think it has something to do with her love of Bob Dylan's songs, the T-shirts she wears that say things like "Green is the New Black," and her obsession with recycling everything.

Ms. Manos is tall and thin, with hazel eyes and brown hair bobbed to chin length. The first day of class, she told us that we could ask her anything we wanted and she'd always tell us the truth. Dub White, who was in my summer school class, jumped right in and asked, "How old are you?"

She answered, "Thirty-four. Anything else?"

Dub asked, "Are you married?"

"No. Does anyone else have a question?"

Dub blurted, "Is it true that this class is a blow-off, and we won't have any homework?"

Ms. Manos replied, "Is that the only reason you took it?"

"Does this truth thing work both ways?" he asked.

"What do you mean?"

"If I tell you the truth, are you going to be mad?"

"No," she said, but I wondered if she meant it.

"Then yeah, I took this class 'cause I thought Mrs. Ray was still gonna be teaching it, and she showed Disney movies once a week."

Ms. Manos studied Dub for a second or two, then said, "Hmm. Anything else? Or preferably, *anyone* else?"

Dub said, "You didn't answer my question."

Smiling, she said, "I guess you'll just have to stick around to find out, won't you?"

It's Ms. Manos's first year as a teacher and her first year in Patience. She'd been a neonatal nurse in Santa Fe, New Mexico, until a baby died in her arms. She told us about it on the first day of school: "My heart broke that day, and I knew I didn't have it in me to continue being a nurse. But I learned a lot from the experience. Sometimes you just have to start fresh. So I packed up my stuff and moved from Santa Fe to Patience. My sister lives here, and I wanted to try out small-town life."

"You came to the right place," Z.Z. Freeman told her. Her full name's Zaquoiah Freeman, who moved to Patience this past summer from Nacogdoches, a college town of about 30,000 people in Deep East Texas. Jasper Freeman, the man who was beaten on the Fourth of July, is her

31

cousin. They live with Aurelia, their granny, and their Auntie Jewel. Z.Z. and I met in English II and became best friends over the summer.

According to the sign at the city limits, Patience has about 3,000 residents. That number seems really high to me, though. I'd say half the kids I go to school with have never even been to Dallas, and it's only two hours away. Around here, Saturday night cruising means the kids get all spruced up and roam the aisles of the Walmart in Six Shooter City, looking for somebody to go out with. But about the only place to actually go out is the Sonic drive-in in Cedar Points, the next town over. When I first got here, a rumor was going around that a Chili's restaurant was moving into Patience, but it never happened.

Cedar Points has a movie theater, but it has just two screens and the owners show only films they don't find offensive. When all the current release movies are too sexy for them, they show old stuff like *Cool Hand Luke* or *Walking Tall*. I've heard that they loop *The Greatest Story Ever Told* continuously from noon Good Friday until midnight Easter Sunday and that every show sells out.

I was already in mental shock when I first moved here, but when school started in the fall, I went into culture shock, too. Here, I met kids who actually hunt and eat possum and squirrel. When Travis Hager told about killing a coyote, eating it, and making a hat out of its head and a rug out of its skin, I watched Ms. Manos's face carefully to see whether she was ready to head back to Santa Fe. But she just said, "Wow, Travis, that must have been some weekend."

Six weeks later, Ms. Manos passed back our first major test. Kevin Cooper was a nervous wreck. It's not that he doesn't try; he's just not the brightest crayon in the box. Kevin's a linebacker on the football team, six feet, four inches tall, with a baby face, big blue eyes, and a heart of gold. He was in my summer school class, too, and he's one of the first friends I made in Patience.

"Kevin, remember when Dub asked me on the first day of school whether this class was a blow-off?" She placed his test face-down on his desk.

He looked up at her. "Uh . . . yeah."

"Look at your grade, and tell me whether or not it's a blow-off class." She wasn't smiling.

He turned the paper over. "72! Yessssssss!"

Ms. Manos patted him on the shoulder and said, "I know it wasn't easy for you to learn all that vocabulary, and I'm proud of you for working so hard."

"You mean you're *happy* with that grade?" T.W. Griffin, another kid from summer school, asked him incredulously. T.W.'s parents, the people who started the brouhaha over *Ironman*, expect him to get A's in everything. His dad is the head football coach at Patience High School, and he's my history teacher. His mom is the secretary at First Church Patience. T.W. pissed off his dad by quitting the football team this year, and I think Coach Griffin blames Bev.

Dub, Kevin's best friend, came to his defense. "That was a hard test, T.W. All that stuff with embarryos and umbrellacal cords and contraptions and—"

Pam Littlejohn sighed loudly and shook her head at them. "Do us all a favor, you two. Try not to spread your intellectually inferior seed."

Kevin looked perplexed, but Dub understood what she meant. "Why do you think we're takin' this class? Kevin's *mom* wanted us to."

Ms. Manos placed Moreyma Rangel's test on her desk and strode back up the aisle to stand between Dub's and Kevin's desks. Hands on her hips, she looked from one boy to the other. "You're taking this class to avoid becoming parents? Dub, you said you took it because you thought I'd show movies every week."

Dub shrugged, but Kevin blushed and volunteered, "My mom said she wanted us to know how much work kids are, so we wouldn't be in a hurry to make one any time soon."

I looked back at Moreyma, who held her test up in front of her face and seemed to be hiding behind it. Moreyma is fifteen years old and has a three-month-old baby boy, Hector Alvarez III, who they call Three. He's named after his father, Hector "Junior" Alvarez. Junior was in the summer school class with me, and he's also on my cross-country team.

I guess Ms. Manos noticed Moreyma's behavior, because she changed the subject. "Okay. Well, class, if your grade on the first marking period's test wasn't what you wanted it to be, then you need to figure out what you need to do differently as far as studying. I'm always available to help if you have any questions. Today, we're starting our study of the family unit. This could be a touchy subject for some of you. I hope you'll keep an open mind."

"Are you going to talk about sex?" asked Pam Little-john. All the boys sat up a little straighter, and Travis Hager howled like a coyote.

Ms. Manos didn't bat an eye. "The subject of sex will come up. We'll cover intimacy, and uniting sexually is a defining reason that many partnerships stay together."

"Why do you say it like that: *partnerships*?" Pam asked as she flipped to the back of a spiral notebook. "Don't you mean *marriages*?"

Ms. Manos shrugged. "Not all couples are in mar-riages. Some are, of course, but some partnerships are civil unions. Culture defines what a marriage is or is not, and that definition is no longer limited to a man and a woman. Let's start with the basics. I want to know what *family* means to you. Tell me in a statement of twenty-five words or less. It's due by the end of class."

My stomach clenched. I wrote my heading and the title "What Family Means to Me." Then I stared at it. My eyes filled with tears as thoughts of my mother zoomed through my mind. I thought about David, Bev, and Ben and how I came to even know them. Less than six months ago, I lived in a whole different family, and even though it was awful sometimes—a lot, actually—it was the only family I had ever known. Asking me to write about *family* felt like ask-ing me to write about what it feels like to be run over by a steamroller, and I'm sure my mom would be driving it. My insides churned, and I, who can usually come up with a poem in fifteen minutes flat, was wordless.

"Ashley? The bell rang," Ms. Manos said. I jumped at the sound of her voice, then looked around and saw that everyone was gone.

"Oh. Sorry," I said as I picked up my things to leave.

"Did you finish your statement?"

"Huh?" I said.

"The 'What Family Means to Me' statement," she said. "Twenty-five words or less?" she reminded me, then raised her eyebrows and smiled kindly as she came around her desk to me.

"Oh. Um, no. Sorry," I said. I started walking toward the door, ducked my head to hide the tears, and hoped I didn't sound as choked up to her as I did to myself.

She reached out and gently touched my upper arm. "Are you okay, Ash?"

"Yeah! I'm great! See ya later," I said, trying to smile.

"You sure?"

I nodded at the floor, and she released my arm. I went into the bathroom to wash my face and see whether I could get control of myself, so I was late to my remedial math class. Luckily for me, Mrs. Bogowitz isn't a hard-ass.

Mrs. Bogowitz retired from teaching college math and, for some reason, decided she'd try to help clueless people like me learn how to solve equations. It wasn't always like this for me—the mathematically challenged part, that is. I was in the middle of fourth grade and a strong student in math when Charlie and my mom got married. Then we moved from LaSalle to Baileyville and he started molesting me.

At my old school in LaSalle, we were still learning to multiply big numbers. But in Baileyville, fourth-grade students were already doing long division. Shortly after I arrived, the teacher threw decimals into the mix. I really didn't get all that tenths place and hundredths place stuff; I had no idea where to move the decimal or why it was supposed to be moved or when to move the damned thing, anyway. My mind was blown by what was happening at home, and finding myself in math hell at school didn't help the situation. I was too shy and too eaten up with shame to speak up and ask for math help, especially when everyone else around me seemed to be catching on so easily. I fell behind and never caught up.

Mrs. Bogowitz is the first math teacher I've had who figured out what I knew at the start of the school year (answer: not much). She works with me from where I am instead of expecting me to automatically know stuff, like how to move decimals around, just because I'm fifteen years old and should have learned that a long time ago.

Oh, and just from being in her class, I've learned another weirdo thing about myself. (Sometimes the list seems endless.) She figured out that I get hard math problems right and easy ones wrong. But she didn't tell me, "Jeez, Ashley, you make such stupid mistakes on easy problems!" Instead, in this gentle way that reminded me of how Nanny used to talk to me before she decided I'm a liar, she said, "Ashley Asher, somebody told you that you weren't good at math and you believed them. And that's a big reason you make the mistakes you do. It's because you're so afraid of making a mistake."

I felt like crying when she said that—because it was true. Charlie used to throw my math book at me and yell, "You're not just crazy; you're stupid, too!" That was in seventh grade, when I told my mother about "somebody" coming in my room at night and doing things to me, and she said that I imagined the entire thing because I couldn't tell my dreams from reality.

It was spooky, the way Mrs. Bogowitz could tell so much about me just from seeing how I worked math problems. She looked at me as if she could see into my head and said, "You're probably a very good reader and writer. I have a feeling you're wired to be a creative person and that you think abstractly." I wasn't sure what she meant by *abstractly*, but she pegged me on the reading and writing. Just knowing that Mrs. Bogowitz doesn't think I'm stupid, I'm able to stay calm instead of freaking out when I don't understand how to solve a math problem.

She handed back our first tests of the year, and I got an 85 on mine. She wrote, "I knew you could do it!" across the top of the paper in great big purple letters.

See? I said to myself. *Things are going to be better now.*

Then I remembered that I was going to have to see Charlie and Mom soon, and the good feelings all fell away.

❧

I've been to Piney Woods Psychological so often that I don't even notice the music that plays softly in the waiting room any more. It's the practice of husband-and-wife psychologists Scott "Dr. Matt" Matthews and Leslie Trevino, and not only does the place look like somebody's living room when you walk in, but it feels like home to me, too.

But it doesn't mean I'm never nervous before my appointments, because sometimes I am. Especially when I'm feeling more like a little kid than a fifteen-year-old. Dr. Matt told me a long time ago that the age you are when you start being abused is the age you kind of freeze at on the inside. Because I was nine when Charlie started abusing me, I stopped emotionally developing at that age and stayed stuck there in a lot of ways until I started getting better. I know it sounds bizarre, but it makes sense. And it also helps me feel a little less wacko when I don't handle things as well as I should. Dr. Matt says that I'm supposed to be patient with myself and to remember that I'm working on getting better as fast as I can, and that beating myself up about it doesn't do me any good.

David went in and talked to Dr. Matt before my appointment started. That's the way it works; first, they talk privately about how things have been going, and then I go in. Sometimes at the end, David (or Bev, if she brought me) comes in again and we talk about a plan for the coming week.

Besides being a little kid in a lot of ways, I startle easily and have intense nightmares. I have flashbacks to when Charlie did things to me, and the flashbacks are set off by things or events called *triggers*. It's part of having posttraumatic stress disorder, or PTSD.

You usually hear about PTSD when people talk about war veterans who went through horrible things on the battlefield. It's the same thing for people who were abused. When something really painful happens to us, emotionally or physically, sometimes our mind protects us from it. It's like there's a switch that senses "Uh-oh, this is some really intense shit, so I'm just not going to remember it right now."

Later on, a smell, a sound, or even a song, a movie, or reading something can trigger something that's buried deep inside and it's like I'm back in that place. It even *feels* like it's happening again, and it totally sucks. Ever since I found out I'm going to have to see my mom and Charlie again soon, the PTSD has been kicking up big time. I've been so restless in my sleep lately and crying out so much that poor Emma has been leaving my room to sleep on the living room sofa, where it's quiet.

❦

"Come in, Ashley." Dr. Matt closed the door behind me and knelt on the floor, scooping up scattered Legos with a small dustpan and dumping them into a plastic box. He snapped the lid closed, then stood. "I forgot to put away my toys," he said, smiling.

Dr. Matt is average height and kind of stocky. He has very short, straight hair and pale blue eyes that seem to see right into my soul. He always wears crew-neck T-shirts in dark solid colors, black or blue Wranglers, a black woven leather belt, and cowboy boots. He looks like he should be working outside instead of sitting in a chair in a psychologist's office.

"How's it going?" he asked. That's the way he usually starts our therapy sessions.

"Okay," I lied.

"Really? Relax your shoulders, then."

Man, he knows me so well. "I . . . can't."

"Don't say you can't. Have you been remembering to breathe?"

I ran my finger along his finished oak desk, in the same place I always do; there's a green smudge on the wood from a marker. I rubbed at it, hard.

"Ashley. Breathe," he commanded. "Take a deep breath in."

I inhaled. It was difficult to obey this simple direction, and my chest shuddered. I stared at the green smudge and rubbed it harder with my index finger. I wanted to make it disappear. *I* wanted to disappear, to run out of his office. The problem was, I would have passed out. Because I couldn't breathe. Wouldn't breathe. Not much, anyway.

He badgered me about breathing until I took a few deep breaths in and out, sighing loudly on the last exhale.

"Good sigh," he said.

"Thank you," I murmured, feeling foolish for being complimented on such a simple thing.

"I don't know how you do it, Ashley. This is what you look like." Dr. Matt pulled his shoulders up to his earlobes, wrapped his arms tightly about his body, scooted his chair closer to his desk, and began rubbing furiously at the edge of it. "No, wait—wait, let me see if I can complete the picture." He wrapped one straightened leg around the other, or tried to. "No, I don't think I can actually *do* that one. Will you *please* try to relax, before you break your legs, tying yourself up in knots like that?"

He wasn't smiling at me, and he was using his no-nonsense voice.

I glared at him, and he gave me The Look, which is this penetrating blue-eyed stare. Sometime, I'll have to closely examine the diplomas he has on his wall, because I'm sure that one of them is a Ph.D. in staring. It's not like a "scary teacher" stare; it's more of an "I can read your mind and you're not fooling me for a minute" stare.

I looked down, breathed in and out deeply, and sighed again. I peeked at him. No compliment this time. He was just waiting. And staring. Clearly, he was serious about this relaxation requirement.

Finally, I closed my eyes, made myself breathe (no sigh this time), and willed my body to relax. It's a lot harder than it sounds when I'm this tense. One time, I asked Dr. Matt why I hold my breath so much. He said, "It's the same response as hiding in your closet. You got in the habit of trying to be invisible."

When I'd lowered my shoulders, unlocked my arms, untwisted my legs, and sighed a few more times, Dr. Matt said, "Talk to me about the phone call David got earlier this week."

"Didn't he already tell you?"

"I want to hear it from you, Ashley."

"Well, I don't want to talk about it. Didn't you even notice I got my cast off?" I demonstrated by straightening and bending my arm a few times, then deliberately crossed my arms and silently dared him to tell me to uncross them.

"What does that have to do with anything?" he asked in a flat voice.

"What do you mean? It's a really big deal!"

"Why is that? You were able to do everything you needed to do, even with the cast on, right?"

I felt myself blushing. "Well, I mean—things are—different now."

"What do you mean, Ashley? How are things different?" He took a sip of water, leaned back in his chair, and crossed his arms.

I raised my arms over my head and flapped them like wings. "Can't you see, Dr. Matt? I'm free now! I don't have that nasty cast on my arm any more! Now people can't tell that—" I stopped, realizing I'd said more than I meant to say.

He uncrossed his arms and leaned forward in his chair. "Finish your sentence, please."

I suddenly felt foolish for flapping my arms and acting like a goof. "They . . . can't tell that my arm was broken. That's all."

"I don't think that's what you meant, Ashley. What did you mean?" When I didn't answer, he prompted, "People can't tell by looking that . . . what? By the way, it's been at least one minute since you've taken a breath, so breathe, please."

I forced myself to take a breath and let it out in a sigh.

"Good sigh," he said. "Now, finish your sentence, Ashley."

I bit my lip and closed my eyes.

"Breathe," he commanded.

I balled up both my hands into fists and slammed them down on his desk, nearly coming out of my chair. Hot tears ran down my cheeks. I took a deep breath in and blew it out angrily.

"Why are you fighting this so much, Ashley? Say it! Just say it!"

"Fine! Without the cast, people won't be able to tell that Charlie broke my arm! Now nobody will know that anything ever happened to me!" I hit his desk again and again, then lowered my head into my hands and wept.

"Do you really think anyone can tell you were raped because you had an arm cast?" he asked softly.

"Don't say it like that!" I cried.

"Don't say that you were raped?" He rolled his chair closer to me. "What's wrong with saying that?"

"I'm not thinking about that any more! I got my cast off, so I don't have to be reminded of Charlie every time I look at my arm!"

Dr. Matt looked thoughtful. "Hmm. But you're reminded of him every time you look in the mirror. Aren't you?"

"No! I don't have to think about him any more at all! It's over! It's all over, and I can just start over now! I don't have to deal with it any more!"

"But you do, Ashley. It won't go away on its own."

"Stop it!" I screamed.

"You know it's true, darlin'. And I know, and David and Bev know, and—"

"I want to forget! Can't you just let me forget?" I begged.

Shaking his head, he said, "It doesn't work that way."

I wanted to throw myself on his floor, kicking and screaming. I looked wildly around his office for something to hurt myself with. I stood up. "I've got to go."

Dr. Matt remained seated. "That is *not* a good idea. Let's work through this, Ashley. Running out the door is not going to make it go away."

"But I don't want to talk about it! I don't want to work on it! I don't want to do this any more. It's too hard!" I put my hand on the doorknob but didn't turn it.

"I'm not going to hold you here, Ashley. David told me what happened after Charlie's lawyer called. He told me that you freaked out when he shook you."

"That's not what's got me freaked out," I whispered, leaning my head against the door.

"Please sit down and tell me what's going on with you," Dr. Matt said. "Let me help you."

I released the doorknob and sat back down, my elbows on my knees and my chin in my hands. I stared at the floor between my feet until the carpet and my shoes blurred. Dr. Matt rolled his chair closer to me, and I saw his boots enter my field of vision. "I'm going to take your hand, okay?"

I nodded. He took my hand and held it. "Ashley, you spent your childhood having to deal with Charlie and your mom on your own. You didn't have anybody holding your hand. But things are different now. You're not alone. You have an excellent support system in your dad, Bev, and Ben."

"And Uncle Frank and Stephen," I added. The "What Family Means to Me" assignment flashed through my mind, and I felt a pang of shame at having such a hard time writing it. *It's the telling the whole story—the truth and the details—that makes it so hard.* Dr. Matt's voice pulled me back.

"Right, Uncle Frank and Stephen," he repeated. "And me. You have all of us to support you now."

I looked at him, then looked at his hand holding mine.

"But even with all of us holding your hand, there are steps on your journey to recovery that you have to take for yourself. And one of those things is being able to accept that some really terrible stuff happened to you, so that you can start to get past it. You've gotta accept that it's a part of who you are. It's a scar that will last a lifetime." He released my hand and rolled his chair back.

"I don't want to be that person. I'm not strong enough," I said.

Dr. Matt shook his head at me. "Ashley, you've already managed to live through much worse things than most people ever experience in their lives. You *are* strong enough. The fact that you're here at all, that you keep at it, is a testament to your strength."

"You really believe that, Dr. Matt?"

"It's five o'clock," the talking alarm clock said, indicating the end of our session.

"Absolutely," Dr. Matt said, rising to open his door for me.

"And you don't bullshit people, so—"

He smiled at me. "See you next time, Ashley."

∾

Every Thursday, our cross-country team runs distance challenges. Coach Morrison chooses a course and marks off four, six, and eight miles. He drops each of us off at the distance we picked to run and returns to the starting point. Then it's back to his truck we go. It really sucks to be the last person back. Seems like I'm always that person.

Coach was standing next to his old Chevy truck—he calls it Old Blue, even though it's black—and he was smiling so big, his eyes were slits. He did his usual Thursday routine, asking each of us, "So? How far can you run today?" Our answer is our ticket to climb up into the bed of the truck for the ride out to the course.

Up until that day, I had only answered "Six" once, and I thought I was gonna die when I ran it. This time, I mumbled, "Four."

"Ya sure, Ashley? Don't wanna try for six this time? Your endurance has probably improved since you got your cast off. I bet you'll do better this time. You might even be able to complete the run without throwing up."

I heard somebody snort and knew without looking that it was Pam Littlejohn.

"Come on, Ashley, don't you wanna go to state?" Z.Z. asked from right behind me. Through clenched teeth, she said, "Remember—our plan?"

At the end of our first distance challenge of the year, Pam, who is also a sophomore, announced that she planned on winning our school's prized track and field scholarship, which is awarded to the girl who medals at state the most times during her high school career. "Shouldn't be hard; it's not like there's any competition," Pam said, looking at Z.Z. I didn't hear her say it because I was throwing up on my running shoes at the time.

That's all it took for Z.Z. to set her sights on beating

Pam for the scholarship. "That stuck-up, know-it-all, whiny-ass bitch don't get to announce that she's the only one with what it takes. No way. We're gonna show her what's what, Ashley. You hear me? Ashley?"

"Mm-hmm," I said, then bent down to throw up some more.

∽

Nearly three months later, Z.Z. had not lost her zeal for showing Pam what's what. But I had other things on my mind.

"I'm going to state, so I'm going for eight," Pam announced as she elbowed her way past Z.Z. and glided onto the lowered tailgate as if lifted by invisible wires. Z.Z. shoved me in the shoulder, and I stumbled forward into Coach Morrison.

"Whoa!" he said, catching me by the elbow. "Steady, there! So? Do you have what it takes to make it all the way, Ash? Gonna push for six?"

A voice in my head said Yes, and then I realized I'd actually said it aloud.

"Well, all righty, then," Coach said, offering me his hand. I looked at it but didn't take it. Then I crab-crawled up onto the tailgate and awkwardly stood up, finding my balance just before Z.Z. bumped into me and we both ended up sprawled on the truck bed. I scrambled up on my hands and knees and crawled over the pine needles that littered the floor, then sat behind the cab.

Z.Z. picked herself up pretty easily for a person who

describes herself as "bountiful, bodacious, and beautiful." She perched atop a wheel well opposite Pam, looked down at me, and mouthed, "Are you okay?"

I just shrugged.

Coach Morrison slammed the tailgate closed and whistled toward the entrance of the gym. Joshua, Dub, and Junior tumbled through the door and raced full speed toward the truck. Joshua and Junior looked like flying reindeer when they jumped up into the back as if the tailgate were a hurdle. Dub, who stands just a hair taller than I am—and I'm pretty short—took a split second longer to make the leap.

Josh knelt on one knee next to me. He brushed some pine needles away, then sat down. I could feel the heat from his body, even though we weren't touching. My stomach did little flip-flops, as if the butterflies inside it were electrified.

"Hey," he said. Not "Hey, how are you?" Just "Hey."

Yet I answered, "I . . . uh . . . f-fine," then choked on my own spit. I did this—why? Because I'm an idiot.

"Come on, Coach! Let's get this show on the road!" yelled Junior. He and Dub stood on either side of Josh and me. I studied the pattern the pine needles made in the space between my feet until the truck heaved to a stop next to an orange cone marked "6."

Coach Morrison slid open the window behind his head and yelled, "Everybody but Pam—out!"

"But what about Josh? He's supposed to run eight with me," Pam said. She tried to take Joshua's hand but he pulled it away from her.

Coach Morrison ignored Pam and addressed Joshua instead. "Nope, I want you to work your way back up to eight. I need that ankle of yours to be a hundred percent. A sprain is nothing to sneeze at." He smiled and said in a thick Southern drawl, "So git out, y'all."

Dub, Josh, and Junior all sprang over the sides of the pickup bed and began running immediately, whooping and hollering. I took my time getting to my feet, and by the time I hit the grass, Z.Z. was running in place with an intense look on her face.

I bent down and tied my shoe. "You don't have to wait for me, Z.Z.," I said.

"Couldn't you have done that in the truck, Ash?" Z.Z. said, hands on her sizeable hips. Z.Z. may be a big girl, but she's solid rock.

"Go on without me if you want," I murmured to my shoe. She bent down and squeezed my shoulder, then waited silently until I looked up at her.

"Hey. I know you're scared about the trial tomorrow. But you're strong. You'll be fine. We've practiced what you're gonna say, remember?" As if that settled the matter, Z.Z. stood up straight and stretched her arms over her head, inhaled deeply, exhaled, then shook her shoulders loose. Her long beaded braids sounded like a rattlesnake's warning. She smiled and said, "Come on!"

The knot on my left shoe didn't match the one on my right, so I untied both shoes and started over. "Just go on, Z.Z. I'll catch up."

Without saying a word, Z.Z. hooked her hand around my left arm and pulled me up. I looked down and to the side, trying to hide the tears in my eyes. But Z.Z. knows me too well, and I didn't get away with it.

"Oh, girl," she said, hugging me tight, then rubbing my back. Z.Z. smelled like cocoa butter. "It's gonna be oooookaaaay," she said soothingly. She took a step back, her fingers still kneading my biceps. "You're gonna feel a lot better when you feelin' all your muscles, and you know that. Right?"

I nodded, my head down.

Z.Z. released my arms, stepped back, arched her eyebrow, and worked her neck at me. She started our routine, the way we got ourselves charged up to try, try again to finish anywhere but at the back of the pack. "Now, *why* do you like to run, Ashley?"

"I don't know," I mumbled, looking down at a fire ant mound by Z.Z.'s foot. By the way, this wasn't the way our routine usually went. But Z.Z. ignored my less-than-enthusiastic participation.

"Unh!" She clucked her tongue and said, "'Scuse me? *Why* do you like to run?"

I shrugged. "There's an ant on your shoe, Z.Z."

Imitating her nearly eighty-year-old granny, Z.Z. made her voice crackle and wagged a finger at me. "Answer me, child! Why do you *need* to run?"

"'Cause . . . I feel strong when I run," I mumbled, swiping at a tear on my cheek.

Z.Z. began jogging in place and sounded like a Marine drill instructor. "I CAN'T HEAR YOUUUUUUUU! Tell me why you NEEEEEEEED to RUUUUUUUUUUN?"

"Because I feel strong when I run." I crossed my arms, sighed, and rolled my eyes at her.

Z.Z. nodded vigorously and brought her knees up higher as she ran in place. She raised her hands to the sky, like someone receiving the Holy Spirit, and shouted, "And WHHHHHHHYYYYY do you need to feel strong?"

I finally started jogging in place. My feet felt like bricks. "Because only the strong survive," I said in a monotone.

Z.Z. continued to ignore my loser attitude. She nodded vigorously, pivoted gracefully, and took off running. She looked like a chunky gazelle. "What did you SAAAAAAAAAAAY?" she screamed from about ten yards ahead of me.

I realized I was facing six miles of solitude and didn't want to be alone with the thoughts in my head, so I began to run after her. "Only the strong survive," I called out.

"I can't hear YOOOOOOOOUUUUU!" she yelled, increasing her speed.

I ran harder to catch up to her, screaming as if my life depended on it: "ONLY THE STRONG SURVIVE! ONLY THE STRONG SURVIVE! ONLY THE STRONG SURVIVE!"

❧

Even though I was exhausted after the distance challenge (last place as usual; I'm nothing if not consistent), I couldn't sleep that night. I'd counted down the weeks and days; the trial was starting in just seven hours.

I had no photo of my mother, and I kept remembering how haggard she'd looked when she showed up unannounced that day in July. She stuck her face in mine and told me, shaking her hands like she was trying to dry them, "This whole—this whole thing is your problem, Ashley."

She looked so awful that day. I felt like it was my fault she was so beaten down and worn out. Now, my mom never goes *anywhere* without putting on makeup and doing her hair. When I was ten and the school called because I broke my arm in P.E., she still took the time to get herself ready, including makeup and curling-ironed hair, before she came to get me. If I hadn't been so slow on the uptake, I'd have realized then that I was low on her list of priorities. But the things she said to me that day last July hurt so bad, I took off running and got myself lost. David found me sitting on a tree stump by the side of the road, examining my blister-covered bare feet.

A few weeks later, Charlie and my mother showed up one night when I was at the house alone. As the trial neared, I kept replaying the night again and again in my head. My thoughts churned like a squirrel on speed, running continuously on a track. Dr. Matt calls this *spinning*.

The night Charlie broke my arm, he looked like his normal scary self: six feet tall, bronzed skin, a mammoth of a man with huge, muscular shoulders from working construction all his life. His bushy auburn hair looked wind-blown even on a calm day. He had almost clear gray eyes, a shiny gold front tooth, and a sizeable beer gut. He always wore sagging blue jeans and a western shirt with only the bottom few snap buttons fastened, and his normal after-work accessory was a 7-11 Big Gulp cup, filled with Wild Turkey bourbon and a splash of Diet Pepsi.

When he and my mom turned up in my dad's driveway in the dark, they gave me the shock of my life. That night, Charlie's drink of choice was Lone Star beer in a long-neck bottle. I remember that because some shards of the glass bottle he threw at me got stuck in my chin and I still have the scars from it.

Standing there, facing each other in the humid East Texas night, when Mom told me she and Charlie wanted to take me back to Northside with them, I asked, "But—but what about CPS, Mom? What about what—happened?"

My mother slammed the car door, laughed at me, and said in an acidic voice, "What about it? There were no charges. You lied, and it didn't work. Lots of kids do that, Ashley. They get into trouble, so they make up some crazy accusation. It got you some attention for a while, but it didn't work. And now you're going to have to face reality."

That's when Charlie bent my forearm backward toward my elbow as far as it would go without breaking, and he put his face so close to mine that I was inhaling his beer-soaked breath. Through clenched teeth, he said, "Things are going to go a lot easier for you if you stop fighting. Now get whatever clothes your father got you to buy you off, and get in the goddamn car." He released my forearm and shoved me hard toward the front door, and that's when I realized that if I did what he told me to do, my life was over. I'd be returned to a life of hiding, and I didn't want to hide any more. Once you know something, you can't unknow it—no matter how much someone else may want you to act like you can. Tasting freedom and living in truth, I couldn't go back into the prison of my closet and a life of lies.

I tried to make a run for the retaining wall that lines our front yard and leads up a short hill to a gate. I knew the gate and the pasture beyond it so well, I was sure I could get away and hide in the darkened woods surrounding the pasture.

Charlie must have read my mind, though, because he grabbed for any part of me that he could catch hold of. I went wild, fighting him with my arms and legs, even trying to bite him. But then he snagged my right arm and folded it behind my back.

I screamed, "No! I'm not letting you two abuse me any more. I won't go back with you!"

That's when he brutally wrenched my arm and I heard it snap. I screamed, fell to my knees, and curled my body into itself, cradling my broken arm with the good one. My mother ran toward me, wigging out, just screaming, "Now look what you've done! Get up! Come with us, Ashley Nicole. *Now!*"

Charlie said, "Shut the fuck up, Cheryl!" then bent low and muttered, "Want me to break your other arm, you little slut? Don't you ever talk to me like that again! I own you."

Through gritted teeth, I sobbed, "Fuck you, Charlie! You'll have to kill me. That's the only way I'll go back with you!"

Charlie stepped back from me as if he was going to kick me. I closed my eyes, turned my head to the side, and braced for the blow. But suddenly, Emma was there. Her vicious snarls sounded like a pack of dogs had descended on us, and she landed lightly on her feet and stood over me, protectively snapping and biting at Charlie and my mother.

"What the fuck?" Charlie said as he stumbled back.

At once, we were all bathed in David's headlights. David lurched to a stop, jumped out of his truck, and roared into Charlie like a tidal wave, easily knocking him down. He punched Charlie again and again, until Bev's and Cheryl's screams to stop before he killed Charlie broke through the fog of his rage.

When I told Charlie and Mom that I wouldn't go back with them to Northside and that they didn't get to abuse me any more, it was the first time in my life I had ever spoken up for myself. Dr. Matt told me that by doing that, I had broken Charlie's power over me and taken a big step forward on my journey toward recovery.

I was starting to understand, in a way, that the reason my mother turns her back on me again and again has nothing to do with me. It's because she's gutless—a gutless wonder. She cannot bear to live in the light of truth, even if it means she has to lose me in order to keep living a lie. And when I realized that, it was like I could see light around the edges of the closet door—the door of the dark closet I'd been hiding in, inside my mind.

But those strong moments didn't last long, and I'd

think, *My mother doesn't love me, so why the hell should any part of life go on as usual?* Then I'd pull the covers over my head and *wallow in self-pity*. That's what Dr. Matt calls it when I fall into my self-pity pit.

I envision it as a dark, deep hole in the ground. There are claw marks carved into the walls of my pit, where I've pulled myself up and out of it before. It takes an incredible amount of work and a lot of time, anywhere from several days to several weeks, to reach the surface again. You'd think that knowing how hard it is to climb up out of that pit, I'd work even harder than I do to stay clear of it. But I'm an expert at feeling sorry for myself and only a beginner at avoiding the pit.

Dr. Matt calls me on it every time, though. "Self-pity is only going to make you weak, Ashley, and you need all the strength you can muster to get through recovery." That's what he keeps telling me.

The emotional pain reminds me of one of those shows on the Learning Channel where a lady is having a baby and she's screaming at the nurse, "I can't do this! I can't do this!"

The nurse always tells the lady, "You don't have a choice. Your baby is coming out, no matter what. Now I know you're tired, sweetheart, but you have to keep going."

Dr. Matt told me once that recovery from sexual abuse is like walking barefoot from Texas to Alaska—and back home to Texas again. "It just stands to reason that on a journey like that, you're gonna run into stuff like thunderstorms, mountain trails that lead nowhere, and searing hot roads. But that doesn't mean you give up," he said.

David, Bev, and Dr. Matt are always telling me how strong and brave I am. But there are times when I feel like lying down on the side of the road and letting the vultures pick apart my flesh.

CHAPTER 3

Friday, October 23. Two months, one week, and six days since I'd seen my mom or Charlie, and there in the courtroom, I didn't know what to do with my eyes. Should I stare at my hands? Study the clock on the wall? Sneak a glance at my mother? I was afraid to look to the other side of the room. I fidgeted with the hem of my skirt and pulled at the neck of my shirt, trying to make sure my bra strap wasn't showing.

Then the bailiff directed, "Please rise for the Honorable Judge Reilly Corn." We stood: Mr. Guzman, the Anderson County prosecutor for the State of Texas; my dad and Bev; Uncle Frank; and I.

On the defense's side stood Charlie and my mom; Nanny and Papaw; and Clyde Sanger, Charlie's lawyer.

"You may be seated," Judge Corn said, plopping down in his seat without looking at us. He addressed Charlie and his lawyer, and they stood. "Am I to understand that Mr. Baker has waived his right to a jury trial?"

"Yes, Your Honor." Mr. Sanger straightened his shiny red silk tie with one hand and ran his hand over his buzz-cut salt-and-pepper hair with the other.

Mr. Guzman stood. "Your Honor, the State of Texas has charged Charles Baker with injury to a child in an incident occurring on Monday, August 10, in which Mr. Baker willingly caused an arm fracture to one Ashley Nicole Asher, a fifteen-year-old girl."

"And how do you plead, Mr. Baker?" asked the judge.

"Not guilty, Your Honor," Charlie said.

Mr. Sanger, a pale, thin man with a big brown mole on his cheek, presented his opening, his deep Texas twang accenting every word: "Your Honor, this is a simple misunderstanding between family members, an unfortunate accident. The defense will show that Mr. Baker loves his stepdaughter and, if anything, his love for her and his desire to see her reunited with her mother so that their family could continue to heal their differences was at the root of what happened that night."

Mr. Guzman asked the bailiff to call the first witness from the hallway. The emergency room doctor who treated me testified that there was no way the fracture could have occurred except by someone purposely forcing my arm backward. I'd promised myself that I'd try hard to be mentally present for the trial, but when Mr. Guzman demonstrated the break by splintering a piece of wood in the same way my arm was broken, *whoosh* . . . filled my head and I didn't hear another word anybody said until Mr. Guzman said, "Your Honor, I call to the stand Ashley Nicole Asher."

I rose, my arms tightly crossed over my chest. I stepped up to the stand, placed my hand on the Bible, and promised to tell the truth, the whole truth, and nothing but the truth, so help me God. Then I sat down and hugged myself tight.

Dr. Matt and I had worked hard in the short time we had to get ready for the trial. He thought it would be a positive thing for me to speak up on my own behalf by making a Victim Impact Statement, or VIS, and we had practiced it in our sessions. Z.Z. had practiced it with me, too. I was going to tell Charlie what his abuse had done to me, and that was supposed to help me move on. Making the VIS was all I could think about; it was as if the trial itself was secondary to what I was going to say when I was given the chance. Even though I knew I was going to have to testify, I still wasn't prepared for what it felt like to be sitting in a chair directly opposite Charlie and my mom.

I almost didn't recognize Charlie. The version of him that smirked at me from the defense table had a short, spiky haircut; his eyes looked blue—was he wearing contacts?— and he had trimmed down considerably. He even wore a black suit with a pink satin tie. *Pink?* The Charlie Baker I knew would have worn his birthday suit to court before he'd wear a coat and tie, much less a *pink* tie. *This* version of the monster who raped me looked like a sharply dressed car salesman.

My mother sat just behind Charlie and to his right. She was sandwiched between Nanny and Papaw. Mom wore a white sweater buttoned only at the neck over a pink blouse that matched Charlie's tie, and she was smiling at me in a way that reminded me of a dog baring its teeth just before it bites.

Her light brown hair was a little longer than when I saw her that night in the summer. She had it highlighted with streaks of blonde and pulled back in clips, looking very old-fashioned. Her makeup was different, too. The circles under her eyes were concealed, and her complexion was healthy instead of pasty white.

I shook my head slightly, trying to clear it. But *whoosh* . . . was all I could hear. I shook my head again and realized I was freezing up, like a squirrel does just before a car hits it.

"Ashley? Are you ready?" Mr. Guzman lightly touched my arm, and I jumped.

"Huh?" I looked at him, hugging myself even tighter.

Leaning over, he whispered to me, "Ashley, you can do this. I know you can. Just keep your eyes on me, and you'll be fine. Okay?"

I nodded, looking down at my lap. I could feel my shoulders up around my earlobes. I was doing the full-body cringe that I do when I'm scared.

Mr. Guzman took a few steps back from the witness stand and addressed the judge. "We're ready to begin, Your Honor." Judge Corn nodded, and Mr. Guzman turned to me.

"Ashley, I need you to tell me what happened on August 10, when your stepfather and mother came to your father's home."

I swallowed, took a deep breath in and out, and focused so hard on Mr. Guzman that his face is the only thing I saw. Everything else—every*one* else—in the courtroom faded into a blurry background.

"I—I'd been waiting for my dad and Bev to get home. I couldn't find Ben, my stepbrother, and finally David called and told me where they were."

"And what time was that?" Mr. Guzman asked, pausing to take notes as if he was hearing my story for the first time.

"About eight o'clock—"

"At night?"

"Yeah. And it was getting dark, and—and then David called and told me that Ben and my cousin Stephen had borrowed a chain saw and that Stephen had gotten hurt while they were using it and they had to go to the hospital."

Mr. Guzman looked up from his notes. "Go on."

I took another deep, slow breath and continued. "I told David I was going to go for a run with Emma—"

"Who is Emma, please?"

"Emma's my dog, who I adopted in July."

"Go on, please," Mr. Guzman said, nodding.

"And so Emma and I went for a run, and by the time we got home, it was completely dark. And we turned up our driveway and . . . " I felt my chest tightening. I looked down and away from Mr. Guzman. *Whoosh* . . . whispered in my mind. I tried taking another deep breath, but it felt like I had forgotten how to breathe.

"Mr. Prosecutor, does your witness need a recess?" the judge asked.

I shook my head, and Judge Corn said, "Please proceed with your testimony, Miss Asher."

My lower lip began to tremble, and I felt my face crinkling. I looked up at the ceiling, then finally dragged my eyes back to Mr. Guzman's. His amber-brown eyes were kind, and he nodded at me. "It's okay, Ashley; you're safe here," he said.

"Objection!" Charlie's lawyer stood. "I have to object,

Your Honor. For the prosecutor to assure the witness that she is safe here implies that she needs reassuring that she is safe, which implies the guilt of my client."

"Overruled," the judge said, then turned expectantly to Mr. Guzman. "Your witness may continue."

"All right, Ashley, what happened next?"

"Emma and I were running up the driveway. It was dark by then. Charlie said, 'Hello, Ash-Hole,' and it startled me so bad that I tripped and skidded to a stop on my stomach—and my face. And he said, 'Oh, did I scare you?' And then he threw an empty beer bottle at my head and told me I was just as spineless as he remembered."

"Objection!" Mr. Sanger sprang to his feet again. "Your Honor, all of this is hearsay, it's simply this child's story—"

"Yes, Your Honor, it *is* this child's story, this child's testimony, which she has sworn will be the truth," Mr. Guzman said, with a bit of an edge in his voice.

"Your objection is overruled, and the witness may continue retelling the events as she recalls them."

"Your Honor, *really*—" Mr. Sanger said.

"Mr. Sanger, your client had the opportunity to tell his side of the story, but he declined to take the stand in his own defense."

"I know, Your Honor, but—"

"But nothing, Counselor. You can't change horses in midstream just 'cause your case isn't going the way you'd like it to. Do I make myself clear?"

"Yes, Your Honor," Mr. Sanger said, sinking into his chair. Charlie narrowed his eyes at me, then leaned over and whispered in his attorney's ear. Mr. Sanger frowned and shook his head.

"Ashley, please continue," Mr. Guzman said.

"So then my mom started yelling at me to get up off the ground, and Charlie came over to me and kicked a bunch of rocks and glass in my face. He poured some beer on my head, too—"

I stole a glance at Charlie and wished I hadn't. He was glaring at me, and his hands were curled into fists. I automatically shrank back in the witness chair. Charlie leaned over to Mr. Sanger and said loudly enough for everyone to hear, "Are you gonna say somethin' or not?"

Mr. Sanger nodded and stood up, his face beet red. "Your Honor, I—I apologize, but I must—I *must* object! This testimony is prejudicial!"

"Mr. Sanger, first of all, instruct your client to refrain from speaking out like that again, and second, you will have an opportunity to cross-examine the witness, if you will stop objecting long enough so that she can complete her testimony."

Mr. Sanger threw himself back into his chair. I began to feel braver and to really feel protected from Charlie, even though he was only about fifteen feet away from me. Maybe he was finally going to get what he deserved.

"Ashley, please continue," Mr. Guzman said.

"Charlie told me to get up. He said, 'Get up, Ash-Hole, get up, you little bitch!' I tried to get up, and when I didn't move fast enough, he yanked me to my feet—"

"By your—?" Mr. Guzman prompted.

"Objection! Leading the witness!" Mr. Sanger said.

The judge gave him a withering look, and Mr. Sanger mumbled, "Withdrawn."

Mr. Guzman nodded at me, and I continued, "He pulled me up by my arm. And then my mom said, 'Hurry up, Ashley Nicole!' She told Charlie that I was just being stubborn and that my dad and Bev had spoiled me—"

"Spoiled you? What do you think she meant by that?" Mr. Guzman asked.

"She said they'd spoiled me because they bought me new clothes. When I—when David came to Dallas to get me, I—I didn't have anything with me except my backpack, and it was empty."

"So what were you supposed to wear, Ashley?" Mr. Guzman asked.

Charlie coughed, and Mr. Sanger sprang to his feet.

"Your Honor, really, I'm sorry, I'm sorry, but I have to object. I do not understand the relevance of this line of questioning," Mr. Sanger said.

"I don't, either!" my mother said.

Judge Corn rapped the bench with his gavel and said, "There will be no outbursts from observers in my court-room!" He looked at his watch, shook his head, and said, "Mr. Prosecutor, would you care to explain your—I mean—what's your point?"

"Your Honor, I am simply establishing the relationship between the defendant and the witness and why the witness was so frightened of the defendant when he and his wife trespassed on the Ashers' property on the night of August 10."

"I'll allow it," Judge Corn said, arching an eyebrow at

Mr. Sanger. Seeing that there would be no immediate challenge to his decision, he said, "You may continue."

"Ashley, what were you supposed to do for clothes, if you had nothing when Child Protective Services placed you with your father?"

Charlie nearly stood up, but Mr. Sanger beat him to it. "*Objection!*" His chair crashed into the railing behind the defense table. "Your Honor, the State is, once again, attempting to influence the outcome of this case by mentioning irrelevant details."

"Sustained. Mr. Guzman, ask your question and get it over with."

"But Your Honor, the witness's clothing and CPS's involvement is relevant because it speaks to the environment to which the witness did not want to be returned!"

Judge Corn glanced at his watch, then turned to look at the clock on the wall. He fiddled with his watch a moment and said, "Last chance: rephrase the question."

Mr. Guzman placed his hands on the railing, leaned toward me, and asked, "Ashley, what did you do for clothes when you lived with your mom?"

"I wore her clothes," I said. "She gave me her hand-me-downs."

"She didn't buy you new clothes? Ever?"

Mr. Sanger looked like a jack-in-the-box when he popped up out of his chair. "Objection!"

"Overruled," Judge Corn said. "The witness will answer the question."

Mr. Guzman nodded at me.

"Well, I mean, she bought me, uh, stuff like bras, because we didn't wear the same size, but she didn't buy me new clothes very often. She usually just gave me her stuff," I said, wondering why Mr. Guzman was asking me about my clothes.

"Did that include nightclothes? Lingerie?" Mr. Guzman asked.

"*Objection!*" Mr. Sanger yelled.

"Sustained. Mr. Prosecutor, approach the bench."

"May I approach, too, Your Honor?" Mr. Sanger asked. Judge Corn nodded at him, and he practically galloped to stand next to Mr. Guzman.

When Mr. Guzman walked away from the bench, his mouth was a straight line and his face was red.

"You may continue, Mr. Prosecutor, with the limits I have set for you," Judge Corn warned.

"Ashley, let's go back to what happened when Charlie told you to get up from the ground. What happened next?"

"I didn't move fast enough, and Charlie jerked me to my feet by my arm."

"And is that when he broke your arm, Ashley?"

"No. I asked them, 'What are you doing here?' and my mom said, 'We've come to take you home. I talked to your father earlier today, and he agreed that it's time for you to leave. He's had all he can stand of you.'" Just remembering what that felt like made me start to cry. Mr. Guzman pulled a couple of tissues from a box on the railing and brought them to me.

I wiped my eyes and wrapped the tissue around and around my index finger, unwrapped it, stretched it over to my middle finger, and then did it again. Staring at my fingers, I softly said, "I told her, 'I don't believe you. David loves me. He would have told me himself if he felt that way. I'm staying here,' and I tried to get away from Charlie."

I looked at David's face for the first time since we'd entered the courtroom. He nodded at me. I continued: "Charlie said, 'You think so, huh? And just who the hell are you to tell us what you're going to do?' And he started twisting my arm really hard, and I was sure it was going to break. And then my mom showed me these papers; they were the custody papers from when I was a baby. She said that my dad had no right to keep me with him, and I said, 'But what about CPS? What about what happened?'"

Mr. Sanger slammed his palms flat on the table and jumped to his feet. "OBJECTION! Your Honor, now the *witness* is trying to bring in prejudicial testimony."

"Sustained," the judge said. "Mr. Guzman, instruct your witness not to speak at all of anything prior to the events of August 10."

"But he—he raped me!" I cried. "That's why I was taken away from my mom!"

My grandfather stood up and yelled, "No, he did *not*!"

Judge Corn banged the gavel three times and said, "Bailiff, remove that man!"

The bailiff walked toward Papaw, but he was having none of it. "I'm going; you don't have to walk me out!" Papaw started toward the door but stopped just short of opening it, turned toward me, and said loudly, "Tell the truth, Ashley Nicole!" The bailiff opened the door and gave him a little shove, then returned to stand to the right of the judge's bench.

Mr. Sanger waited for the door to close behind my grandfather and said, "Your Honor, there were *no charges* in the CPS investigation; the witness's charges of rape were unsubstantiated, and as far as the legal system of the State of Texas is concerned, nothing happened. Period."

Judge Corn said, "Miss Asher, you may speak of nothing but the events on August 10 as you recall them. *Nothing matters* prior to August 10." Turning from me to address the lawyers, he said, "Can we get on with this? I have a tee time at one."

I stared at the railing of the witness stand, with its intricately carved edges, and imagined the curving pattern as waves on the ocean. I focused hard on the scalloped shapes and making them move in my mind.

Mr. Guzman sounded to me as if he were underwater. "Ashley?" He bent down, his face close to mine. He waved his hand in front of my eyes.

Finally, I said in an emotionless voice, "I don't know what else to tell you. They told me I had to go back with them, and I told them I wouldn't. Charlie twisted my arm back until it broke, and—and he was going to kick me in the head, but Emma protected me. Then my dad and Bev got home, and my dad beat up Charlie. That's it. Charlie broke my arm—because I wouldn't do what he wanted." I focused harder on the railing, the numbness filling me up as the judge's words echoed in my mind: *"Nothing matters prior to August 10."*

"Thank you, Ashley. Your Honor, I have no further questions for this witness."

"Mr. Sanger? Your witness."

"The defense has no questions for this witness, Judge," Mr. Sanger said, not looking up from his notepad.

"Mr. Prosecutor, do you have any other witnesses?" Judge Corn asked, glancing at his watch.

"Your Honor, I do not," Mr. Guzman said.

"Defense Counselor, are you calling any witnesses?"

"No, sir."

"I see. Then we'll move on to closing arguments."

∾

Mr. Sanger went first, pacing back and forth in front of the judge. "Your Honor, what we have here is a case of a rebellious teenager with a fertile imagination and a flair for the dramatic. Unfortunately, her parents—her mother, Cheryl, and her stepfather, Charlie Baker—the only father she has ever known up until this past May—are the ones paying the price for the stories she tells. Charlie Baker has provided a home for Ashley since she was eight years old and has been a devoted family man. His in-laws will testify to his generous heart and his love for his wife and the girl he loves as if she were his own child. Now, you'd think that if he was the kind of monster who would break a child's arm on purpose, his in-laws and his wife would be the last people on earth who would come to his defense."

Bev moved her arm from around my shoulders and took hold of my hand. David, who sat on the other side of me, crossed his arms over his chest and breathed in and out slowly and deeply—his way of keeping his anger in check. He caught me looking at him and gave me a little nod, which I read as *Don't worry, Ashley*. I leaned my head against his shoulder and could feel his muscles flexing.

Mr. Sanger continued, "It should be plain to Your Honor that while Ashley's story may have been engineered to garner favor from her long-absent biological father, this tragic episode in the life of the Baker family should not be allowed to continue beyond today. There is Mr. Baker's reputation in the community to consider. He is a leader in his church and a member of the Northside Chamber of Commerce. I respectfully request that you find Mr. Baker not guilty of injury to a child and that this family be able to move beyond the past and into healing."

He lowered his head, backed away from the judge to the defense table, and patted Charlie on the shoulder as he sat down. Charlie, his hands clasped before him, bowed his head like he was praying. My mother sniffed loudly and wiped her eyes with a white linen handkerchief. Nanny put her arm around my mom and leaned her head on her shoulder.

Mr. Guzman stood, ran his hand over his wavy brown hair, and took a few steps over to a lectern. He cleared his throat before beginning. "Your Honor, the defense has resorted to the lowest tactic: attacking the victim and painting her as a liar while attempting to elevate the status of the defendant to sainthood. The facts are the facts. On the evening of August 10, Charlie and Cheryl Baker trespassed on the property of David and Beverly Asher with the sole intent of taking the victim, Ashley Nicole Asher, back to their home in Northside. In the process of attempting to remove Ashley from the care of her father, David Asher,

Charlie Baker did in fact willfully injure Ashley, breaking her right arm by forcing it into a position so it would be fractured. Those are the facts. On behalf of the State of Texas and Anderson County, I present indisputable evidence of injury to a child and request that you find Mr. Baker guilty. Thank you."

Judge Corn announced, "The court will recess for one hour for lunch. When we return, I will have my decision." The bailiff told us to rise, so we did. The judge walked out through a door in the paneling behind his bench.

David told us, "I want to talk to Mr. Guzman for a few minutes. Y'all go on, okay?" Uncle Frank didn't budge from his spot, but Bev took me by the hand. We went out to the front lawn of the courthouse and sat on a cement bench beneath a huge oak tree. The first cold front of the season was starting to blow in, causing crisp, rusty-looking leaves to flutter down around us. About ten minutes later, David and Frank emerged from the courthouse.

"So what's going on?" Bev asked. She pushed her sunglasses back on top of her head and squinted at David.

He shook his head. "Guzman's not real optimistic. He told me that because we couldn't bring in any prior history, Judge Corn's not likely to go hard on Baker, if he finds him guilty at all. On top of that, there's the judge's tee time at one. I hope that's not influencing his decision, but who knows?"

"Well, let's not get ahead of ourselves," Bev said, using both hands to push my hair back behind my ears and looking at me reassuringly. "Let's not give up."

None of us really felt like eating, but we got sandwiches at a Subway across the street, then trooped back to the courthouse for the judge's decision.

When Judge Corn entered the courtroom, the smell of sunblock came with him, and I caught a glimpse of his purple and green plaid golf pants as he ascended the steps to the bench. It was 12:45.

Papaw was allowed back into the courtroom for the reading of the verdict. He, Nanny, and my mother were all leaning forward on their bench behind Charlie and Mr. Sanger, as if by reaching for him, they could keep Charlie from going to jail.

The bailiff commanded, "All rise."

We had barely stood before Judge Corn said, "Be seated. This shouldn't take long." He sank into his seat, squinted, and grumbled, "Sunblock in my eyes." The bailiff stepped over and handed him a handkerchief, and he rubbed his eyes with it for what felt like forever. Finally, he said, "Uh, Mr. Baker, I need you and your attorney to stand. I have carefully considered the evidence before me. I am inclined to believe that this was, indeed, an unfortunate accident. Mr. Baker, you did break your stepdaughter's arm, and even though your attorney says you didn't mean to, well, fact is, ya broke it; therefore, I do find you guilty of injury to a child." With that, Judge Corn banged the gavel.

My mother choked out a sob. I turned in her direction and saw that Nanny had enveloped her in her arms. Papaw stood, his hands on Charlie's shoulders.

David put his arm around me and gave my shoulder a little squeeze.

Mr. Guzman stood. "Your Honor, the prosecution requests that the court hear a Victim Impact Statement prior to sentencing—"

My stomach felt like it had hit the floor. Was it that time already?

Judge Corn snapped, "Now, Mr. Prosecutor, you know good and well that you can't present a VIS until *after* sentencing."

"Yes, Your Honor, but in light of the time . . . and the State believes that if you knew how the victim has suffered as a result of Mr. Baker's actions—"

"Sit down, Mr. Prosecutor."

Mr. Guzman sat and began scribbling notes on his legal pad, his brow furrowed.

I felt a wave of relief at having more time before I had to tell Charlie what I thought of him.

Mr. Sanger stood. "Your Honor, the defense invokes its right for the court to hear testimony on behalf of Mr. Baker prior to sentencing."

❦

My grandfather took the stand, his eyes seeming to burn through me. "My daughter was a struggling single parent when she met Charlie Baker seven years ago. Due to *David's* abusive behavior, Cheryl left him when Ashley was only three months old, and we celebrated the day they came back home to us. We never looked back. David didn't show the slightest interest in seeing Ashley. The only evidence of his existence was the child support payments he was bound by law to send. Charlie Baker is a great provider. I've never seen a man work as hard as he does, and I know that if a child I was supporting made allegations like Ashley has, it would take an act of Congress to get me to stay around. The fact that Charlie is even still willing to be part of our family after the public humiliation this incident has caused—well, it speaks to his devotion."

Watching Papaw on the stand, it was hard to believe that this was the same man who had taught me how to ride a bike. I remembered my shaky first try without the training wheels and how Papaw ran alongside me, promising me that he wouldn't let go of the seat until I was ready. As he walked back to his seat behind Charlie, my grandfather looked like he wanted to spit on me.

Unlike Papaw, Nanny wouldn't look at me at all. The scent of Estée perfume trailed behind her when she walked up to the stand. She sat, and I remembered being a little kid and stomping around in her high heels, wearing her big straw hat and her "Kiss the Cook" apron over my T-shirt and jeans. She'd sit at her vanity putting on makeup, and when she'd finished, she would spray Estée on her wrists and at the hollow of her throat, then turn to me and spritz a tiny bit on my wrists.

Nanny stared at the back wall of the courtroom. "You may begin," Judge Corn prompted. She dabbed at her eyes with a tissue, and seeing her cry made my eyes fill with tears, too. In a choked voice, she said, "My daughter . . . loves Charlie Baker with all her heart. He is completely devoted; he's wonderful to her. He's just . . . he's just a good man. I am begging you, Your Honor, not to take my son-in-law away from my daughter. She's already lost—" She looked at me at last. "So much."

Nanny's composure collapsed. She closed her eyes, and her face looked as if it was folding in on itself. She rose, but she held onto the railing for a moment before going back to her seat. Nanny was so close, within ten feet of me, and part of me wanted to run into her arms and tell her I was sorry for all the trouble I'd caused.

My mother nearly fell, teetering a moment on her high heels. She usually only wears flats; I guess the shoes were just part of her costume. Watching what happened in court that day, I felt like I was watching a play. I look back on it now and still can't believe it was real.

Mom kept her eyes on Charlie the entire time she spoke, her voice shaky. "I have *not* been . . . a perfect mother. I tried to save money by sharing a wardrobe with Ashley, and maybe that makes me a bad parent for not buying her every little thing her heart desired whenever she wanted it."

I looked over at Charlie, and he had tears running down his cheeks. He wasn't even wiping them away; he was just letting them fall. I'd never seen him cry before.

"Your Honor, please don't make my husband pay for my failures as a mother. Everything that happened is—it's all my fault. If only I had been a better mother to Ashley Nicole—more firm with her—from the time she was a baby until she was eight, when Charlie came into our lives . . . I hate to think where we'd be today, if it weren't for him."

Images of hurting myself scrolled through my mind, like I was watching some kind of bizarro movie. I envisioned stabbing myself in the chest with a knife, running out in front of a tractor-trailer rig, and shooting myself in the head. I know that this always happens any time my mom shows me what kind of mother she is. It's as predictable as pulling a chain on a ceiling fan and seeing the blades turn. Dr. Matt tells me to separate facts from crap when I start having self-destructive, spinning thoughts at times like this. But it's easier said than done.

I found something to focus on: the stained-glass window in an archway above the judge's bench, and I allowed the numbness that began in my chest to move on up my body, through my upper arms and shoulders to my neck, and, finally, my head, which was buzzing with *whoosh*. A few more minutes and the suicidal mental movie blips might or might not be there. But either way, at least I wouldn't feel the pain that causes them.

Judge Corn said, "I will now pronounce sentencing. The defendant will rise."

My mother whimpered.

"Mr. Baker, I think what you did was an honest mistake; therefore, I am sentencing you to deferred adjudication. If you stay out of trouble for five years, it will be as if this unfortunate incident in the life of your family had never happened. I strongly recommend that you, your wife, and your stepdaughter seek family counseling so that I don't see any of you in my courtroom again."

David put his arm around me and pulled me close to him. Bev patted my leg. Uncle Frank grumbled, "Unbelievable."

My mom and grandparents stood up, making happy sounds and hugging each other. Papaw patted Charlie on the back, and Nanny kissed him on the cheek. Mom cried and laughed at the same time. She kept saying to Charlie, "I was so afraid I was going to lose you!"

Judge Corn banged his gavel. "Order! This proceeding has not adjourned! Be seated, or I'll clear the courtroom of observers. Mr. Guzman, Miss Asher may now present her Victim Impact Statement."

"A moment, please, Your Honor?" Mr. Guzman said, and then he leaned in to speak to David, Bev, and me. "Ashley? This is your chance. Your stepfather has to listen to what you say. You can say whatever you want to him. Sentence has already been pronounced, so what you say won't change it. This is your chance to vent, to have closure. He can't leave the room while you are speaking."

I heard what Mr. Guzman was saying, but it wasn't registering with me as real.

As Dr. Matt and I had worked through writing my Victim Impact Statement, I'd imagined myself being this strong, victorious person, finally getting justice as Charlie was dragged away to be locked up. I'd convinced myself that my mother would finally see him for who he is and that she would feel sorry for not protecting me from him. Dr. Matt had tried to pull me off my cloud; he'd said that the VIS was for me and that I shouldn't expect my mother to change because of it. But I didn't believe him. I just knew that once I told Charlie in front of my mom how much he'd hurt me, she'd see how much she'd hurt me, too, and things would be different. She'd want to make it right. My grandparents would sandwich me in a hug the way they used to, and Nanny would ask, "Who loves their Ashleykins?" I know it's a stupid nickname, but it was part of my life before Charlie came along. I still don't understand how my grandparents and mom can just delete me from their lives when what happened to me wasn't my fault. Why wasn't Charlie the one outside their circle?

I felt myself breaking apart on the inside, like a mirror that's been hit with a hammer until it's tiny slivers of glass. It felt just like that day back in May, in the kitchen of my mother's house in Northside, when I told her that Charlie'd been molesting me since I was nine and she told me, "We're just going to move on. Go to your room."

That was before I went through the rape exam at the hospital and definitely before the puzzle pieces of that night started flying around inside my head. But it didn't seem to matter to my mom. Nothing happened to Charlie then, and nothing was happening to him now.

Everyone seemed to be moving in slow motion. I looked over at my mother, Charlie, and my grandparents. Heads together, they were smiling and whispering to each other. I narrowed my eyes, trying to read their lips. Were they deciding where to celebrate?

"Ashley?" David said. He touched my upper arm. I turned my head slowly, seeing his hand on my skin but not feeling it. "Ashley, honey, if you don't want to say anything to him, you don't have to. Okay?" I looked at him. My throat felt like it was being squeezed by giant hands.

David told Mr. Guzman, "I don't think it's a good idea for her to make a statement. I think it'll do her more harm than good at this point."

"I'm inclined to agree with you, Mr. Asher," said Mr. Guzman. He straightened and said, "Your Honor, Miss Asher is waiving her right to make a VIS."

"In that case," said Judge Corn, "we are adjourned."

⟳

David, Bev, and Uncle Frank gathered around Mr. Guzman in the aisle on the far right side of the courtroom, their voices low murmurs. They all shook hands, and then Mr. Guzman exited through a side door.

I was sitting by myself on the bench, staring at the swirl pattern in the floor tile, when a pair of feet in wobbly high heels appeared in my field of vision.

"Ashley, I'd like to talk to you," my mother said. Suddenly, three more pairs of feet appeared: David's boots, Bev's closed-toe flats, and Charlie's shiny black dress shoes. "I'd like to speak to my daughter alone, David," Mom said tersely.

"I don't think so," Bev said, stepping close to my mother. I looked up and saw that they were nose to nose. Charlie stood a few feet behind my mom, with his arms crossed over his barrel chest. My eyes got as high as the knot in his pink tie, but I couldn't make myself look at his face. I swallowed hard and looked back at the pairs of feet on the floor in front of me.

David's boots took a step toward my mother, and Charlie's black shoes backed up. "If you want to speak to Ashley, you can say whatever you need to say in front of us," David said in a voice that sounded like a warning growl.

"Really, now, isn't this just a little melodramatic?" Nanny's off-white heels joined in. "Cheryl is Ashley's *mother*. What possible harm could come from a mother speaking to her daughter in private?"

"Ashley, do you want to talk to your mom alone?" David asked the top of my head.

I shook my head and mumbled, "No."

"What is it, Cheryl?" David asked in a clipped voice.

Mom sighed loudly. "Fine, David; you may as well know that I've changed my mind about fighting you for custody. Charlie's attorney told us that it would be very messy because Ashley would probably keep up with the lying, and it's just not worth it to us to go through all that."

"Is that *it*?" David asked her through gritted teeth. I could see his fists clenching and unclenching.

I glanced down and to my left and saw that Uncle Frank's worn eelskin cowboy boots had sidled up to stand beside me. I felt his rough hand resting gently on my rounded shoulder. I smelled Aramis cologne and knew that the pair of brown dress shoes that stepped up to my mom's heels belonged to Papaw.

"Is that it?" Papaw boomed. "I would think that you'd be grateful, David. We were willing to support Charlie and Cheryl financially—"

"And emotionally—" Nanny cut in.

"For as long as it took to settle this. We believe in Charlie's innocence," Papaw said, and I could feel him glaring at me, even though I was trying to lose myself in the floor tiles. "You need to know that, Ashley. We believe that Charlie is completely innocent of the horrible things you accused him of. You have hurt us all so—"

"You're done! You don't get to poison her any more. That's it. Come on, Ashley," David said, as he left the group and turned toward me. Uncle Frank gently lifted me at the waist, then David wrapped his arm around me and pulled me to my feet the rest of the way. We started toward the exit. "That's it, you're done," he said more softly, as if to himself this time. We picked up speed as we neared the door.

Just outside the courtroom, he stopped suddenly and turned around. "Oh. There you are, Bev. Take Ashley to the car. I have something to say to Charlie."

Frank followed David, not waiting for an invitation.

Bev took my hand and started to lead me down the hallway into the foyer. The floor was covered in colorful patterns from the stained-glass window in the dome atop the courthouse. I stopped in the midst of the mosaic images, temporarily transfixed by the way they appeared to move and by the way the beams of midday light made them dance. I heard my mother's voice, then Charlie's, but I couldn't make out what they were saying. Then I very clearly heard David yell, "If you ever set foot on my property again, I will kill you. Do you get that, Baker? I *will* kill you."

Bev tugged my arm and led me out through the front doors of the courthouse and into the blinding sunshine. Two squirrels chased each other across the courthouse lawn as the chilly wind marked the changing of seasons, of life going on like it's supposed to. Goose bumps rose on my arms. But I couldn't feel a thing.

CHAPTER 4

We drove back to Patience in silence—no radio, none of David's Eighties-era CDs blasting Def Leppard or Van Halen—but my mind was broadcasting my mother's voice: *"Ashley would probably keep up with the lying, and it's just not worth it to us to go through all that."*

I felt myself starting to cry. I held my breath, squeezed my eyes closed, and pinched the bridge of my nose until the pain went back down—kind of like swallowing real hard when you feel like you're going to throw up.

Uncle Frank, next to David in the front seat of Bev's Ford Focus, tried to make conversation. "Hey, Dave, did you call Mr. Wheeler to give him an estimate on the engine overhaul for his backhoe?"

When David didn't answer him, Frank just said, "We can talk about it later."

I stared through a rear passenger window at the East Texas countryside between Palestine, where the courthouse is, and Patience. Huge pine trees rooted in rust-colored sand lined the two-lane highway. We'd blast along at seventy-five miles per hour until we came upon a tiny town. Then

David would slow to thirty-five, I'd blink, and we'd be flying toward home once again. Half an hour later, I could see
the rusted white water tower with "PATIENCE" painted on
it and the faded outline of a black panther on its side.

We exited the highway and pulled in at a gas station.
Jasper Freeman came out of the building and started spray-
ing window cleaner on our windshield as David removed
the gas cap and started filling up the tank.

David exchanged pleasantries with Jasper; watching
David's face from my seat, I thought, *His voice sounds just
like nothing's wrong, but his face sure doesn't look like it.*

David noticed me looking at him. He winked at me and
gave me a little closed-mouth smile, but when we broke eye
contact, his smile faded away.

"Ashley," Bev asked, "do you want to go for a run
when we get home? We have time before your therapy appointment, and it might help you feel better if you get in a
little practice for your meet tomorrow." It was the first time
she had spoken since we left the courthouse. I figure she
spent most of the ride home staring blankly out her window, too.

"Mmm, I'll have to think about it," I said. The next
day's cross-country meet was the last thing on my mind.
All I wanted to do was go home, crawl into bed, pull the
covers over my head, and never come out again.

An old Buick pulled in on the other side of the gas
pump island. The driver killed the engine, and the car continued to shimmy, growl, and fart before it sighed into silence. A middle-aged woman in a red T-shirt, rolled-up blue
jeans, and red Keds got out, mumbling. She hugged herself

against the cold and left the driver's door open when she went to pump the gas.

An electric guitar appeared to slide itself from the back seat to the front passenger side. Then I saw what looked like Taylor Swift, but dark black and minus a face—just a mass of hair—sit up in the back seat.

Meanwhile, the driver pulled the hose and gas nozzle to the rear of the car, started it pumping, then returned to the open car door and stood in my line of sight. She leaned over and appeared to speak to The Hair, then closed her door and turned to walk into the station.

The Hair leaned forward over the seat, and I could see very pale, chubby arms. One hand held the neck of the guitar while the other pulled the shoulder belt across it. Suddenly The Hair shook, and I found myself being glared at by narrowed eyes in the round white face that had been hidden under a cloud of long, dark curls. I immediately looked down, but as soon as I dared, I peeked again. The Hair—I mean, the person in the back seat—must have lain down, because he, she, or it was gone again.

I was so focused on the scene in the next car that I jumped when David got in and slammed his door. As if Uncle Frank had asked him just a second before, David replied to the question of several miles ago: "No, Frank, I haven't called Wheeler about the backhoe; I've been waitin' to get a price on the overhaul kit first."

"Oh, man, I forgot to tell you. The John Deere place in Dallas called." Frank and David talked shop the rest of the way home.

When we got back, Emma met me at the front door. I

bent down and kissed her in the center of her head, right above her eyes, like always. I'd read once that mama dogs show their puppies they love them by nuzzling them in that spot; I don't know if it's true, but Emma sure likes it. She followed me to my room and jumped on my bed. I closed my door and lay down, lined my body up with hers, and tried not to notice how heavy and weighed down I felt, like I had an anchor in my chest.

I'd just started to relax when David called me. "Let's go, Ashley. Your appointment with Dr. Matthews is at four."

It was one of those days when David and Bev both went with me to therapy. When they came out of their short meeting with Dr. Matt, David told me to go on in. I found my shrink already sitting down, which wasn't how he usually started our sessions.

Dr. Matt leaned back in his chair, swiveled it toward the large window behind him, and parted the blinds with his fingers. "Looks like a norther's blowin' in," he said. "The wind's kickin' up all the leaves. There's even a dust devil out there."

"Yeah, it was really windy on our way here," I said, grateful he wasn't going to start off by asking me how it was going. I rose from my chair and joined him at the window, where I parted the blinds too and watched a miniature tornado of leaves and dust as it hopped and skipped across the wide lawn. It spun freely until it ran into the huge pine tree that dominated the yard; then, in the blink of an eye, the dust devil vanished. The only evidence of it ever having existed was the leaves fluttering to the ground.

"That's nature, right there," he said, releasing the blinds and turning his chair back toward the chair I always sit in, which is right next to his desk. I took that as my cue to sit back down.

"Yep, that's nature," he repeated, watching me carefully.

I kicked off my shoes and crossed my legs in my chair, then stretched my arms over my head and realized how tired I was. Not sleeping all night will do that to a person. So will doing a pretzel imitation for twenty-four hours straight. I inhaled and exhaled without even thinking about it, then said, "Hey! I'm breathing! At least one thing's working right."

"You sure are." He smiled at me. "Good job. Do you know why I love nature, Ashley?"

"No. Why?"

"I love it because what's supposed to happen, happens. That dust devil out there wasn't meant to keep on twisting, and you and I aren't meant to stop our bodies from breathing or sleeping. Eventually, nature takes over and we need to yield to it. We need to respect the process."

He picked up his mug and took a sip of water. "People get thirsty; they gotta drink. People get tired; they need to sleep. The body can be trusted. It instinctively keeps us alive, even when we fight it."

"At least some things can be trusted to do what they're supposed to do," I said, with an edge in my voice.

"What are we talking about here, Ash?"

"I didn't make the Victim Impact Statement. I went off into la-la land instead, so David and the district attorney thought it would do more harm than good for me to say what I'd rehearsed. I'm still just a chicken shit, I guess. I can't believe I ever thought I'd be able to talk to Charlie like that."

"That's okay. You're allowed to be human, you know."

"Aren't you disappointed in me, Dr. Matt?"

"No, not at all. But I think you're disappointed in the way the trial ended up."

"Well, nothing bad happened to Charlie, and that sucks," I said, looking down.

"What did you want to see happen to him, Ashley?"

"I wanted him to go to prison. And I wanted him to get beat up when he got there, too. Bev told me that child rapists are despised, and—"

"He wasn't on trial for raping you, Ashley," Dr. Matt said quietly.

"Yeah, I know. But I wanted him to go to jail. I wanted him to have a big ugly cellmate who would—who would—" My throat was getting tight. I knew what I wanted to say, but I acted like I had lost my train of thought.

"What? Who would what?"

"I forget," I said, looking around Dr. Matt's office for something to focus on. I chose my usual "avoid this" object: the sandbox with toy tractors in it. Next to the sandbox was a poster with different feelings on it, and I stared at it until the images all blurred together. My mind whispered, *Whoosh.*

"Bullshit!" Dr. Matt said sharply.

"Huh?" I closed my eyes and put my feet down on the floor. I straightened out my posture but felt myself wanting to curl my body into a knot again.

"I said, 'Bullshit,' Ashley. You didn't forget anything." He rolled his chair closer to me and leaned forward. "Say it."

"Say what?" I asked.

"Don't play games with me. Say what you wanted to have happen to him in jail. Say it." He leaned back in his chair but didn't roll it back.

I closed my eyes tighter and felt my face getting hot. Tears gathered at the corners of my eyes, and my throat constricted. I gritted my teeth against the tears and the words.

Dr. Matt waited, and the silence between us felt like something I could reach out and touch. It became clear to me that this was like a staring contest with him—a contest that I never win—and I knew I had no hope of outwaiting him, either. I can be stubborn, but Dr. Matt is the god of stubbornness.

Choking with tears and rage, I said, "All right, fine! I wanted him to be—to be raped, too. I—I wanted him to know what it feels like to have somebody's dick shoved up his ass. I—I wanted—I wanted—" I pressed my fists into my eyes, bent over, and felt every muscle in my body lock down. I shook with anger and sobbed.

Dr. Matt didn't say anything. He just waited quietly for me to stop. When I did, I heard the sound of tissues being pulled from the box—*one, two, three*—and held my hand out. He placed them in my hand, and I curled my hand back into the bent-over shell I'd made of myself and dragged the tissues roughly across my eyes.

"Did you honestly expect *justice* to happen in that courtroom today?" he asked, punctuating his question with a little laugh.

I sat up abruptly and said bitterly, "Well, *excuse me* for wanting him to get what he deserves."

Dr. Matt sat back in his chair and shook his head at me, frowning. "There *is* no justice in cases like this."

"Then why bother having a trial?" I wailed. "Why did I even have to see them again?"

"Ash, the judge could have sentenced him to life in prison and that still wouldn't have been enough for you. Would it?"

I glared at Dr. Matt, who raised his eyebrows at me but said nothing in response to the go-to-hell look I knew full well I was giving him. I breathed hard and felt like I was filled with lava. Finally, I managed a response: "So?"

"So? What do you mean, 'So'?"

"So don't I have a right to want justice?" I was twitching with rage.

"What does that have to do with anything?" Dr. Matt asked.

"What the fuck do you mean, 'What does that have to do with anything?' What have we been talking about in here for the past five months?"

He shook his head at me again and threw his hands in the air. "Well, we sure haven't been talking about you getting justice through the court system for what the perpetrator did."

"Arrrrrggghhh!" I banged my fists on my temples, stuck my elbows onto the edge of the desk, then growled through clenched teeth, "What in hell do you want from me?"

He rolled his chair closer to me and softly said, "It's not about me, Ashley. It's about helping you fully recover from what happened to you."

I said sarcastically, "I know you don't take notes or anything, *Scott*, but maybe you don't really get the full picture here. My mother, my grandmother, and my grandfather all hate me for telling on Charlie. They were so convincing, talking about what a great guy Charlie is, *I* started to believe what they said about him. And I guess I need to remind you that *I'm* the one who was raped. *I'm* the one whose mother turned her back on me again. So excuse me if I'm just a little pissed off about that right now."

"How's all that self-pity workin' for you, Ashley?"

"Fuck you!"

"Oh, that's helpful," he said flatly. "I don't think you're as pissed off that Charlie didn't get jail time as you are that your mother has no interest in challenging David for custody. She's not willing to fight for you now any more than she was willing to protect you from Charlie when you lived with her. *That's* what you're really pissed about."

"No shit, Sherlock!"

"So where's the justice, Ashley?"

I scowled at him.

"Where's the justice?" he asked again.

"Gee, I don't know, Dr. Matt. You tell me, seeing as how you're the one with all the answers; it was your fucking idea for me to do the VIS in the first place, but I'm the one wallowing in self-pity." I glared at the irregularly shaped green smudge on the desk and began rubbing hard at it again.

Softly, he said, "Ashley, do you remember what that dust devil looked like when it hit that pine tree?"

Without looking up, I nodded.

"That's nature, darlin'. Today, what happened in court? That was your pine tree. Your mom turned her back on you again. That'd make anybody hurt. It'd make anybody cry. Any dust devil runs into a pine tree like that, it's gonna fall apart for a little while. It's natural."

My eyes filled with tears, and I rubbed the smudge so hard that my fingertip felt like it was on fire. Snot started to run out of my nose, and I angrily swiped at it with the back of my hand. I had an overwhelming urge to gouge my eyes out to stop the tears and to claw my nose off to stop the snot.

Dr. Matt continued in a gentle voice: "What you have to do now, Ashley, is make a choice. Are you gonna stay in a million little pieces, or are you gonna pick yourself up and use what you've learned these past few months to keep moving forward on your journey to heal?"

My face crumpled, and I laid my head down on his desk. I ignored his question and said in a thick voice, "*You* seem to know everything. Where *is* the justice?"

"It's five o'clock," announced Dr. Matt's talking alarm clock.

"That's something you'll have to figure out. We'll work on it together," he said, crossing to his door and opening it for me. "You hang in there."

93

I went to him, my head down, and hugged him. He seemed surprised at first, then hugged me and briefly patted me on the back. Then I turned to go.

David, Bev, and I were driving out of the parking lot when I looked over at the pine tree again. On the other side of the tree, as if it had picked itself up and started over, the dust devil was dancing.

CHAPTER 5

I was supposed to leave for my cross-country meet at 7 a.m. on Saturday, but I wouldn't get out of bed. Z.Z. called a few times, and I pretended to be asleep each time. *Screw the meet. My mother doesn't love me.*

Ben got so disgusted with trying to talk to me and getting only a sarcastic "Who gives a shit?" in response that he gave up and went to Uncle Frank's to hang out with Stephen.

David and Bev seemed to understand that I wanted to be alone, and they gave me space all weekend. But knowing that they never considered letting me miss school so I could stay stuck within myself, I didn't bother asking. Even though my life felt like it had skidded to a stop, I still had to get up and go to school on Monday. I'm not allowed to quit the stuff I *have* to do—like school—even when I just want to curl up in a ball and let my thoughts race around inside my head like squirrels on speed. If there were Olympics for mental spinning, I'd be wearing so many gold medals, it'd be impossible to stand up straight.

On Monday morning, I emerged from my self-imposed exile. Ben stood by the kitchen counter, looking like his usual morning self: his stick-straight brown hair stood up at odd angles all over his head, and there was crusty stuff in the corners of his eyes from being asleep. His black T-shirt read, "Stop Looking at My Shirt," and it looked like it'd been slept in. He was still wearing his red and green Christmas boxers that he wears all year long; Ben usually waits until Bev is in the car and honking the horn for him to hurry up before he rummages through the pile of clothes on his floor for a pair of jeans.

"Hey," I said as I poured Raisin Bran into a bowl. Ben didn't answer, so I said, "Hellooooo, did you hear me?"

Ben reached into the cabinet above my head for a drinking glass. "I'm sorry; I didn't know you were talking to me. I thought the only thing you could say was 'Who gives a shit?'" He poured milk into the glass and added heaping spoonfuls of chocolate powder to it, scattering it on the counter as he stirred.

I sighed wearily and added milk to my cereal. "Jeez, Ben, do you have to make such a mess?"

"Mmph," he replied as he chugged down the tall glass of light brown liquid. Ben thinks of himself as a chocolate milk expert. If the bottom quarter of the glass isn't dry chocolate mix, he thinks he made it wrong. That's because, according to him, the best part is the dry stuff oozing down the sides of the glass when all the milk's gone.

He tilted his head back and held the glass above his wide-open mouth as bits of mix trickled onto his tongue.

Bev hurried into the kitchen, snatched her lunchbox out of the fridge, and asked, as she does every school morning, "Ben, where are your jeans?"

"On my floor," he said and placed his glass in the sink.

"Well, you need to get them on. I have to get to school early to make copies," Bev told him as she gathered graded essays from the kitchen table.

&

Z.Z. nearly ran me over when I followed Bev through the front doors of Patience High School. "Ashley! Girl, what happened to you over the weekend? How did the trial go?"

Bev glanced back at me and raised her eyebrows, but she continued on her copy-making mission. I just rolled my eyes at her and made a face at her back. Then I moved out of the crowd of kids and stood by the entrance to the office.

I acted like I was trying to adjust the strap on my backpack, hoping Z.Z. would go on to class, but she wasn't giving up that easily. "Why wouldn't you come to the phone when I called you?"

Feeling my cheeks getting warm, I looked at my feet and exhaled loudly. "I just didn't feel like talking," I said flatly.

"Oh," Z.Z. said. "Well, I was tryin' to call you to, you know, check on you, see how the VIS went, since we practiced it and all."

I stared at her feet, remembering the hours she'd spent with me, coaching me as I read the Victim Impact Statement aloud until I could do it without shaking. Z.Z.'s the only person in Patience outside of my family who I've told anything about what happened to me before. I told her all of it—well, all of it that I'm able to remember, anyway.

"So? Did ya read it to 'im?" she asked.

I said nothing, just shook my head, bit my lip, and closed my eyes.

Z.Z. touched my shoulder softly and said, "Okay, if you don't wanna talk about that, then tell me why you wouldn't get out of bed for the meet—"

I cut her off. "I don't *owe you* an explanation!"

"Oh. You don't, huh? Well, I had to listen to that damned ole snot, Pam, talkin' shit about you, sayin' how she *knew* you wouldn't stick with it. How she could tell all along that you're a quitter. Said I should hang with her if I wanna go to state. I jus' 'bout popped her upside the head!"

"There are worse things in life than not going to state, Z.Z.," I said, then started to walk away.

Z.Z. grabbed my arm roughly. "Hey! Wait a minute, Ash—"

"Let go of me!" I jerked my arm back from her and allowed my backpack to slide to the ground. I glared at it, as if that would make it crawl back up my arm. Hot tears stung my eyes.

"Know what, Ashley? You need to grow up!" Z.Z. stormed off in the direction of her locker.

I sighed, "Great." As I knelt to retrieve my backpack, a foot in a clunky wooden-soled sandal barely missed squishing my fingers. A cloud of Chantilly perfume told me that the toes belonged to Marvella.

"Ashley, you're just the person I was looking for." Marvella's ornately painted toenails were coated with brown polish and embossed with tiny oak-leaf shaped rhinestones in alternating colors of burnt orange, mustard yellow, and forest green.

I raised my eyes from her feet, stood up, and slid my backpack over my shoulder again. "Why did you want me?" I asked warily.

Marvella smiled at me and said in her typically loud, twangy way, "Well, we have a new student who's goin' to need a tour guide today."

She stepped to the side and pushed open the office door. That's when The Hair from the gas station joined us in the hallway. Seeing The Hair from head to toe, I could see that "Cousin It" was female. She was about my height and wearing a too-tight dark green Nirvana T-shirt, faded blue jeans with rips in them, and Doc Marten boots. Her hair was parted in the middle and black curls reached to her waist. Her hair and skin were shocking opposites of dark and light.

"Oh. Hi," I said flatly, not even trying to disguise my foul mood.

"Krystle, this is Ashley Asher. Her stepmom is Mrs. Asher, your English teacher."

I said, "I saw you on Friday at the gas station; you had this guitar, and you were putting it—"

"It wasn't me," she said, cutting me off and shaking her head.

"No, I'm sure it was," I said, angered that she was arguing with me about what I knew I saw. Thoughts of my mother not believing me zipped through my mind at the familiar feeling.

"I doubt it," she said, shaking her head again.

"Ooo-kay," I said, making my eyes huge and looking at Marvella. "Whatever."

Marvella blinked as she looked from me to Krystle and back, a smile frozen on her face but her eyes saying, *Uh-oh.* "So . . . here's a copy of Krystle's schedule, Ashley; and Krystle, you have your own copy—"

"It's K.C.," Krystle interrupted.

"K what?" Marvella said, her smile fading a little.

"K.C. I go by K.C.," she said.

"All righty then, K.C., Ashley will show you to your first-period class. Ashley, you and K.C. have the same lunch period, so be a dear and make sure K.C. gets some lunch, 'kay, hon?"

I screwed up my face in an ugly smile and said in a syrupy twang, "Okey-dokey, Marvella."

Her smile faded at the look on my face and the sound of my voice. She'd never seen this side of me—the pissed off, who-gives-a-shit one.

"Come on, K.C.," I said as I started toward one of the three main hallways. "So where're you from?" I demanded, cutting my eyes to the side and noticing that she was lagging behind me.

K.C. didn't answer, and it seemed to me that she was purposely dragging her feet.

I snapped my head around and said roughly, "I asked where you're from."

She made a face and said, in a tone that sounded like mine, "I heard you."

"So you're not going to tell me where you're from?"

She snorted and shook her head. "Jesus H. Christ, what's your problem?"

At that, I whirled around and she ran right into me. I

could feel my eyebrows low over my eyes and knew without a doubt that I was wearing my go-to-hell look. K.C.'s expression reflected mine.

She stepped away from me, and Travis Hager ran into her. "Hey!" she said, shoving him aside.

"Bitch!" he called as he bounced off a locker. Then the first bell rang.

I looked at her schedule and said, "Okay, your first-period class is American History with Coach Griffin. I have him, too."

"Oh, joy," K.C. said. "You know what?" She snatched my copy of her schedule out of my hands. "I'm not a moron, and it's not like this school has three floors like my old school. I'm fairly certain I can find my classes without a"—she mimicked Marvella's Deep East Texas twang—"tooo-er gahde!"

"Fine!" I said as I watched her drift slowly away, glancing side to side for room numbers. I spun on my heel and said to no one in particular, "You're on your own, bitch."

～

I slid into my seat in Coach Griffin's American history class as the tardy bell rang. His room is in a portable building between the school and the football field, and it's easy to be late to his class.

Coach Griffin turned off the lights, and a newsreel from the 1940s appeared on the projector screen. "Everybody Joins WWII Effort," the title read. A voice-over said,

"In democratic America, everybody is doing his bit. . . . " Then sunlight cut across the images, and a log-shaped outline topped by fuzzy hair appeared in the doorway: K.C.

The newsreel froze on Clark Gable in a pilot's uniform, and the lights flickered on.

"May I help you, young lady?" Coach Griffin asked. Although he's the head football coach, he isn't one to play. He's never without his yardstick, and if he thinks a student isn't paying attention, he slams it down on the student's desktop.

"Yeah, um, I'm—" K.C. stammered and blinked rapidly.

"Excuse me?" he interrupted.

"I said, 'Yeah, I'm—' "

"I'm sorry, young lady, but unlike our resident English III teacher, with her 'anything goes' attitude"—as he said this, he looked pointedly at me—"I do not recognize the word *yeah* as proper English in my classroom. And in this room, we use what, class?" he said, turning to all of us and swinging the yardstick back and forth like a pendulum.

"Proper English, Coach," we said.

"And what is that, class?" he asked, raising the yardstick as he leaned slightly forward, his sharply angled features appearing even more hawkish than usual.

"Proper English is a dialect representing English speech that includes no slang and that can be understood by anyone, anytime, anywhere, Coach," we recited. From the first day of school, we were required to learn Coach Griffin's definition of proper English. We had weekly quizzes on it until everyone in class got a 100.

"Is the word *yeah* proper English, class?"

"No, Coach."

Raising the yardstick toward her like a sword, Coach Griffin pivoted back to K.C. "Would you like to try again, young lady?"

"Um, yes? I mean, yes . . . uh, you can—I mean *may*—help me. I'm K.C. Williamson, and I'm new . . . here?" K.C. looked at him hopefully and held out her schedule to him. He glanced at it without taking it and pointed his yardstick at an empty desk directly in front of his desk. She sat.

He started to turn from her, then locked his eyes on her jeans until she asked, "Wh-what's wrong?"

"Are you aware that this school has a dress code? The jeans you're wearing are ripped. They look to me like they are intentionally ripped."

"Yeah, I mean *yes*, that lady in the office told me not to wear these again. I wore them at my old school, but—" K.C. began.

Coach Griffin cut her off. "You know, I long for the good old days, when young people had a modicum of respect for societal standards. People of that time would never have purposely defaced a perfectly good pair of trousers. It would have been un-American to do so. No intentionally destroyed clothing on any of these upstanding citizens . . ." He walked along one wall of his classroom and pointed with the yardstick at posters of smiling military men, white-capped army nurses, and everyday people from the 1940s. Coach Griffin's classroom is wall-to-wall World War II.

Wartime poster replicas fill the space above the white-board at the front of the classroom. They have slogans like

"Work on a farm this summer. Join the U.S. Crop Corps!" "Another American Naval Victory! Stay on the Job, Keep 'em Launching, Don't Slow Up the Ship!" "The Navy Needs You! Don't Read American History! Make It!"

Maps of Europe and the Pacific that detail major battles cover another wall, and past student projects are displayed on the back wall. Coach Griffin teaches American history by starting in the back of the book and working his way to the front. He explained why he does this on the first day of school: "Otherwise, we don't get to spend as much time on World War II as we need to, and I believe that there are countless valuable lessons to be learned from intensive study of that period in our nation's history."

We spent a couple days covering the election of the first African American president, globalization, and the New Economy, and about a week on Iraq and the George W. Bush presidency, with one day each devoted to the September 11 attacks and Hurricane Katrina. Then there was Clinton, W.'s daddy Bush, and Reagan. That took another week. Carter, Watergate, and the oil crisis were knocked out in just four days.

Coach Griffin told us there wasn't that much to see in the Sixties and gave us the option of completing the reading and questions for those thirty pages of the textbook for extra credit. I, along with a few other Invisible Outsider Nerds, worked on it in class every day that week while everybody else joined Coach Griffin and his assistant coach as they watched films from the previous weeks' football games and strategized for the upcoming game against Patience's arch-rival, Cedar Points. The Patience Panthers haven't been doing as well as anyone in Patience would like (those who care about that sort of stuff, that is). T.W.'s defection from his dad's team—he was going to be a running back—is a constant topic of armchair quarterback speculation. People talk about it all the time, just not in front of Coach Griffin.

The coach became grouchier and grouchier as the football season got under way, reminded every day that his own son would rather write a short story than watch while his dad drew up plays. But the closer we got to World War II in the textbook, the more Coach Griffin's usually sour mood improved. He had a spring in his step that week as he paced back and forth, reading to us from PowerPoint slides about Eisenhower, the Cold War, nationalism, and the Korean War. The test for the marking period covered fifty-five years of history and had 150 questions. The decade from 1960 to 1969 was completely absent. There was no mention of the struggle for civil rights, Martin Luther King, Jr., John F. Kennedy, the Vietnam War, or the student protests about it. And nothing about the Kent State shootings.

Bev told me that she had stopped him one day in the teachers' lounge and asked him, "How can you do that? How can you even consider leaving out such a socially relevant era as the 1960s?"

"I provided an opportunity for the students to engage in independent study of district-approved curriculum, Mrs. Asher. Maybe you should try that sometime," Coach Griffin replied.

"Back in the 1940s, the war brought out the best in people as America struggled valiantly for its very survival. Just think, if the Japanese had never bombed Pearl Harbor on December 7, 1941, we might never have discovered our hidden capacity for survival."

Kevin Cooper asked, "Were you even born back then, Coach?"

Coach Griffin closed his eyes and shook his head. "Alas, Cooper, I was born in 1960. It's one of my greatest regrets, not getting to experience the miraculous coming together of all Americans in our country's time of need." He walked down the center aisle, beneath models of vintage fighter planes, and happened to be standing next to K.C. again when she stretched her arms over her head and yawned. It wasn't even a loud, obnoxious "God-this-is-so-boring" yawn; it was just a garden-variety, normal yawn. I hoped Coach Griffin hadn't noticed.

He had.

"Stand up, Miss Williamson."

"Why?" K.C. asked, remaining seated.

A wicked smile spread across Coach Griffin's face. "Excuse me?" He slowly brought out the yardstick.

"Huh?" she looked confused. I noticed that most of the other students were wearing pained expressions, as if fingernails were being dragged down a chalkboard.

"Just stand up!" hissed Roxanne Blake, another summer school student, who was seated two rows over from me.

"O-kay." K.C. slid out of the desk and self-consciously pulled her too-tight shirt away from her pudgy middle. "Now what?"

Coach Griffin looked like a cat who has a mouse pinned by the tail and enjoys watching it struggle. He laid the yardstick behind him on his desk, crossed his arms, and relaxed his rigid stance enough to lean against his desk. I breathed an inward sigh of relief. When he slams that yardstick, it makes me jump a foot. "Young lady, you owe this class an apology."

"For what?" K.C. asked, her voice high.

"You yawned without covering your mouth," he said.

"Yeah—I mean—*yes*. So . . . ?"

"So?" The yardstick reappeared in his hand so quickly, I didn't even see him pick it up. "So? Did you say, 'So?' to me, young lady? Turn around and face the class, please."

He said 'please' but did not wait for K.C. to turn on her own. Instead, he used the yardstick to direct her movements, the way a person might herd a sheep, the stick hovering in midair beside her body.

K.C.'s eyes grew huge, then filled with tears. Her lower lip quivered.

From behind her, Coach Griffin explained, "Even though this is a first-period class, people rarely yawn, because my teaching inspires rapt attention. However, when a student is compelled to yawn, he or she at *least* has the decency to cover his or her mouth. To do otherwise is . . . *rude*." The yardstick lowered on his last word until he held it, cane-like, before him.

"I'm sorry," K.C. said, her voice thick. A tear ran down her cheek, and she raised a shaky hand to wipe it away. She began to sit down again, but he stopped her with the yardstick.

"No, no, no, Miss Williamson, you have not made proper amends to the people you've offended. Look around the room at your classmates, who were subjected to the full view of the inside of your mouth," he said, as if it were the most disgusting thing on earth.

K.C. moved her eyes from side to side. When she glanced at me, I looked down. A second later, I sneaked a peek around the room and saw that almost everyone else had averted their eyes from having to see her face, too.

"Miss Williamson, you will apologize to your classmates as a proper young lady should, by saying 'Pardon me' and curtsying."

K.C. whirled to face him. "Are you for real?" she asked, her voice squeaky high.

SLAM! Coach Griffin flattened his yardstick on her desktop, and I jumped a foot, as did a lot of other people. Immediately, K.C. bent her knees into an awkward, tiny curtsy. But that wasn't good enough for him. I wondered whether he was like this when he was at home with T.W.

"Face your classmates, Miss Williamson. I did not give you permission to vary your position. Now, you will go up and down each row, stopping at each of your classmates. He looked around until his eyes landed on Pam Littlejohn. "Miss Littlejohn, please demonstrate for Miss Williamson the way I require this to be done."

"Yes, Coach!" Pam said. She rose from her desk, walked right up to K.C., took her hand, and curtsied—and I mean a deep knee bender of a curtsy. "Pardon me," Pam crooned.

"Thank you, Miss Littlejohn," Coach Griffin said.

"You're more than welcome, Coach," she said in a little-girl voice, then practically skipped back to her seat.

The yardstick poised to strike again, Coach Griffin glanced at his watch. "The sooner you perform your act of contrition, the sooner the Japanese can attack."

"Huh?" K.C. looked around wildly.

"Our lesson, Miss Williamson. Pearl Harbor. December 7, 1941. The impetus for the United States joining World War II. I'm waiting. We all are."

I wondered where K.C. was in her mind right then—fight, flight, or freeze?

Most creatures have those three basic instincts when they find themselves in the position of being someone else's prey. Until that night in August when I fought back against Charlie and my mom's attempt to take me back to Northside, I had always frozen.

I didn't look at K.C.'s face when she came to my desk, picked up my right hand, shook it, and said, "Pardon me." I sure didn't watch her curtsy. I peeked at her after she had passed me, though, and noticed how she kept pulling at her shirt, as if it was getting tighter and tighter. At that moment, I hated Coach Griffin for showing off his power as the authority figure in the classroom. I sensed K.C.'s feelings of helplessness, and rage gurgled inside me.

When she had performed her "act of contrition" for everyone in our class, K.C. sat at her desk in the front row, reminding me of, well, *me* when I lived with my mom and Charlie and I'd have to sit on our brown imitation leather sofa—I called it *the sticky leather seat of doom*—and listen to Charlie tell me what a waste of flesh I was. Even though

K.C.'s back was toward me, the way her body curved in on itself told me that she was in that same mental place of waiting for the hell to end.

◇

I saw K.C. sitting by herself at lunch, and I joined her. Didn't ask whether I could sit down; I just sat. "Why aren't you eating?" I asked. "It's my job to see that you get fed, remember?"

"Not hungry," she said, her hands visor-like around her eyes. I heard her sniff and could tell she was crying.

"Hey, I'm sorry about the way this morning went. I was just in a shitty mood," I said.

She covered her face with her hands and sniffed loudly. I picked up a napkin from my tray and tapped her hand with it. She took it and wiped her eyes. "Thanks. Me, too. I—hey, that lady in the office? Ms. Brown? Jesus, I felt like I'd stepped into another dimension or something. Is she for real? I mean, those glittery things on her toes and . . . man, that accent!"

"Ah, Marvella's okay; she's just country." I pushed my tray toward K.C. "Have some of my nachos, okay? They're one of the less disgusting items on the menu."

She said in a shaky voice, "Seriously, I'm not hungry. I think I'll be sick if I eat anything."

"Okay," I said and, noticing Z.Z. exiting the serving line, called out, "Z.Z.! Hey, sit over here!"

Z.Z. looked my way, but when she saw that it was me, she turned the other way.

"Shit," I said.

"What?" K.C. asked.

"Oh, my best friend's pissed at me."

"Your day sucks about as much as mine does, huh?" K.C. sniffed again and swiped at a stray tear. Her fingernails were covered in black polish, but it looked like she had been picking it off.

"I guess." I spied Roxanne Blake and Kevin Cooper. "Roxanne! Come over here!"

Roxanne nodded and turned back to Kevin. She jerked her head toward our table, and Kevin followed like an obedient puppy.

When Roxanne was ten years old, her parents were killed in a car crash that threw her through the windshield. She was left with a jagged scar that cuts diagonally from the left side of her upper lip, across her lips, then sideways and down across her cheek and jaw on the right side of her face. She's also only four feet, six inches tall. When people see her with Kevin Cooper, who she met in summer school, they do a double take.

Roxanne failed her seventh-period English II class last year because the other kids in her class were so cruel to her. She skipped it every day and went home early. The first time she ever had friends was when she, Z.Z., and I met and became tight in summer school.

"Hi!" Roxanne said to K.C. and introduced herself and Kevin.

"Hey," K.C. said. I watched her face to see how she was going to react to Roxanne's scars up close. Her eyes widened a bit at first, but she covered her shock.

"Oh, my God," Roxanne said, "I felt so sorry for you this morning. Coach Griffin is such a douche."

Kevin nearly choked on his burger and said, "Roxy—not so loud!" He looked around to see whether anyone else had heard. He took another bite and said through his food, "I don't wanna run suicides till I puke, if you don't mind."

"What's a suicide?" I asked, since I've never thought of running as a way to off myself.

"It's basically a run that you start at one end of the field; run a quarter of the way downfield and run back; turn around and run half the field and back; turn again and run three-fourths of the way, and then you run the whole thing again. Oh—and you have to touch the ground every time you turn around, too." Kevin chugged his chocolate milk in one big gulp and took another bite of burger.

"He'd make you do that because of what someone else said about him?" K.C. asked in disbelief.

Kevin dipped a French fry in ketchup and crammed it into his mouth. "You bet your ass he would."

"Wow. What an asshole," K.C. said.

Kevin ducked, as if he could make his huge body less visible by doing so. "Shut up, will ya? And it doesn't help being part of the Summer School Seven."

K.C. arched an eyebrow. "Summer School Seven?"

I named and held up a finger for everyone in our summer school class. "We were all in my stepmom's English II class for summer school, and . . . " I told K.C. about the big stink T.W.'s parents—Coach Griffin and his wife—had made about *Ironman.*

"Yeah, and Coach is major-league pissed about T.W.

quitting football. He was supposed to be our star running back. Coach told us we'll have practice twice a day until we win again." Kevin leaned down and whispered, "He's outta his fuckin' mind. He's never been like this before."

"The coach's own kid quit the football team? Jesus," K.C. said.

"Don't do that, either!" Kevin said.

"Don't do what?" K.C. made a face.

"Take the Lord's name in vain, for Christ's sake," Kevin said.

"Did you mean to do that?" I asked him.

"Did I mean to do what?"

"You said not to take the Lord's name in vain and then you—" I nodded at him and made the "come on" motion with my hand.

"Huh?" Kevin asked, his brows furrowed.

"Never mind." I shook my head at him.

"Oh, Kevin, relax." Roxanne placed a tiny hand on his massive arm. "So, K.C., what does *K.C.* stand for?"

"Her first name's Krystle—" I said, and K.C. shot me a look. "Isn't it?"

"So what's the 'C' for?" asked Roxanne.

K.C. picked up one of my nachos and studied it a moment, then set it back down. "I don't tell anybody my middle name." She picked up the nacho again, held it sideways in front of her face, and observed, "The facsimile of melted cheese on this chip is not moving—at all. Scary." She slid the chip into her mouth, then turned around to see the wall clock. "What time does the bell ring?" As if on cue, it began ringing.

"So where are you headed next?" I asked her.

She pulled her schedule from her pocket, unfolded it, and said, "English III. That classroom is actually inside the building, right? Not in a portable like Mr. Manners' room? That's why I got lost."

"Way-ell . . . " I imitated Marvella's twang. "Would yew li-ike ay tooo-er gahde?"

K.C. smiled at me. "Sure. That'd be cool."

It probably seems obvious to say that our English III class is different from the summer school English II class. At the start of the school year, I was really excited about us all being together again because I just assumed it would feel the same as English II.

I didn't take into account that the class would be a lot bigger than the Summer School Seven and that some kids would bring preconceived notions about what Bev was like based on what they had heard or what their parents thought about her after the whole *Ironman* scandal. Those kids seemed to be looking for things about her to tattle about.

And then there's the drill-and-kill workbook that Mr. Walden insisted—through Marvella, of course—that Bev use. Every day of our first marking period, we trudged through sentence revision exercises. Bev made it fun, although the way she did it sometimes gave the tattletales something to jot down on the lists they kept of what happened in class. It drove me up the wall. I was very protective of Bev, and my anxiety was tripping the switch that engages my mouth before I activate my brain.

"Ashley, you're going to create problems for me if you don't control your mouth. I don't need you to be my guardian or to try to stop the notes those kids are taking about what's happening in my classroom. I can handle it, honey. I'm a big girl, and I've been teaching a long time."

"Yeah, but it's not your fault that every time we diagram sentences on the board and you ask for a subject with an adjective, Dub shouts out, 'Drunk Uncle Cletus'! Don't you see Pam Littlejohn making that face and scribbling notes in the back of her spiral notebook?"

"Well, don't you think it's better than always having *brown dog* for a subject and an adjective? I mean, that's soooo boring," Bev said.

"Arrrrgggggghhh!" I groaned, putting my head in my hands.

◌◌◌

As we walked into English, K.C. followed me to Bev's desk, where my stepmom was emptying boxes of books. "Bev, this is K.C. Williamson. She's from . . . where are you from?" I asked K.C.

"Houston," K.C. said.

Bev offered her hand to K.C., and they shook. "Nice to meet you, and welcome to Patience. I'm Mrs. Asher." She scanned the room and pointed. "There's an empty desk there . . . and one over there, too. It's your choice." She went back to unpacking books.

"Come on," I said, pointing to the empty desk next to Z.Z.

"I have exciting news, guys!" Bev announced right after the tardy bell rang. She held up one of the paperbacks she'd been unloading from the cardboard box. "After six long weeks of drills about drunk Uncle Cletus and brown dogs, we're taking a break from the workbook. Today, we're going to start our first book of the year."

"Is it a Chris Crutcher book?" Kevin asked.

"No, Kevin. I tried, but I couldn't get his books put on the approved books list, so we won't be reading one of his."

I glanced over at Pam Littlejohn and noticed she had flipped to the back of her spiral notebook and was scribbling in it. I sighed, and in my mind, I heard Dr. Matt say, *Good sigh, Ashley.*

"So what are we reading, Miss Asher?" Roxanne asked.

"*Farewell to Manzanar*, by Jeanne Wakatsuki Houston and her husband, James Houston. You have two weeks to read it and then we'll start discussing it."

"What's a Manzanar?" T.W. asked.

"Manzanar was the name of the internment camp where Jeanne Wakatsuki Houston and her family were sent when Jeanne was seven years old. It's a true story, a memoir of her time there."

"Sounds boring," Kevin said. "Can't we just read another Chris Crutcher book and not tell anybody?"

"Kevin. Look around you, man," Dub said.

Kevin did so, and his face fell. "Oh. Yeah."

Bev ignored the stink eye that Kevin and Dub were

giving the tattletale kids and read the book's back cover to us: "Jeanne Wakatsuki was seven years old in 1942 when her family was uprooted from their home and sent to live at Manzanar internment camp with 10,000 other Japanese Americans. *Farewell to Manzanar* is the true story of one spirited Japanese American family's attempt to survive the indignities of forced detention and of a native-born American child who discovered what it was like to grow up behind barbed wire in the United States."

"Why did they have to go live in an internment camp? And what's an internment camp, anyway? It sounds like a prison or something," I said.

"That's basically what it was, Ashley. Internment camps were prison camps where some Japanese Americans were forced to live during World War II," Bev said.

"Here? In the United States?" T.W. asked.

"Yep," Bev said.

"Nah, that can't be right," T.W. said. "America doesn't do things like that."

"America certainly *did* do that, T.W. It's one of our country's dirty little secrets," Bev said.

"Well, there had to be a reason. They must've done something wrong," Pam Littlejohn said.

"Oh, yeah. And there were weapons of mass destruction in Iraq, too," I said, my acid tongue unable to resist.

"There were? I thought they didn't find any," Kevin said.

"That's the point, Kev—they didn't! You're—you're just playing dumb, right?" T.W. asked.

But Kevin's expression was blank.

"Ashley, T.W., and Kevin, let's stay on topic," Bev said. "After Pearl Harbor was attacked on December 7, 1941, the American government became concerned that Americans of Japanese ancestry might be spying for the Japanese government. Here, I'll show you the chronology."

Bev placed a copy of *Farewell to Manzanar* under the document camera. "See? 'December 7, 1941: Surprise attack on Pearl Harbor by the Japanese . . . February 19, 1942: President Roosevelt signs Executive Order 9066, giving the War Department authority to define military areas in the western states and to exclude anyone who might threaten the war effort.' "

"Could you say that in English, please?" Kevin asked. The class laughed.

"Sure," Bev said. "What it meant was, if you were living on the West Coast of the United States—closest, relatively speaking, to Hawaii and Japan—and you were of Japanese ancestry—not just if you had been born in and emigrated from Japan but if you were born here in the United States and were as little as one-sixteenth Japanese—you were removed from your home and relocated to internment camps farther inland. See? It says, 'By August 12, 1942, the evacuation was completed. 110,000 people of Japanese ancestry were removed from the West Coast to ten inland camps.' Two-thirds of those people were American-born U.S. citizens."

"But that's not fair!" Z.Z. said. "Just 'cause they had a Japanese family tree doesn't mean they helped the Japanese bomb Pearl Harbor."

"That's one of the things we're going to look at as we read this book," Bev said.

"Are there any swear words in this book?" Pam asked, her pen poised.

"No, Pam. There are no swear words in *Farewell to Manzanar*. And yes, before you ask, it's on the district's list of approved books. Any other questions, before we read the foreword?"

"What about dirty stuff? Any dirty stuff in there?" Travis Hager asked.

Bev's eyes got larger for a moment. "Noooo, unless by *dirty stuff* you are referring to the way the Japanese Americans were treated by their own government."

"I meant sex," Travis said, sounding disappointed, and the class laughed. He grinned and worked his eyebrows up and down.

Pam Littlejohn bent over her notebook, and I bit my tongue so I wouldn't yell at her. It wasn't like Bev said the word *sex*, but Pam would probably edit that little factoid right out of her report.

"What religion were they?" asked Marcus Merriweather.

"Wh-what? What religion were *who*, Marcus?" Bev asked.

"You know, the Japanese—"

"The Japanese *Americans*, you mean?" Bev asked as she walked over to Marcus's desk and stood next to him, her arms tight across her chest.

Breathe, Bev, I thought. *Don't forget to breathe.*

"Yeah," he said and leaned back in his chair, his hands folded across his bulging stomach. "I mean, maybe they were being punished if they weren't God-fearing people.

Like when Hurricane Katrina hit the Gulf coast and when the Twin Towers fell, you know—"

I couldn't stand it any more. "Marcus! What difference does it make what religion they were? They were taken from their homes and placed in prison camps for no reason other than their race. Doesn't that strike you as, you know, fu—I mean *wrong*?"

Marcus shrugged. "I'm just saying—"

Roxanne chimed in: "And where do you get off saying that Hurricane Katrina was God punishing those people? My great-grandmother lost her home in Mississippi, and she goes to church every Sunday!"

Marcus maintained his serene smile, hands clasped atop his belly. "All I'm saying is—"

"What? What are you saying, Marcus?" My heart was pounding in my ears, and I was shaking with anger. I was surprised at how furious a class discussion was making me.

Bev made a "T" sign with her hands, signaling for a time-out, and calmly said, "Don't answer that, Marcus. Ashley, go get a drink of water. Let's start the book, okay? And Marcus, when we have finished reading it, if you still think that their religion had anything to do with why Jeanne Wakatsuki's family was relocated to Manzanar, I'll give you a whole class period to explain it."

After class, I caught up with Z.Z. at her locker. "Hey, Z.Z. Didn't Marcus piss you off? He's such an asshole!"

She wouldn't look at me; she just kept digging through

her locker. "You know what's not fair, Ashley? What's not fair is that I was as nervous about the trial as you were. I helped you practice that statement. I was there for you. I'm your best friend—at least I thought I was—and you blew me off all weekend. I was so worried about you."

I touched her arm. "I'm sorry, okay?" But there was an edge in my voice. I didn't feel sorry; I just wanted the tension between us to go away. I tried playing on her sympathy. "My mom . . . turned her back on me again."

"Oh, well. Speaking of family trees," she said, still not looking at me.

"What?"

"Cutting people off. I guess you learned from the best," Z.Z. said. She grabbed a book and shoved it into her backpack, then slammed her locker door and walked away.

"Yeah? Well, fuck you, too, Z.Z.!" I yelled, not realizing that Mr. Walden was standing behind me.

"Miss Asher! To my office! Now!"

"Oh, shit," I said, as my Monday went from bad to worse.

⁂

"Whatcha need, Ashley?" Marvella asked as I walked past her on my way to the wooden bench outside Mr. Walden's office. I didn't answer her.

I sat down and ran my finger over the words carved into the armrest. *Walden = priklus wunder.* Those words were on the bench the first time Bev brought me to Patience High School, the morning after CPS removed me from my mom's home and placed me with my dad. I wondered why Mr. Walden didn't have the bench sanded to get rid of them.

"Why are you sitting there?" Marvella called from her desk.

"I'm in trouble," I croaked. My throat felt like someone was choking me, and I knew that if I said any more, I'd start bawling.

"You? *You're* in trouble?" Marvella wiggled her way out of her chair and stood over me. "What did you do?" she hissed.

Mr. Walden swung the office door wide and charged through it. "I'll handle this, Marvella. You get back to work."

Marvella did not return to her seat but instead took a step back from me and stood there, hands on her hips.

Mr. Walden glared at me and pointed to his door. I rose from the bench and trudged into his office. He pulled the door almost closed behind me and remained in the hallway. I heard him say to Marvella, "You are *not* to tell Bev about this. Do you understand me, Marvella? Bev is not to be disturbed. I will handle this as if Ashley were any other student."

While I waited for him to come in, I looked around. His office, apparently, was a place where wildlife go to die. Taxidermied animals stared blankly from the walls; a catfish hung above Mr. Walden's university diploma. He'd made a makeshift ruler out of the diploma frame so visitors would know for certain that the catfish was fifteen inches long. Next to the fish, a small picture frame held a yellowed newspaper photo and article. I stepped close to it and saw that the photo was of Mr. Walden—he actually had hair in the picture—and the catfish, just after he'd caught it. The caption read, "Terry Walden snapped this sucker out of Lake Palestine, July 13! Water moderately clear, temperature 82–88 degrees. Caught on crawfish."

The mounted head of a deer had a baseball cap on its head between the antlers. The cap read, "Fish *tremble* at the sound of my name!" A pair of hip waders were draped over an umbrella stand, a fishing pole stood in one corner of the office, and a pair of hunting boots peeked out from under Mr. Walden's desk. A long board lay across his desk calendar; a rattlesnake skin, covered in tire tracks, was stretched out over it.

Mr. Walden came in and closed the door. "I see you're admiring my wife's handiwork. Have a seat."

"Your wife killed that snake?" I asked as I sat down in the small wooden chair across from him. The legs wobbled a little, and I glanced down to see that they were uneven. They'd been shortened, and I felt like I was peeking at Mr. Walden over the edge of his desk.

"Oh, yes! It was in the paper and everything. She and the kids were driving home from Walmart, and she swerved to avoid what she thought was a rock in the road. That 'rock' uncoiled and struck at the passenger side of the minivan, so she went back and rolled over it five times, just to make sure it was dead." He smiled at me.

I was surprised that he was being so nice. "So, you're going to hang it—that snake—up in here, too?" I tried not to make a face, but I guess I did.

His tone abruptly changed. "Oh, do you have a problem with that, Miss Asher?" His elbows were on his desk, and his index fingers touched so that his hands resembled a gun—one that was pointing at me.

My voice high, I said, "No! No, sir, no problem." My chest was tight, and I forced myself to take a breath in and then let it out slowly.

Still pointing at me, he said, "Are you allowed to use that kind of language at home?"

"Do you mean the word *no*?"

Mr. Walden sneered at me and leaned back in his chair. He stroked his jet black goatee with one hand and studied me. "Oh, so that's the way you want to play it, is it?"

I felt as if I'd missed something and bit my lip, my mind zooming backward, trying to figure out what he meant. *Oh. Duh.*

"Ooooooh, you mean what I said to Z.Z. in the hallway, right?"

He said nothing but made a face as if he had smelled something bad. I realized he was waiting for me to tell him whether I was allowed to curse at home. Well, yes, I am. But I wasn't about to tell him that. I didn't want to lie, but I didn't want to make more problems for Bev, either. So I shook my head and murmured, "No."

"I don't believe you, Miss Asher; do you know why I don't believe you?" Without waiting for me to answer, he said, "Your parents clearly have no problem with children using profanity, or else Bev would not have chosen the novel she used this past summer. Have you ever counted how many times the main character said the word *asshole*?"

"No, sir, I—"

He gestured at the mounted catfish and his ballcap-wearing buck. "Do you know why I have these animals mounted on my walls, Miss Asher?"

"Because you . . . like looking at dead things?" I shrugged and looked at my feet.

He slammed his hand down on his desk, and I jumped a foot. "NO!" He stood up and came at me. I instinctively drew my knees up to my chest and wrapped my arms around my knees.

His face contorted in rage, and I got the feeling that he was mad about a lot more than just me saying the F-word in his school.

I lowered my head and closed my eyes as he stood over me; through gritted teeth, he said, "You see that fish? I fought that fish. He didn't want to give up, and he fought me until I broke him. You see that deer? I conquered that deer, Miss Asher. I tracked and I stalked it, and I pursued it through the forest. And then I killed it."

His face was inches from the top of my head, so close that I could feel his hot breath. I started crying softly.

Whoosh . . . filled my head. Then he grabbed my shoulder and shook it. And I was so out of it, I thought Mr. Walden was Charlie.

"Stop crying!" he said through gritted teeth. "Stop that crying right now!" He dug his hand into my shoulder and neck as he tried to pull my head up so I'd have to look at him.

But I just burrowed farther down inside myself, like the time Emma had an armadillo cornered in our back yard and it started digging straight down into the earth.

Mr. Walden kept trying to get a better grip while I curled myself up, trying to fend him off as puzzle pieces of Charlie trying to turn me over in my old room raced through my mind.

Then I heard a rapid knock on the door; it flew open, and Bev stormed in. "What are you doing, Terry?" she demanded.

"This is an administrative matter, Beverly!" Mr. Walden spat.

I remained in lockdown and held my breath to try to stop the sobs that were rocking my body. I was trembling all over.

"Get your hands off her!" Bev said, and I felt Mr. Walden's claw-like grip release me. I locked my head against my shoulder, blocking his hand from returning. "Get out!" Bev ordered him.

"But this is my—"

"GET OUT!"

"This is *not* over, Beverly!" Mr. Walden said, but I heard him leave, slamming his office door behind him.

The door reopened, and I smelled Marvella's Chantilly perfume. "Is she okay, Bev?"

I slowly opened my eyes but did not release my grip on my legs. Bev touched me, and I cringed.

"Ashley, it's okay now. It's okay. Sit up," she said matter-of-factly. But I didn't move. My breath was hot in the little space against my thighs.

Marvella babbled, "Oh, Bev, I should've come for you when this first started, instead of waiting a few minutes. I'm sor—"

"Ashley, take a breath," Bev said firmly. She laid her palm against my back. "I want to feel you take a breath. Come on, Ashley. Do it."

At last, I inhaled slightly.

"Through your mouth, Ash. Sit up, and let's take some breaths."

"Come on, sweetheart, you can do it," Marvella said.

Finally, I uncurled myself, sort of like one of those stop-action movies of a butterfly emerging from a cocoon.

"Marvella, get someone to cover my classes the rest of the day, please," Bev said. "Ashley and I are leaving as soon as I get my things."

"You got it," Marvella said. I heard the rustle of her skirt and felt the coolness of her hand when she patted my shoulder as she walked out.

Bev had me sit in the nurse's office behind the privacy screen while she retrieved her purse from her classroom. She told Marvella that she didn't want Mr. Walden to know where I was, if he asked. I'd never seen Bev so stoic before or seen her so businesslike and formal with everyone.

A couple of kids saw us as we were leaving. I must have looked pretty bad, because they asked Bev, "What's wrong with Ashley?"

Her arm tight around me, she replied tersely, rather than in her usual friendly way of talking to students: "She's not feeling well, and I'm taking her home."

We walked rapidly to the car, where Bev unlocked my door. She helped me on with my seat belt—my hands were shaking too hard to do it myself—then closed my door and quickly got in behind the wheel. She started the car and drove in silence until we stopped at a traffic light, and then she exhaled as if she had been holding her breath for a long time.

"What happened?" She shook her head, not looking at me, and I got scared.

"Tell me what happened, Ashley!" She hit the steering wheel in frustration, and I crossed my arms over my chest and started curling in on myself. Turning my head away from her, I closed my eyes.

"Why were you in his office in the first place?" Bev asked. Then the light turned green, and the car behind us honked.

She asked me again, with an edge in her voice. "Huh? Talk to me, babe. Why were you in his office? Were you in trouble?"

I opened my eyes the tiniest bit and watched the fields and pastures go rushing by. I didn't want to confess that the out-of-control mouth she'd been warning me about had finally landed me in hot water.

CHAPTER 6

"He did *what*?" David asked from beneath the truck he was working on.

"Yeah. I can't believe it either, David." Bev shook her head and continued pacing back and forth next to the old black Chevy, stepping over David's legs each time she reached them.

"Bev, there's gotta be more to the story than Walden just up and takin' Ashley to his office," Frank said from the mustard-colored recliner next to me.

I was perched on a ladder-back chair in such a contorted position that I looked like someone had stood a twisted pretzel on end and told it, "Stay." Anxiety filled me from head to toe as Frank gave me a sideways look and raised his eyebrows.

"What'd you do to end up in there, Ashley?" he asked.

"I said the F-word in the hallway," I mumbled, my arms crossed over my chest and my head down.

David slid out from under the truck on his rolling creeper. "Huh? I couldn't hear you. What did you do?" He sat up and dragged the back of a grease-covered hand across his forehead. Bev yanked a paper towel out of a box on the hood of the truck and handed it to him. He wiped his forehead with it, then wadded it up and tossed it in the trash. "I'm waiting, Ashley."

"I . . . got in a fight with Z.Z., and I said, 'Fuck you' to her. I'm . . . sorry."

Bev calmly said, "Sounds like you need to be apologizing to Z.Z., Ash, not us. What were you two fighting about? The track meet you wouldn't get out of bed for?"

I sighed and rolled my eyes, shook my head, and stared at the ancient Coke machine on the far wall of the shop.

"Was that a response?" David asked.

I bit my lip and continued staring, crossing my feet at the ankles and hunkering my body down until it felt like my back was the shape of a turtle's shell. I sighed again and thought to myself, *Good sigh, Ashley.*

Frank heaved himself up out of the raggedy old recliner. "Well, break time's over. That tractor's not gonna find its own oil leak," he said, then shuffled out of the bay door into the waning afternoon sunlight.

David shook out a newspaper section to unfold it, laid the paper across the seat of the recliner to keep from dirtying it, and sat down heavily in it. Field mice nest in the springs of the recliner, and I watched to see whether any panicked residents would race out when he sat down.

"Ash, could you look at me, please?" David said.

I dragged my eyes away from his chair and forced myself to make eye contact with my father.

"Thank you," he said softly. Bev stood an orange crate on end to make it a stool instead of a table, then sat down between David and me.

She exhaled loudly, and I said, without even thinking about it, "Good sigh, Bev." She regarded me with raised eyebrows but didn't say anything.

"Honey, what's goin' on with you? Talk to us. Please," David said.

"What do you want me to say?" I shrugged and looked at my lap. "I cussed in the hall at school, and Mr. Walden heard me. I'm sorry I got into trouble."

"Well, here's the thing, Ashley," Bev said. "I've been trying to talk to you about your mouth getting away from you lately. Like today, in my classroom, with Marcus—"

"That guy's an asshole, okay? He's a goddamn jerk who thinks that his way of thinking is the only way, and I can't stand him!"

David broke in, "Okay, that's fine, you don't have to like him. But you can't keep losing your temper and shooting your mouth off. If you're going to break the rules at school, you have to face the consequences. Regardless of what you're going through right now with your mom—"

"My mom has nothing to do with this, David. As far as I'm concerned, she's dead!"

"Well, you didn't act like this before the trial," Bev said. "You—"

"So now that you're stuck with me, you wish I'd leave. Is that it?" I sprang off the chair and looked down at Bev, my upper body still twisted. I hated that I was starting to cry and swallowed a frustrated scream.

"What are you talking about?" Bev asked, making a face. I read her expression as hatred, yet I knew I was wrong. I just couldn't seem to shut up.

"Oh, yeah, that's just great, why don't you just give me a detention or something while you're at it?!" I knew I wasn't making sense or being reasonable, but I didn't care. My hands unclenched enough that I could dig my fingernails into my upper arms. I screamed, "I know you hate me! Just go ahead and say it, Bev—you hate me!"

She stood up and tried to reach out to me, but I stumbled backward. "Honey, why would you say that?" she asked.

"You were mad at me in the car! Do you think I couldn't tell how mad at me you were? Like how mad you are now?" I was blubbering, snot was flowing, and that made me even angrier at myself.

"Ashley, sit down. Calm down, and let's just talk, okay?" David said.

"Oh, yeah, right. I saw the way you looked at me! You don't want me, either! You think I need you to tell me what a worthless piece of shit I am?"

Bev sat and put her head in her hands. David sighed, rolled his head back on the recliner's headrest, and stared at the ceiling. The only sounds were the wind blowing through the bay doors, the birds in the shop's rafters, and me sniffling when the snot started pouring onto my upper lip again.

I started to turn and walk out of the shop. "We're not through talking about this, Ashley. Come back here. Now," David said in a no-nonsense voice. I'd heard him talk to Ben that way, but not me—until now. I froze in place, still facing the bay door.

My upper arms throbbed, and I was surprised when I glanced down to see that I was still digging my nails into my flesh. I released my arms; then, clenching my teeth, I clawed at my neck, driving my nails into my skin from my jaw line to my collarbone. Then I immediately dug them in again, even harder and with more fury than before. I focused all my energy on trying to rip my skin. I felt as if rage was swallowing me, and behind my tightly closed eyes, I saw red.

My mother's words from the courtroom—*"Ashley would probably keep up with the lying"*—boomed in my mind. My chest felt tight; I knew I was holding my breath, and although I kept clawing and scratching myself, it didn't hurt at all. I was numb, yet I was panicked with the desire to hurt myself.

I did not realize that Bev was behind me, and when she touched me softly on the shoulder, I jumped; then I locked my fingernails into my upper arms again. Bev said nothing, but came around in front of me. Her eyes widened when she saw what I was doing to myself, and she looked past me to David. Something in her gaze must have alerted him because suddenly he was there, too. I was now sandwiched between two people I was sure hated me as much as I hated myself.

"Ashley, what are you *doing* to yourself?" Bev asked softly. She tried to pull my hands away from my upper arms, but I held onto myself even tighter. I felt David's enormous rough hands on mine, and he easily broke my grip. He held my hands tightly in his own and bent down, his face close to mine

"Look at me, Ash," he commanded.

My eyes closed, and I shook my head. I couldn't do it.

"Look at me," he said again. I felt his breath on my face. Softly, he said, "We know you're hurting and angry. We're here to help you. We love you! Do you hear me?"

I had to take a breath now. I gasp-coughed and started crying. I immediately thought of how ugly I look when I cry and tried to hide my face from them, but there was no place to hide.

No closet, no pine wardrobe, no place to hide from the hurt.

&

I didn't go to school the next day. My neck was covered with jagged lines from clawing the shit out of myself, and my forearms were bruised and swollen. Bev took the day off, and I think she and David were afraid I was going to try and off myself or something. They called Dr. Matt and told him I'd wigged out and made an appointment for later that morning.

David and Bev had their own hour-long session before I went in. I guess I was putting them through so much that the usual ten or fifteen minutes before my appointment wouldn't do it this time. I tried to read a magazine, but I couldn't concentrate. I was worried about what Dr. Matt was going to say about what I'd done to my neck and arms.

A lady came in with two kids, a teenage boy and a little girl. The boy, who I guessed to be about fourteen, looked angry. He scowled at the woman, but she didn't seem to notice. He wore oversized jeans, an enormous hooded sweatshirt, and Vans shoes. He plopped down on the sofa next to me, then took two throw pillows and stacked them between us, constructing a wall. That was fine with me.

The girl was decked out from head to toe in pink, from her ruffled headband to her ballet slippers. She looked like she'd come straight from her dance lessons. She planted herself at a child-size table, put her chin on her hands, and stared at the boy.

The woman sighed heavily as she wrote out a check and folded it. She offered it to the boy, but he ignored her as she repeatedly waved it at him, trying to get him to take it. Finally, she tossed it onto his abdomen, where he left it. She opted to sit on a hard wooden bench, withdrew her checkbook and a small calculator from her purse, and appeared to be figuring her bank balance. She looked toward the boy and shook her head, frowning. He didn't seem to notice her, engrossed as he was in finding just the right song on his iPod. He inserted his ear-buds, leaned back, and closed his eyes as heavy metal music blasted.

The inner office door opened, and Dr. Trevino, Dr. Matt's wife, said, "Hi, Ian."

I glanced at Ian and noticed that he had turned his iPod off when Dr. Trevino came in. He waved at her and gave a small smile.

"Wait here just a few minutes, Ian. Margie? Would you please come in for a few minutes?"

The lady looked surprised. "I-I'm not his mother, Doctor. I'm his stepmother. Usually his father brings him, but—"

"I know, but I'd like to visit with you for a moment, if that's okay," Dr. Trevino said, smiling.

"Oh. Well, I guess so. Um, Halle, come on," the woman said. The little girl was at her side immediately.

"No, Margie; Halle needs to wait out here," Dr. Trevino said firmly, her smile ever-present.

"But—who'll watch her?"

Dr. Trevino gestured to Ian. "I'm sure Ian won't mind keeping an eye on her."

Margie said, "*Him*?" The look on her face showed that Margie didn't like Ian much. Halle whined and buried her face in the small of her mother's back.

"We'll just be a few minutes," Dr. Trevino said reassuringly. "It'll be fine."

Halle stuck out her lower lip and sat down hard on the child-size chair. She crossed her arms and narrowed her eyes at Ian. Margie looked worriedly from Halle to Ian, but she followed Dr. Trevino and closed the door behind her.

Ian reinserted his ear-buds, and once again, metal music pounded the sides of his head. He leaned his head back and closed his eyes.

I doubt Margie even had time to sit down in Dr. Trevino's office before Halle was standing in front of Ian, hands on her hips. "I want a drink of water," she demanded.

Ian, eyes closed, did not respond. Halle pinched his cheek, and Ian sat up. "Ow! Cut it out, you little shit!"

"I'm telling!" Halle yelled.

Ian sighed loudly, rubbed his cheek, and leaned back again as an extended drum solo rumbled from his ear-buds. He closed his eyes.

"I'm tel-ling," Halle sang, daring to put her face right up next to his. She poked him in the forehead with a tiny frosted pink fingernail, and I noticed Ian's arms move ever so slightly through his oversized jacket. He sprang forward and stood up, and in doing so, his shoulder caught Halle on the chin. She flew back and landed square on her butt. Her eyes grew huge and her mouth dropped open, but no sound came out at first. Then she began shrieking and screaming for her mother.

Ian looked horrified. "Oh, my God, Halle, I'm sorry. I'm sorry. I didn't mean to—"

The inner office door flew open, and Margie came barreling out, followed closely by Dr. Trevino. Halle ramped up the volume and pointed at Ian. Through sobs that anyone could tell were fake, Halle choked out, "I—didn't—do—any-thing—to—h-h-h-himmmmm!"

"What did you do?" Margie yelled at Ian. "What did you do to her?"

"Margie, I'm sure that there's a reasonable—" Dr. Trevino said from the doorway, but Margie wasn't hearing it.

"I told you! I told you I couldn't trust him with my baby!" Margie pointed at Ian and railed, "He's bad! I told you—he's just bad! The worst day of my life was the day his mother died and he came to live with us!"

"If you'll come into my office, I'm sure we can—" Dr. Trevino spoke calmly, but I noticed that she wasn't smiling any more. I looked at Ian. He sat on the sofa with his arms crossed, staring into space. His eyes were full of tears, and he wasn't even trying to keep them from running down his cheeks. He still had the ear-buds in, but the cord dangled freely. His iPod was on the floor where it had landed when he stood up.

"No! No more! I've been telling his father for months

that this is a huge waste of money! His problems are costing us money that could be spent on more important things!"

"Margie, this is a discussion we should be having in my office," Dr. Trevino said firmly, moving to stand in front of Ian as if to protect him from his stepmother's words.

I had assumed my usual "Oh, shit" position of curling in on myself. With Ian on one end of the sofa and me on the other, we probably looked like the poster children for Fucked-Up Teenagers.

"He's not my child! He's not my child, and I don't know what to do with him! I can't take his anger any more!" Margie yelled at Dr. Trevino, then stepped past her and assailed Ian directly. "You! You have to go someplace else. You're destroying my marriage and the life that your father and I had before you moved in! Everything was fine until you came along! I'm telling him tonight, Ian. It's either you or me and Halle. He can't have it both ways. Now stand up, give Dr. Trevino her check, and we're leaving."

Ian looked like an animated corpse. He had no expression on his face at all. He held out the check to Dr. Trevino, but when she tried to talk to him, Margie interrupted.

"No! No more talk! We're leaving. Period." She grabbed Halle's hand, and they walked briskly to the front door. Ian took a few steps after Margie, then stopped and looked back at Dr. Trevino. He raised his hand in the tiniest of waves, then turned and followed Margie out the door.

Dr. Trevino was turning to go back to her office when the inner office door opened and David, Bev, and Dr. Matt emerged. They all looked questioningly at Dr. Trevino, but she made a quick exit.

Bev looked beaten down, and David's eyes were red from crying. He shook Dr. Matt's hand and said, "Thanks, Dr. Matthews."

I stood up, but Dr. Matt said, "I'll be with you in a few minutes, Ash," and closed the door softly behind him.

Bev told me, "Your dad and I are going to go pick up a pizza for dinner, but we'll be out here waiting for you when you get out of your session, okay?"

A feeling of gratitude for Bev being the way she is filled me up so much that I thought I would burst. "I love you, Bev," I said, hugging her tightly.

She hugged me back and murmured into my hair, "I love you too, Ashley. We'll get through this together. I know we will."

❧

I should have known better than to expect sympathy from Dr. Matt. No friendly "How's it going?" from him this time.

"Well, I can see for myself what you did to your neck. Let me see your arms," he demanded.

I sat on the edge of the chair I always sit in, my back so rounded that my shoulders were nearly touching in front of me. I stared at my feet and didn't even bother wiping away the tears running down my cheeks. I made no effort to comply with his instructions.

"Show me, now," he said. "And sit up, Ashley. You're not four years old, so stop acting like you are."

I slowly sat up and pushed back one sleeve, then the other so that he could see the pattern of bruises and crescent-shaped stabs on my arms.

Dr. Matt rolled his chair closer to mine and looked closely at the injuries I'd inflicted on myself. He abruptly pushed his chair back and rose out of it, then strode to his bookcase and picked up a teddy bear. "This is what you're doing to yourself," he said as he took a pair of scissors and mimed cutting gashes in the teddy bear's neck and arms.

I pulled my sleeves down, crossed my arms, and went into lockdown in my chair.

"Look at me!" he yelled.

"I am!" I said, glancing at him, then quickly lowered my eyes to my feet again.

"I said, look at me!" His face was all red and contorted in rage. He set aside the scissors and pounded the teddy bear, then drop-kicked it across his office. "This is what you're doing to yourself!"

I forced myself to maintain eye contact with him and meekly said, "What did that bear ever do to you, Dr. Matt?"

He sat back down and growled, "I'm not amused. There is nothing funny about what you're doing." He crossed his arms and stared at me until I began to squirm. After what seemed like forever, Dr. Matt rose from his chair and retrieved the teddy bear from the floor. He cradled it in his arms like a baby and stroked its head, then put the bear up on his shoulder and rubbed its back as if it were a baby.

I watched him and felt a smirk growing on my face, seeing a grown man being so tender with a stuffed animal. He turned to me and handed me the bear as if it were a real baby.

"Ashley, this little bear has not been taken care of like it should have been. Hold this poor little thing the way you'd want to be held."

I imitated his tenderness for a moment before I noticed a loose string on the bear's nose. I picked at it; then I saw that the bear's fur was matted on one arm and I pinched it, trying to make the fur stand up.

"What are you doing? Why are you doing that?" Dr. Matt demanded.

"It's—there's—it's not—its nose has a loose thread," I said, not looking up from trying to pull the string off the bear's nose.

"*Stop it!*" He snatched the bear from me and drop-kicked it again. "That's what you're doing. I didn't tell you to pick out the imperfections, Ashley. I told you to hold the bear the way you would want to be held."

"I'm sorry, I just feel stupid holding a teddy bear like that, okay?"

"*Not* okay!" he said, and picked up the bear from the floor again. He sat in his chair and settled the bear in the crook of his arm as if it were a baby. We sat, he with his bear and me with my wounds, until the silence was more than I could take.

"So . . ." I said.

"So?" he shrugged.

"So what's the deal with the bear, again?"

"We'll talk about it when you sit up straight and relax your shoulders," he said.

I did so, sighing heavily and rolling my eyes.

SLAM! Dr. Matt held his hand above his desk, poised

to hit it again. "Don't you roll your eyes at me, young lady!"

"I'm sorry!" I said sheepishly, curving my spine over again. He cleared his throat, and I sat up straight, but I crossed my arms tight across my chest. I glanced down and noticed that my sleeves weren't even, so I pulled the right one down to match the left one.

He waited for me to look him in the eye, and then he said softly, "You're treating that bear like your mom treats you, Ashley. That bear is not good enough for you the way it is, and your mom treats you the same way."

Dr. Matt waited for a response; I didn't have one. I looked at my sleeves again, as if by magic they might have become uneven in the past thirty seconds. They were still even, but I tugged at them anyway. The teddy bear sailed past me and landed face-down on the floor by my feet.

"Have at it, Ashley. Maybe you can stomp it while it's down, treat it like your mom's treating you."

My chest felt heavy, and my throat tightened with the effort to not let out the sob I was stifling. A tear rolled down my nose and tickled the tip of it. I didn't just brush it away—I clawed at it and growled savagely.

"Why are you doing *that*?" Dr. Matt asked.

I shook my head vigorously and shoved my sleeves up, studied my forearms a second, then pushed my fingernails into their undersides as hard as I could, trying to scratch right through to my veins.

Dr. Matt rolled his chair next to me and said, "You feel like screaming right now, don't you?"

I bent at the waist and ground my top and bottom teeth

together, making a noise that I don't think I even realized was coming from me. The pain was intense, and I dragged my nails from the crook of my elbow down to my wrists along the long blue veins.

He yelled, "You feel like screaming, don't you?"

I squeezed my eyes tightly, trying to stop the tears, and nodded.

Bending down to my ear, he commanded, "Well, god-dammit, scream, then! Sit up and SCREAM!"

I didn't just sit up; I stood up. I might have even stood on the chair; it all happened so fast that I can't remember. But it *felt* like I was standing on a mountaintop, screaming with every cell in my body. When I opened my eyes (and, apparently, closed my mouth), Dr. Matt had rolled his chair away from me.

He was wearing a smile that stretched from ear to ear. He applauded enthusiastically, pumped his fist in the air, and said, "YESSSSSSSSS! Good scream, Ashley!"

I looked down at my hands in surprise. They were re-laxed. I wasn't digging my nails into my forearms. I felt like a tight knot that had been untied. I breathed in deeply and released the breath slowly.

I looked at the bear on the floor and knelt down, picked it up, and sat down with a loud sigh. I laid the bear on the desk beside me and pulled my sleeves back down over my throbbing forearms, making sure the cuffs were even.

"Ashley, look at your arms."

"I don't want to," I said, picking up the bear instead.

"Please, just do what I asked you to do," he said.

I sighed, pushed up my sleeves, and made a face at the mess I'd made.

"What did you do just a few minutes ago, when I told you to scream?"

"I . . . screamed," I said, looking up at him. "Very loudly."

"Yes, but you've been screaming a lot longer than that," Dr. Matt said.

"No, actually. I've never—"

"Trust me, Ashley, you've been screaming for at least as long as you've been treating your skin like a scratching post."

I started to roll my eyes but caught myself. "You've lost me."

"You've been expressing how helpless you feel. Instead of screaming, you've turned the rage you feel at your helplessness into ripping yourself up. I have one question for you. . . . Ready for this?"

I exhaled loudly and bit my lip. When Dr. Matt asks me if I'm ready for a question, I've learned that it's going to rock my world. *Oh, well, why not?*

"Sure," I said, not feeling at all sure that I was.

"How's it working for you?"

I rubbed one eye and said, "Huh?"

"How's it working for you? You told your mother what Charlie was doing to you, and she didn't act on your outcry. Hell, she even blamed you for it. That motherfucker broke your arm and went to trial for it, and she was still on his side. You said he raped you—said it under oath on the witness stand—and she *still* chose him over you. She *still* says you're a liar," he said as calmly as if he were reading a grocery list.

"Please, stop. Please, Dr. Matt, I can't take this," I begged. I clutched the teddy bear to my chest with my left hand and rubbed hard at the green smudge on his desk with my right index finger. He took a sip of water from his mug, and I started to relax, thinking he was through. I was wrong.

He set the mug down and continued, "She's not going to change, Ashley, and there's nothing you can do about it. You cannot force her to become who you wish she would be, and it's eating you up inside."

"But she *has* to," I said. "She's my mother; she *has* to love me."

"That woman is not a mother," he said simply. "She's not. In one of our first sessions, I told you that the job of parents is to love and protect their children. It's not your fault that she chooses not to do that for you."

We stared at each other for a moment, and I felt a whimper deep inside me grow into sobs. An emptiness in the pit of my stomach was moving into my chest, and I hugged the bear with both arms. I bent my head over its ears and stroked its back with my fingers.

Dr. Matt came to me and put his hand on my shoulder. "Ashley, that little bear is lovable just the way she is. She always has been, even if she has loose threads and matted fur. You, darlin', are lovable just the way you are. You always have been, whether your mom acted that way or not."

My shoulders shook, and I couldn't stop crying. He placed a box of tissues on my lap and said, "Ashley, I'm very proud of you. You did a lot of hard grief work today. I know it wasn't easy."

145

I managed to nod behind a handful of tissues. I stood up and handed him his teddy bear, breathed in and out as deeply as possible, and discovered that, as much as I wanted them to stop, my tears kept falling.

❧

First thing next morning, Mr. Walden met Bev and me as we came into school. His eyes widened at the sight of me, but he quickly recovered. He held open the door for us and gave us a cheery "Good morning, ladies!"

"Good morning, Mr. Walden," Bev said, again assuming the professional veneer she'd worn when she'd walked me out to the car a couple days before. I remembered Mr. Walden's last words to us: "This is not over!" and felt myself die a little on the inside.

"And how are you two on this fine autumn morning?" he practically sang as he gestured for us to follow him into the office.

"Are you feeling all right?" Bev asked flatly.

He laughed. "Of course I'm all right!" Then, suddenly serious, he took her by the elbow and tried to pull her closer. She dug in her heels, and I nearly ran into her. He leaned into her and said, "Mrs. Asher—Bev—may I please see you and Ashley in my office? It won't take long."

Bev took a step back and said, "Of—of course, Terry. Come on, Ashley."

My stomach felt like it was going to fall right through the soles of my feet. Mr. Walden held open the main office door and said, "I'll be right with you, ladies. Please make yourselves comfortable in my office. I brought doughnuts for you!"

Something caught his eye, and he assumed his usual scowl, took a step into the foyer, and yelled at Travis Hager, who'd just walked in wearing his coyote-head hat and the matching skin rug. "Mr. Hager! Halloween is not until Saturday!"

Travis didn't stop, and Mr. Walden took off after him. Bev and I exchanged wide-eyed looks.

Marvella called out from her desk, "Good morning, ladies! Beeea-utiful day, don'tcha think?"

Bev said, "All right, what's going on here?"

"Whatever do you mean?" Marvella asked with a smirk.

"Did you put something in Terry's coffee this morning, Marvella? He's acting way too nice, especially in light of what happened the last time we were here."

"Me? Never!" Marvella grinned. She heaved herself out of her chair and casually ran a long, pumpkin-colored fingernail along the edge of her desk.

"Come on, spill it," Bev said. "Did he finally get the school board to agree to fire me? That'd make him happy—"

Marvella pulled Bev and me into a huddle and said in a loud whisper, "Maybe *someone* called Trini Cooper and told her they'd *heard* that Mr. Walden had lost control of himself and manhandled a female student in his office with the door closed. . . . Maybe."

Bev's jaw dropped; mine did, too.

Bev finally sputtered, "Kevin Cooper's mom, Trini? The reporter for the *Patience Press* who leaked the *Ironman* scandal to the Dallas paper, so that all hell broke loose?"

Marvella nodded and spoke rapidly. "Trini called Mr. Walden and asked him whether he'd like to comment on the matter!"

I finally regained my voice. "But who called her, Marvella?"

Bev and Marvella gave me a look. *Oh. Duh.*

Marvella looked past us to the foyer. "He's coming!"

Bev and I scurried to Mr. Walden's office and sat down.

CHAPTER 7

Mr. Walden sat behind his desk and held up a box of doughnuts for us. "Please, help yourselves. I hope you like chocolate with sprinkles."

"I don't care for anything, thank you." Bev sat back in her chair and folded her hands in her lap.

Mr. Walden tried to hand me the doughnuts. "Um, no, no . . . thanks," I said, trying to imitate Bev's relaxed appearance. The chair wobbled, reminding me of when I was balled up and Mr. Walden was trying to pull up my chin. My stomach clenched, and my shoulders crept skyward.

Mr. Walden smiled, but it looked like he was in pain. He glanced down at his folded hands and grimaced. "I—I called you in today because, well, I've thought about—the way I-I handled the, uh, the situation—and—" he looked up at the ceiling as if the words he was trying to find were somewhere up there.

"I—" He raised a finger in the air. "I cannot, *cannot* condone the language you used in the hallway, Ashley—"

"And you shouldn't condone it, Terry. My husband and I have spoken to Ashley about her choice of words, and we understand that she faces consequences," Bev said.

"Well, I appreciate that, Bev. I do. However, because Ashley has never been in trouble before and I'm sure this was an isolated incident, was it not?" He raised one eyebrow at me.

Bev nudged me with her elbow, and I said, "Oh! Oh, yes, Mr. Walden. It—it won't happen again. I'm—sorry."

"Good, I'm glad to hear that. I hope that we can all just let bygones be bygones and not bring up—or discuss—this incident with, well, with anyone, and I mean absolutely no one. Can we agree to do that?"

"I'll consider that, Terry." Bev stood up, and I did, too. "I do have your assurance that you will never touch a student like that again, then?"

Mr. Walden looked like he had been hit in the face with a brick. "Yes, yes, of course. I'm . . . sorry." He smiled weakly.

"Then I'll tell my husband that there's no need to visit with you today. Thank you for the apology, Terry. It means a lot," Bev said and then ushered me out of his office ahead of her.

"I hope you realize that just because you're not being punished for what you did, it doesn't make it okay to do it again," Bev whispered to me when we were almost to her classroom. We rounded the corner and found Z.Z. waiting at Bev's door.

"Oh, my God! Did Mr. Walden do that to you?" Z.Z. blurted.

I grimaced and covered my neck with my hand. "No," I said. "This was all me."

"Tell you what, girls. I'm gonna run to the teacher's lounge for a Diet Coke." Bev unlocked her door and pulled it open for us. "You two go on in. Maybe you have some stuff to work out? I'll lock my door so nobody comes in and bothers you."

"Thanks, Miss Asher," Z.Z. said.

"Yeah, thanks, Bev," I said.

We settled on an old love seat in Bev's classroom library area. I picked up a book and started paging through it, then set it down and forced myself to look Z.Z. in the eye.

"Z.Z., I'm sorry for what I said to you the other day. You're right. I have been cutting you off. You didn't deserve the way I treated you."

Z.Z. took my hand and held it. "Yeah, well, I talked to my granny about what happened, and she set me straight for not trying to understand where you're comin' from right now . . . with your mom, you know, the way she is and all the stuff that happened—to you."

She looked away and said, "I made that stuff with Pam more important to me than it should be. I shouldn't be worryin' so much about what she's doin' or not doin'. Granny told me I need to be the best I can be, and trust the Lord to take care of the rest."

"Yeah, well, good luck with that," I said with some

bitterness, then wished I could take back the words. Sometimes I forget that not everybody has trust issues with God. I shook my head and said, "So are we friends again?" I squeezed her hand.

"Girl, we more than friends, we sistahs!" She hugged me, then abruptly sat back and said, "Oh, Ashley! Guess who was askin' 'bout you yesterday?!"

"Hmmm, I don't know, Marcus Merriweather? What did the backwoods redneck Bible-thumper say?"

"Nooooo, silly! Joshua Brandt! At practice!" She worked her neck side to side, closed her eyes, and snapped her fingers as she danced from the waist up to music only she could hear.

"What, did he wonder why you set a new personal best since I wasn't there to slow you down? Or did he just miss the sound of someone blowing chunks behind Old Blue?" I sat back and crossed my arms, then winced.

She stood up, still doing her dance moves. "I think he was worried about you. Word got around about what you looked like when Bev was taking you home early the other day."

I put my head in my hands. "Oh, great. Just great. And now I've got these." I gestured to the scratches on my neck, threw myself back, and closed my eyes. "I wish I had a shirt that, like, came up to right here," I said, indicating my eyebrows.

We heard Bev's key turn in the lock, and Z.Z. held out her hands to me. I took them, and she pulled me up and put her arm around my shoulders. "Come on, my sistah. Just tell anybody who asks, 'No comment.' That's what Mr. Walden told Ms. Manos when she asked about you after school. I was there."

～

I mostly said, "No comment" and "No, Mr. Walden didn't do this to me" all day long. I guess I could have said, "Well, see, my mom's a selfish bitch, and when I get really angry about that, I think it's a good idea to beat the shit out of myself. So tell me about *your* hobbies." Mmmm . . . no.

～

Joshua Brandt was standing by the door when I emerged from the gym that afternoon. I was wearing one of Bev's old long-sleeved White Rock Marathon road race shirts and a pair of running shorts. A cold front was moving in, and the sky appeared threatening.

"Hey, Ashley!" he said, smiling.

"Hey," I said, quickening my pace.

Joshua took two long strides and easily caught up with me. "Are you okay?" I cut my eyes to the side and could see the concern on his face.

I stopped. "I'm—I'm fine," I said, straightening my neck but trying to cover the scratches with my hand.

"What's that on your—?" he asked, tilting his head. I lowered my hand, and his eyes widened. "Jesus, who did that to you?"

"No com—" I started to say, but he seemed so sincere, I couldn't brush him off like that. I took a deep breath in and let it out slowly. "I—It's a long story, Joshua."

"I'm sorry, I didn't mean to be nosy, I just—man, that looks really painful," he grimaced. Thunder rumbled, and he looked up. "Looks like we may not have practice today after all."

"Yeah, maybe not," I said, grateful for nature's timing. We sat on Old Blue's tailgate.

"Listen, Ashley, I'm inviting the team to my house for a Halloween party Saturday night." He took a folded paper from his back pocket and gave it to me. "I'm hoping you can come."

I unfolded the paper—a simply drawn map. He scooted closer to me on the tailgate. "I live between Patience and Cedar Points, off this road," he said, pointing over my shoulder at the map. "Do you know where that is?" He lowered his arm but kept it right behind me.

"No, but my dad or stepmom will," I said. My heart was racing, and I scooted to the edge of the tailgate to get away from his arm.

He withdrew his arm but kept talking as if I wasn't acting weird around him. "It's not gonna be a big deal. We're just going to order some pizzas and watch old horror movies. No costumes, unless you just want to wear one," he grinned.

"Well, I'm wearing my zebra outfit, as you can see," I gestured to my neck and sort of snorted, then grimaced at my stupidity.

He smiled at me and shook his head. "I'm just—glad you're okay, Ashley."

"Thanks, I—"

Lightning flashed in the distance as Coach Morrison stepped out of the gym and yelled, "Practice is off! You two get in here before you get electrocuted!"

"Great! I hope you'll come," Josh said, hopping off the tailgate. Lightning flashed again, closer this time. He grabbed my hand and pulled me toward the gym.

～

The next day in Human Ecology, Ms. Manos leaned against her desk and said, "The book defines *family* as 'two or more adults related by blood, marriage, or affiliation who cooperate economically, share a common dwelling place, and may rear children.'" She moved down the center aisle of the classroom and scanned the room. "Can anyone tell me what a nuclear family is?"

"Like *The Simpsons?* Homer Simpson works at a nuclear power plant," Kevin said, straight-faced. Everybody laughed. "What?" he asked, genuinely puzzled.

"Thanks for trying, Kev," Ms. Manos said. She strode to her desk, picked up a marker, and wrote on the whiteboard, "Two Parents + Kids = Nuclear Family." She circled it.

"Oh," said Kevin. "That makes no sense to me whatsoever."

Ms. Manos pointed to the circle and said, "*Nuclear family* does not have the same meaning as traditional family. Can anyone tell me what a *traditional family* is?"

Pam Littlejohn raised her hand and said, "It's when the mom doesn't work and the dad does." Then she made a face at Kevin and, in a voice that mocked his, said, "Like *The Simpsons*."

"Right, Pam. But parents who stay at home also have jobs, even though they aren't paid. Marge Simpson works hard, too. Anyone care to guess what percentage of families are traditional, nowadays?"

"Twenty?" I guessed.

Ms. Manos wrote on the board: "8–11% of all families." She turned back to us and said, "Okay, here're some more numbers for you." She spoke as she jotted figures on the board. "According to the last census, 50 percent of children live with natural parents and siblings; 23 percent live in single-parent families, 15 percent in blended families, and 12 percent live with extended families and relatives."

Turning back to the class, she said, "Most of us fall somewhere in there, right?"

Dub raised his hand. "I don't. I live with Kevin's family, and we're not related at all."

"Ah, so you live in a foster family," Ms. Manos said.

"Ms. Manos, you know my last name's Cooper, not Foster!" Kevin interrupted, shaking his head and smiling. "God, it's October and you still don't know my last name?"

Dub sighed and looked at his hands.

Ms. Manos studied Kevin for a second, trying to figure out whether he was kidding around, concluded he wasn't, and moved on. "Today's assignment is a genogram."

She began passing out sheets of white paper as she talked. "On one side of this paper, draw your family. Look on page 79 of your book to see an example of a genogram. It's basically a diagram of your parents, grandparents, great-grandparents, and so on. On the other side of the page, use images only—no words—to draw what a family is. I mean, I want the entire page covered in what a family is. Please use map pencils as well; color is very important when expressing emotions, which are an important aspect of family."

Well, shit, I nearly said out loud. *Do I have to be reminded of my mom every single day?* I turned to page 79 and gave the genogram a hard stare. It was quickly blurred by angry tears. When the bell rang, my paper was still blank. I crumpled it up and tossed it in the trash as I walked out the door.

The scratches on my neck were still visible, but I told myself they were not as horrible as they had been.

Bev took me shopping Saturday morning and bought me a new sweater and some jeans for Joshua's Halloween party. I'm still accumulating a wardrobe, seeing as how I came to Patience with just the clothes on my back. I don't have a lot of experience with shopping, since my mom used to just give me her old stuff. Once a month or so, Bev takes me to the Tyler Mall and we look for bargains and go out to lunch. Sometimes we take in a chick flick that David and Ben wouldn't go see if their lives depended on it. It's fun. I think it's like how having a mom is supposed to be.

I was a mixture of nerves and excitement about the party when Bev and I arrived home around 3 p.m. We found

Stephen and Ben were perched atop large floor pillows in front of the TV, right where they'd been when we left four hours earlier. They hadn't even bothered to get dressed. The answering machine was beeping repeatedly.

"Hey, Ash," Ben said while he kept playing The Legend of Zelda: Twilight Princess. "Z.Z. left a message for you on the machine."

"Why didn't you just answer the phone, Ben?" Bev asked. He ignored her.

"He's almost to the next level, Aunt Bev!" Stephen said.

A musical chime equivalent to "Sorry, you lost" sounded. "Arrrrgggghh!" Ben let out a defeated growl and bowed his head.

"My turn!" Stephen said happily as he took the controller from Ben.

I played back Z.Z.'s message.

"Ashley, I can't go to Joshua's party tonight. I have to stay home and hand out candy," she said in a disgusted voice. A voice in the background said something I couldn't understand, and even though Z.Z. tried to cover the phone, I heard her say, "Well, it's true, you are making me! Yes you *are*!" Into the receiver, she said impatiently, "Anyways, I can't go tonight, okay? Sorry. Bye."

"Aw, man! That sucks. Now I don't wanna go," I moaned.

"What? Oh, come on, Ashley. You'll have fun!" said Bev.

"But the only other girl's going to be Pam," I said, tossing my hair the way Pam does, as if she's posing for a camera.

"Just give it a try, okay? You can take my cell phone, and if you're not having fun, just go into the bathroom and call me to come get you. That way, nobody will know you're bored or want to leave," Bev said.

"Oooo-kaaaaay," I said. I put my hand to my throat, felt the scabs on the deepest of the claw marks, and shuddered. "God, I'm such an idiot," I whispered to myself.

❧

Joshua lives off one of the gazillion county roads between Patience and Cedar Points. Where he lives, like where we live just outside Patience, very few lighted areas break up the miles of asphalt roads running through thick black forests. I'm still pretty spooked from Charlie and my mom surprising me in the dark the way they did, so I don't ever go outside at night by myself.

Dr. Matt's trying to get me to appreciate the cool things about nighttime in the country, like how the stars are much more visible than they were where I lived in Northside, just outside Dallas. But when I'm outside in the dark, my chin tends to be glued to my chest. So I haven't developed much of an appreciation for stargazing just yet—that'd mean actually looking up.

"The map says to turn left at the sign advertising goats for sale, right?" Bev asked.

I flicked on the interior light and double-checked the map Josh had given me. "Yep."

We drove until we saw a yellow sign reading "Goats Fer Sell" and hooked a left onto a gravel road.

After several more miles of nothing but rolling hills and pastures, we saw signs of life or, more accurately, the formerly alive. "Third house past the cemetery?" Bev asked.

I consulted the map again. "Yeah. Says it's the white two-story on the right."

"Then this must be it," Bev said. She pulled up and parked in front of an old, tired-looking farmhouse. Three jack-o'-lanterns, each with a different hideous expression, sat on the porch steps, and it looked like every light in the house was on. I could hear Green Day's "Christian's Inferno" blasting from inside.

"Hmm. Green Day." Bev nodded her head to the beat. "Joshua has good taste in music." She reached into her purse and handed me her cell phone. "Call when you're ready to come home. If we don't hear from you before eleven, we'll be here then, okay?"

I took a deep breath and let it out slowly. "Okay. Thanks, Bev."

"You're going to have fun, Ashley!"

I sighed again and nodded, bit my upper lip, and got out of the car.

"Smile, silly!" Bev called after me. She watched until I reached the front porch, then drove away.

I slid the phone into the front pocket of my jeans and knocked on the door. "Last Night on Earth" was starting up. I knocked again, checked to make sure my shoulders weren't up around my earlobes, took a deep breath, and forced myself to smile through my nerves.

A heavy-set but attractive woman who looked a little older than Bev opened the door. She wore a long-sleeved black sweatshirt with a witch on it. The caption under the witch said, "Witchy Woman."

"I'm so sorry, honey! This music's so loud I can barely hear myself think!"

"It's okay," I said. She held the door open for me, and I went inside.

"I'm Lily, Joshua's mother," she said.

"Hi, Ashley!" Josh came up behind his mom. This time I didn't have to force my smile.

❧

The party was really small. Junior Alvarez wasn't there. He's supporting Moreyma and their baby, so if he's not at school or a track meet, he's working as a dishwasher at *Mi Abuelo's* restaurant. Z.Z., of course, was stuck at home handing out candy to trick-or-treaters. Pam's family does not celebrate Halloween, so she was at her church's "Fall Festival." I have to admit, I relaxed considerably when I found out Pam wasn't coming. And I was glad to see that Dub had brought his girlfriend, Veronica.

The four of us mostly listened to music and talked. Lily tried to keep Joshua's twelve-year-old brother Cody and his friend Robert upstairs with her, but the boys kept coming up with schemes to try and scare us. They failed miserably each time, mostly because they gave themselves away by giggling from their hiding places.

Around nine o'clock, Lily came downstairs and said,

"Cody is driving me crazy, begging me to take him and Robert to the Tour of Terror. Now, I'm sure it's too—what is it y'all say? Lame?" She cocked her head and squinted at Joshua, as if to check her terminology. Without waiting for his response, she nodded and said, "Yeah, I'm sure it's too lame for you guys to want to go, but—"

"Oh, yes! That place rocks!" Dub sprang off the sofa, then pulled Veronica up, too. In a Count Dracula-esque voice, he said to her, "My dear, you don't . . . scare easily, do you?"

Veronica said, "I grew up chanting 'Bloody Mary' in the mirror at midnight with my cousins. Takes a lot more than some people in costumes to freak me out." She looked at me as if she was waiting for my story of bravery. I didn't have one.

"Wanna go, Ashley? It'd probably be better than just sitting around here. Sorry this party kinda sucks," Josh said.

"No, it doesn't," I said. But everybody else clearly wanted to go to the Tour of Terror.

"What time does it close?" Lily asked.

"They don't close until the last person has gone through the woods and come out the other side," Dub said.

"You're sure it's not too scary for Cody and Robert?" Lily asked Josh.

"Awww, Mom!" Cody whined. "Everybody in my class has gone except me."

"And me," Robert volunteered.

"And this is the last night until next year!" Cody put his arm around his mother. "Pleeeeeease?"

Lily rolled her eyes and sighed, "Fine. Load up, y'all. Hope it's not too lame."

We piled into Lily's old Suburban and drove all the way through Cedar Points, past the movie theater, until there were no buildings in sight. I thought about calling home and telling David about the change in party location, but Michael Jackson's "Thriller" was playing so loud on the radio, I knew I'd have to wait until we arrived at the Tour of Terror to be able to call.

"There it is!" Dub yelled above the music. He pointed to an orange glow in the distance. We joined the line of cars at the entrance. Ten minutes later, we parked and lined up with a bunch of other people who were gathered around a large white sign lit by a kerosene lantern.

WELCOME TO THE *TOUR OF TERROR*
ENTER AT YOUR OWN RISK!
EXPECT TO BE GRABBED BY GHOULS!
The Tour of Terror is an interactive experience
that you will never forget!

"Boys, I want you to stay with me," Lily said, taking Robert and Cody each by the hand.

"Mom!" Cody yanked his hand back, wiped it on the back of his jeans, then karate-chopped her hold on Robert. "We're not babies, and it's just for fun!"

"Well . . . " Lily read the sign again under her breath.

"Mom, it'll be fine," Joshua said, shaking his head at her anxiety. "The people who run this thing have been doing it for something like twenty years." He glanced at me and smiled.

I nodded and tried to look like I wasn't freaking out at the idea of being grabbed by "ghouls." I turned away from the others and faked being interested in my surroundings, thinking, *I gotta get outta here!*

I pulled the cell phone from my pocket and turned it on. No signal. *Shit.* I turned it off and turned it on again, then tried waving it around above my head. Still no signal bars. My stomach clenched.

An old man in overalls pulled up on a tractor, hauling a flatbed trailer covered in square hay bales. He smiled and said, "Happy Halloween! Are y'all ready to have some fun?"

"Yeah!" Dub, Veronica, Joshua, and just about everybody else yelled. Cody and Robert emitted the kind of eardrum-bursting screams that only twelve-year-old boys can.

I managed a weak, "Yeah." Lily just said, "Oh, dear."

We climbed onto the trailer and settled ourselves on the hay. Joshua sat next to me, and his leg touched mine. I took a deep breath in and out, then did a shoulder-earlobe check.

Good, good. I can do this. Then it dawned on me: *these people think I'm just like them!* I squared my shoulders and made up my mind that I was going to have fun, come hell or high water.

∾

"Everybody off!" our driver said. He stepped down from the tractor and said, "It was nice knowing you." Lots of people laughed. Lily looked as worried as I was. I just hoped my feelings weren't as obvious as hers.

The grounds of the Tour of Terror appeared to be on fire. From the front gate to the decrepit-looking mansion, fire was everywhere. The roofline was edged with shooting forks of flames, and there were blazing barrels placed near the trail leading up to the building, making the blackness of the woods beyond the trail seem even darker, if that's possible.

Workers on either side of the front doors counted off and let in ten people at a time. I tried to keep count of how many people were ahead of us and how much longer it would be before we had to go in. I wrapped my arms around myself. *Don't think of it like that! You* want *to go in, remember?*

"I heard that the house really is haunted!" a scared-looking girl in front of me said.

"Probably is," Veronica said. She eyed our surroundings, shook her head, and said matter-of-factly, "My cousin Julio haunts *mi abuela*'s house. You put the toilet seat down, and"—she mimed the movement—"Julio don't like it that way. Puts it back up every time. I go to the bathroom in the middle of the night and fall in. Ghosts are real, man."

"Oh, dear," Lily said and looked worriedly at Cody and Robert.

The theme from *The Addams Family* began to play, and the crowd cheered wildly, snapping their fingers at the appropriate times. Joshua whistled and grinned. Then the music stopped abruptly, and a scream filled the air. Immediately to our right, a scaffold was suddenly lit up by a spotlight and a body in a long black cape fell and hung from a noose. The crowd went wild.

Before we'd had a chance to recover from that, snarling surrounded us and someone in a werewolf costume chased a young woman through the crowd. She was covered in fake blood, and her clothes were ripped. She ran in and out of the stunned crowd before disappearing into the woods, screaming at the top of her lungs. The werewolf followed close behind, and the young woman began wailing, begging him to stop, and moaning as if she were dying.

Whoosh . . . whispered in my mind. I gritted my teeth and willed the sound away. *What was it Dr. Matt told me? "You have a choice of whether to give in to the panic. Even when you're afraid, you can fake being brave until you really feel that way. It's your choice: fake it till you make it. Got it?"*

"Got it," I nodded once, saying it out loud.

"Got what?" Joshua asked.

"Um, nothing."

Then we stepped forward in line.

"Seven, eight, nine, ten," the zombie at the door counted off, ending with me. I looked back at Lily and the boys.

"Y'all go ahead," she said. "We'll be right behind you."

"You sure, Mom?" Joshua said.

"We'll take care of her," Cody said, crossing his arms and nodding toward his mom.

Robert said, "Yeah, we got it."

The first stop inside the mansion was Dracula's crypt. Dracula got right up in our faces, close enough that we could smell the burrito he'd had for dinner on his breath. He closely examined the neck of the girl who'd wondered whether the mansion was really haunted.

"Hmmm," he said in his best burrito-tinged Transylvanian accent, "you . . . look like . . . my type." He bent in and actually put his mouth on her neck; she screamed and tried to push him off. Then he lifted his head, stepped back, and told us, "What can I say? I like . . . girls."

Suddenly, a dozen vampire girls ran in from behind us and swarmed our group. The lights flickered on and off as these vampires ran their hands over people's faces and along their necks and upper bodies. I tried to block their hands, but they came at us one after another; then they all exited as quickly as they'd appeared. Then a door creaked open on the other side of the room. Dub, Veronica, Joshua, and I stumbled toward the light, and as we entered the next room, we found a slippery floor and felt blasts of cold air. The walls were icy and damp, and just when my eyes had adjusted, the light went out. Then a black light illuminated a sign that read, "13th Street Morgue."

"Oh, yeah! This part is awesome!" Dub whispered loud enough for all of us to hear. What looked like a body in a steel drawer rolled out from the wall, stopping just short of slamming into Dub and Veronica. She was wrapped around him so tight, there was no space between them. He was grinning from ear to ear.

Next, a man in surgical scrubs and a white lab coat appeared from the shadows, smiled at us, slipped on safety glasses, and pulled on a surgical mask. Then he reached inside the drawer cabinet, yanked out a chain saw, and pulled the cord. The chain saw roared to life, and he began cutting the body on the drawer, showering us with fluids and tissue that sprayed all over us. The gruesome sounds that filled the room were indescribable, and a man next to me threw up.

"Aw, it's just pig parts," Veronica said. Whatever it was, it smelled horrible. Then five doors in the wall opened simultaneously, and the surgeon switched off the chain saw. He said, "Exit by twos. Thank you for coming to the Tour of Terror."

Veronica said sarcastically, "That's it? Some tour!"

The guy flicked a wad of fatty skin off his cheek and said, "The Freddy Krueger–type guy who usually does this has the chicken pox, okay? Anyways, you still have to find your way to the exit. Now get out."

❧

The door Joshua and I chose opened onto a twisting hallway. Organ music blasted from the ceiling, and as we made our way through, the lights became progressively dimmer and the floor increasingly uneven. There were doors lining the hall, but they were locked. As the floor tilted downward, the hallway narrowed and darkened until we had to feel our way along the wall.

"Hey! It's an opening!" Joshua said. "But it's really short and narrow." Holding my hand, he ducked down and moved sideways to get through.

On the other side, the floor continued its steep descent, and the sound of dripping water began and grew louder and louder. It was now completely dark, and we fell onto a conveyor belt moved by huge rollers that carried us along until we heard an evil laugh echoing all around us. Suddenly, it was over and we were dumped outside. I fell right on top of Joshua and immediately scrambled to my feet and crossed my arms over my chest. Remembering my manners after a second or two, I said, "Sorry!" and offered him a hand to help him up.

A blazing barrel was nearby, and shadowy shapes fell out of the building through exits spaced out along the wall. "I'll bet Dub and Veronica are over there," I said, pointing to the figures stumbling around in the dark.

"Oh, they'll be fine," Joshua said, looking around. "But I'm worried about my mom and the boys."

"I'm sure they'll be out soon."

"Yeah, you'd think so. But I just wonder where they'll come out."

~

Ten minutes later, another set of screaming people was regurgitated from the building, but none of the shadows resembled a short, chubby woman with two kids. We walked up and down in front of the five exits and asked people whether they had seen them, and they all remembered Lily and the boys.

"Yeah, those two little kids lost it when that dude started in with the chain saw!" laughed a guy wearing a shirt that read, "Mud makes me horny." He pulled a flask from his pocket and took a swig, then handed it to a girl wearing a *Twilight* T-shirt.

"But did you see them leave the room with the rest of the group?" Joshua asked.

"I didn't see whether they did or not, man. Sorry."

Joshua turned to me. "Wait right here, Ashley. I'm going to go see if I can find them."

"No, Joshua, I don't—" I said. But it was too late. He was already gone.

❧

I pulled the phone from my pocket again and saw that it was 11:15. Bev had told me they'd be at Joshua's at eleven to pick me up, so I held the phone above my head and said a quick prayer to God/Jesus/Allah/Jehovah/Somebody Up There that I'd get a signal. But there was nothing. I nearly threw the phone into the darkness, but I stopped myself and shoved it back into my pocket.

"Shit," I said aloud; I didn't even try to pull my shoulders down from my earlobes. Once again, I crossed my arms tightly over my breasts and wanted to curl myself into a ball on the ground. But I gritted my teeth and resisted the urge.

A tall figure in the darkness moved toward me, waving his arms.

"Joshua?" I tried in vain to focus in on the face, but at once, the figure was upon me. He lit his face with a flashlight under his chin and roared at me. He had wild hair, and to me, in that moment, he looked just like Charlie.

I gasped, ducked, and began running away from him. He grabbed me by the shoulder, and I felt my sweater pull and stretch. Then I jerked forward, and it slipped from his fingers.

He continued yelling and chasing me, nearly catching me again. I didn't focus on anything but getting the hell away from him, even though thorns and brambles tore at my skin, scratching my face and hands. Branches slapped at me, and my right foot caught in a tree root, but I stepped out of it and kept running. A branch snagged my sweater; I pulled at it frantically until it tore. My heart pounded in my ears, and I could hear myself make a sound like a dog whining. Flight was now running this show.

My mind was whirring with images of Charlie tackling me last May, back at Mom's. I'd blacked out, and when I came to, there was bright red blood on my thighs and butt. A thorn pierced my right foot, startling me, and I shrieked in anguish. But I thought I heard Charlie close behind me and scrambled to my feet, forcing myself to charge ahead.

Suddenly, there was no ground beneath my feet; after what seemed like minutes, I landed with a thud in shallow, icy cold water. The shock of it snapped me out of my fog, and at once, I knew that I was in the present and that Charlie was not the one who'd been chasing me.

I felt creek water rushing past me; it was very loud, and I grabbed wildly for a handhold. The sharp point of a branch stabbed my left palm, and I screamed, pulling my hand back. Terrified that I was about to fall off into deeper water, I used my good hand to feel around for the bank. I found it, dragged myself out, then collapsed face-down in the dirt, gasping and sobbing.

I don't know how long it took me to sit up and try to figure out where I was. I looked around for the orange glow of the Tour of Terror but saw only blackness; there wasn't even starlight. I put my hand over my mouth, trying to quiet myself so I could listen for the sounds of people. All I heard were coyotes and owls and some leaves crunching now and then.

I began to shiver, and I pulled my arms out of my sleeves to hug myself under my sweater. My right foot was throbbing now, and I remembered the cell phone. Gingerly working my fingers into my pocket, I pulled the phone out and checked the time: 12:01 a.m. and still no signal bars. I screamed in frustration, but my throat was raw and the scream was hollow—just the way I felt.

I stared hard into the darkness, and my mind was flooded with memories of watching for the early morning light from behind my clothes in my hot closet. I no longer heard the night sounds of the forest. *Whoosh* . . . had taken their place. The last of the hiccups after such hard sobbing finally stopped, and I sat there, completely silent and invisible, in a wordless, unmoving daze.

Suddenly, I heard a car horn; it jolted me out of my disengaged state, and I got to my feet. I listened for a few more seconds and could hear cars on the road. I started making my way toward the sounds, stopping from time to time to check whether they were getting closer or farther away. After several changes of direction, I could see red taillights and began limping toward them.

It was hard to keep my balance on the uneven forest floor with my arms still inside my sweater, and I winced when I forced my arms back into the sleeves. When I reached the top of a hill, the moon came out from behind the clouds, letting me see a two-lane road in the distance. I took the phone from my pocket, closed my eyes, and hoped for a signal.

When I opened my eyes, I saw "6 Missed Calls, 2 Voicemails" and four signal bars. I looked up at the night sky and said "Thank you!" to Whoever Was Listening for Once and called home.

Ben answered. "Oh, my God, Ashley, you are sooo busted!"

"I need to talk to David!" I said.

"He's sooooo pissed; I can't believe you pull—"

"Goddammit, Ben, would you put David or Bev on the phone?"

"They're not here, Ashley. They're waiting for you at that guy's house. You know, where you were *supposed* to be?"

"Is that her?" I heard Stephen say.

"Yeah, she *finally* called," Ben said.

"Does she sound drunk?" Stephen asked.

I hung up on Ben and dialed David's cell.

"Where are you, Ashley?" David said. He sounded angry, and I burst into tears, babbling nonsense. David handed the phone to Bev.

"Now, sweetie, let's try again. Where are you?" She put me on speakerphone.

It took me a minute to calm down enough to tell them that I didn't know where I was, except I knew I was near a road; that the cell had had no signal till now; and that I had been at the Tour of Terror with the others.

"Are you alone now? Are you hurt?" Bev asked.

"Yes," I choked out. "I mean, yes, I'm alone, and I just have some scratches and got jabbed pretty bad on thorns, but at least nothing's—nothing's broken this time."

"Listen to me, Ashley. We're going to find you," David said, no longer sounding angry.

"But how?" I wailed. "It's so dark, and—"

"Because we *will*, Ashley. The phone is GPS-equipped, so you just need to call 911 and they can track your cell's GPS," he said.

Panic gripped me. "But what if I lose my signal again? How will you find me?"

He spoke calmly, slowly. "The GPS will let the police triangulate your location. I need you to call 911 and stay on the line with them. I'm going to call the sheriff's department, too. Don't worry, Ash. We'll find you."

"But what if—?" I was terrified of getting off the phone and losing the connection to him. "Don't—don't hang up on me, pleeeeeeeease."

"Ashley, you're just going to have to trust me. Can you try to trust me, please?"

My chin dropped to my chest. I gritted my teeth; every cell in my body was screaming, *He's leaving you! He's leaving you!* But I whispered, "Okay, yeah, I'll try."

"Good. I'm going to hang up now. I need you to call 911. And—Ashley?"

I took a deep breath and let it out. "Yeah?"

"Once you call 911, stay right where you are. No matter what, don't move; don't go anywhere else. Can you do that for me?"

"Yeah."

"I love you, Ash," David said. "It's going to be okay."

"I-I love you too, Dad," I said—for the first time in my life.

❧

"Ashley, can you hear sirens yet?" the 911 operator asked.

"Yeah."

"Okay, can you see the rescue vehicles?"

"Not yet. Oh—wait! Yeah—I think I see some flashing lights. Yeah! Is that a fire truck?"

"Yes, ma'am, you should be seeing a fire truck, an ambulance, and some patrol cars. We've triangulated your position between cell phone towers. Please hold."

I stood up and started to limp toward the vehicles, then remembered what David had told me about staying put.

"Ashley?" the operator said.

"Uh-huh?"

"Tell me when it looks like the flashing lights are directly in front of you. I'll stay on the line with you until they reach you."

"They sure are moving slow," I said, shifting my weight from the outer edge of my injured right foot back to my left one. I kept hugging myself, as if it would make me feel less chilled to the bone.

"Yes, ma'am, they don't want to take a chance on pas—"

"There! They're right in front of me!"

"Please hold."

The trucks and cars abruptly stopped and cut off their sirens, and I saw bright spotlights turn on and move up the hill toward me. "Ashley, I need you to keep the phone open and hold it up as high as you can. Wave it around with the light facing toward the road and yell as loud as you can. I'll stay on the line with you."

I waved the phone around and tried to yell but choked on my own spit. I cleared my throat and tried again. "HEYYYYYYYYYY! I'M HEEEEEEEEEEEERE! Hey! Hey! I'm here!"

Then the spotlights blinked on and off. I said, "The lights blinked. Do they see me?"

"They do see you, ma'am. They're coming for you now. I'll stay on the line with you."

CHAPTER 8

The paramedics wanted to take me down the hill on the stretcher, but David just picked me up and started carrying me down, holding me tight in his arms. He was so warm, and I felt so safe there; I snuggled up against his chest and breathed in his scent.

Against a background of flashing red and blue lights, David set me down gently and Bev took me in her arms. My shoulders shook with sobs.

A paramedic set down his crash kit and told David, "Sir, if you don't want us to take her in the ambulance, we recommend that you have her evaluated for shock at the E.R. Those puncture wounds on her hand and foot look pretty serious, too. At the very least, she'll need a tetanus shot and some antibiotics."

"Will do," David said.

"Honey, why are you crying?" Bev said into the top of my head.

"You—you're here. You came to g-get me. I just—it means a lot that you tried so hard to find me," I choked out.

Bev bent her face down to mine and said, "Well, of

course we did, Ashley. We love you. That's what moms and dads do."

I nodded, unable to speak.

❧

By the time we got home from the emergency room, it was 4 a.m. Bev insisted that I have a soothing bath before getting into bed, and she even washed my hair for me. I don't even remember putting on my Happy Bunny pajamas that read, "Wake me when the boring stops."

❧

Emma nudged me with her doggy nose. I cracked one eye open and groaned, "What time is it?" She nudged me again, and I rubbed her head, then sat straight up as pain shot through my hand. "Oh, my God!" The bandage reminded me of the night before; I closed my eyes and fell back on my pillows.

Tap. Tap. Tap. There was a knock at my door. Emma yawned loudly, looked at my bedroom door and then back at me. The knock came again.

"Ash, you wanna try wakin' up?" David asked from the hallway.

"Not really," I mumbled.

"Then can I come in?" he asked.

"Well, I'm not coming out there—ever." I yanked my covers over my face.

He came in and sat down gently on the end of my bed.

I uncovered my face to just below my eyes and looked at him.

"So how's Miss Ashley today?" He used his fingers to pull up the corners of his mouth into a smile.

"Ugh," I grunted and yanked the blanket over my head again.

"You can't stay in here forever, you know," he said in a singsong voice.

"Why not?" I moaned.

"Because life goes on. You had a rough night. You—"

I sat up abruptly, the blanket still over my head. "Rough night? Rough NIGHT? David, I freaked out and got lost in the woods. My whole body looks like a voodoo doll. Everybody and their brother knows what a complete spazz I am, and—"

"How's that self-pity workin' for ya?" he asked quietly.

"Jesus, have you been taking lessons from Dr. Matt?"

David sighed. "All I know is, there have been times in my life that I messed up. Like when you were a baby and your mom took you and I didn't even try to stop her."

I threw the covers off but covered my face with my hands.

"And look what I lost, Ashley—what we lost. We lost years that we could have had together, just because I let shame and embarrassment rule my life." David's voice was thick, and I forced myself to look at him. My eyes filled with tears, just like his.

"Yeah, but I'll bet you've never gotten confused about where you were or who was chasing you. I'm crazy, David.

And I don't mean in a good way. I mean," I twirled my finger next to my head in the signal for somebody who is looney tunes.

He pulled my good hand into his and held it gently. "Everybody, Ashley, *everybody* gets lost sometimes, whether it's in their head or out in the world."

"Or both," I said, just on the edge of letting out the sob I was holding in.

"Right—or both," David agreed. He gently tilted my chin up with his finger so I had to look at him.

"I am so . . . grateful that I got a second chance to be your dad, Ashley." Tears ran down his cheeks, and he didn't even try to stop them. "Not everyone gets second chances, you know. But—" He seemed to be trying to choose the right words. "I'm asking you to be kind to yourself right now, to treat yourself the way you'd treat a friend if she'd gone through what you did last night. Would you want your friend to be beating herself up like this and hiding under the covers?"

The knot in my throat was so big, all I could do was shake my head. Emma's moist brown eyes looked like she was crying, too. I ran my finger over her head, tracing the outline of her ears. She shook her head, jumped off my bed, and walked out of the room.

"Looks like Emma's got the right idea," David said. He stood up, rubbed his eyes, and stretched. "So are you gonna get up, or are you gonna sleep your life away?"

I breathed in and out deeply, then sighed. "Well," I said, swinging my legs out of bed and putting my feet on the floor, "I guess I'll—" I stood up and suddenly remembered the hole in my right foot. "Oww—yikes!" I said, sitting down again. David extended an arm to me. I took it and allowed him to help me up. "One way or another . . . " I took a hop-step. "I guess I'm getting up and going on."

Ben actually paused his video game when I hobbled into the den. "Hi, Ashley."

"Hey, Ben. Sorry I yelled at you last night when I called," I said as I reached into the cabinet for a bowl. Lucky Charms: the midday breakfast of champions.

He restarted Zelda: the Twilight Princess but said nothing. I said, "Fine, don't talk to me."

He paused the game but kept looking at the TV screen. "It's okay. I probably shouldn't have assumed you were at a pasture party or somethin'."

I laughed and said in an exaggerated East Texas accent, "*Me*? Sittin' on a tailgate in somebody's pasture, drinkin' some bubba's daddy's beer till I'm shit-faced and stupid? Jeez, Ben, I have enough trouble thinking straight without doing that kind of stuff!"

"So is that guy your boyfriend?"

"Who, Joshua?"

"Yeah."

"No, he just invited the whole cross-country team to his party, that's all." I limped over and sat down on the sofa next to him with my bowl in my lap.

Bev came through the front door, carrying bags of groceries. "Hi, Ashley. Ben? Some help with the groceries, please?"

He moaned, then paused his game and went outside.

"Did your dad go to Frank's to work on the heater?" Bev asked.

I placed my now-empty bowl on the counter. "Yeah."

"Good thing. Now that Halloween's passed, our first freeze will be here soon. Frank's house is so old, they have to resuscitate the heater every year about this time."

Ben kicked the door to indicate that his arms were too full of groceries to open it himself. When I opened it for him, Joshua was standing behind him, equally loaded with groceries. Ben stated the obvious: "Ash? That Joshua guy is here to see to you."

My jaw dropped. I looked down at my Happy Bunny pajamas, then up at Joshua. He said, "Hi, Ashley. I—"

I closed the door in their faces and stood there, frozen. Bev said firmly, "Calm down, honey. Go get dressed." When I didn't move, she took me by the shoulders and turned me toward my bedroom, then gave me a little shove to get me going.

"But—I don't wanna talk to him," I groaned as I hop-walked to my room.

"Ash, you're going to have to talk to him sometime. May as well do it now as later," Bev said. She opened the door and said, "Sorry about that, guys! Hi, Joshua, thanks for helping with the groceries. Come on in."

❧

I looked out the window. Joshua was sitting on the porch swing, and our orange-striped tabby, Orange Kitty, was weaving in and out of his legs. He bent down and scratched her head.

"You'll probably need a jacket. It's pretty chilly out there," Bev said. She placed a pot of water on the stove and added salt to it. When she looked up to find me not moving, she jerked her head toward the door. "Go."

I slipped my hoodie over my head. "Where's Ben?" I asked, hoping to take him outside with me as a buffer.

Bev smiled as if she knew what I was up to. "I sent him to Stephen's to tell the guys we're eating dinner early. Do you want to invite Joshua to stay? I'm making spaghetti."

I looked at her like she was crazy. She grinned at me, then allowed the smile to fade and said in her teacher voice, "Ashley Asher, get yourself out there and talk to that boy. He told me he didn't sleep at all last night, he felt so bad about losin' you."

* * *

I went out on the porch and closed the door quietly behind me. Joshua immediately stood up. "Hey, Ash." He shifted his eyes away from me and put his hands in his pockets.

"Hi," I said and hobbled over to him.

He talked fast. "Ashley, I'm so sorry about last night. I don't know what happened. I couldn't find you—"

I grabbed the chain and eased myself down on the swing. "It's not your fault."

He sat on the other end and said, "Are you . . . okay? I mean, your hand. And—" He pointed. "Your foot."

I wiggled the fingers on my bandaged hand and said, "Yeah. I'm okay."

"I'm glad—That's good." He pushed back, and the swing began to rock. I wrapped my arms across my chest and looked at my legs. He seemed to need to fill the silence. "So did your family build this log house?" he asked.

"Uh-huh."

"Was it really hard to do?"

"Probably. But I wasn't here then." I used my good foot to push the swing, too.

"Oh. So . . . where were you?"

"Last night?" I glanced at him.

"No, when the house was built."

"I lived with my mom in Northside; it's a suburb of Dallas."

"Oh, okay. Well, yeah, that, too. I mean, where were you last night? Where'd you go?"

I looked at him and said flatly, "I don't know where I was. That's why it's called *getting lost*."

He blushed. "Yeah, you're right." He laughed uneasily. "I guess what I meant is, what made you take off like that into the woods?"

I closed my eyes and sucked air in through my teeth. Then I opened my eyes and looked up at the ceiling fans. I watched the blades rotate slightly from the cool breeze, and I hugged myself tighter.

"Are you cold?" Joshua took off his green school jacket. He scooted closer to me and put it around my shoulders. I nodded my thanks, and he moved back to the other side of the swing.

I realized I was holding my breath and exhaled loudly. Finally, I looked at him and said, "I'm—I've got—I—I get scared. Easily."

Joshua nodded at me and said, "Yeah, a lot of people do."

"I mean, I get scared—like freaking-out scared—and this . . . whatever-you-call-it, this ghoul guy came running up at me and got right in my face and screamed."

"Yeah, I know the guy you're talking about. He told me he felt responsible for you running off the trail, but I didn't know what he was talking about. And that's what made you run off? I told you I'd be right back; I had to go find my—"

"I know, I know. Like I said, it's not your fault." I studied the links of the chain next to my face.

"If you didn't want to go to the Tour of Terror—"

"It wasn't that I wanted to go or didn't want to go, Joshua. I just wanted to be like everyone else for once."

"Well, you are; I mean, you're not the fastest runner, but—"

"It's not about *running*! My God, do you know how much I wish that my biggest problem was a sucky *pace*?" I laughed bitterly.

Joshua had never seen the quick-tempered side of me. He swallowed hard; I shrugged off his jacket and pushed it toward him.

Barely above a whisper, he asked, "Well, what *is* it, then?"

"I'm not like other girls," I whispered.

"I know." He took my good hand and held it on top of his jacket on the swing. "That's why I like you so much."

"You don't even know me," I shot back.

He wove his fingers through mine and retorted, "Yeah, I do. I know enough about you to know that you're *not* like other girls. You're not loud or stuck-up. You don't talk shit about other people."

"Well, not to you, I don't. You've never heard Z.Z. and me, we—"

"Why do you have such a hard time believing that I could like you, Ashley?" he asked softly.

I took my hand out of his and pulled my sleeves down, then crossed my arms and looked down. "Joshua, the reason I ran away when that guy scared me was . . . he reminded me of my stepfather."

"So?"

I stared hard at Orange Kitty, who was stalking a cardinal hopping around in the grass. "He did some stuff to me that really messed me up. It's the reason I moved to Patience." Inside my sleeve, I dug my fingernails into my good palm as hard as I could stand, and I watched Joshua for his reaction.

His eyes widened, and he said softly, "I'm sorry, Ash. That really sucks."

I narrowed my eyes at him, surprised that he was still sitting next to me on the swing. I had expected him to take off once he heard me mention Charlie. *Oh, yeah. That's right: I'm the one who does stuff like that.*

"Yeah," I whispered. "It did."

We rocked on the swing for a while longer. Finally, Joshua said, "Those scratches on your neck . . . do those have anything to do with . . . you know . . . what happened?"

I pulled the neck of the hoodie up higher but said nothing. I could feel my cheeks turning red and my throat getting tight.

Joshua said, "Hey, I'm sorry. I didn't mean to—" His words hung between us, and I noticed I was holding my breath. I forced myself to inhale, then let it out in a sigh. We rocked again in silence.

"So I guess you found your mom? Last night?" I asked.

"Huh? Oh, yeah. Yeah, um, Cody and Robert flat-out refused to go any farther inside the Tour, so my mom had to take them back out through the front to wait for us. Dub and Veronica were with them, too. When I went back to get you, you were gone. We searched everywhere. We even had all the ghouls out looking for you. Then the police showed up, said they had things under control, and closed the place down. I wanted to stay, but—"

I burst out laughing.

"What's— You're laughing?" Joshua asked.

"*All the ghouls* were looking for me? That's funny. Even Dracula, with his burrito breath? He was wandering around out there, too?" I glanced at Joshua, who was looking at me like I'd lost my mind. I started laughing again and couldn't stop.

"Jeez, I'll bet the forest looked like a bad horror movie, with all those monsters stumbling around in the dark!"

He smiled the tiniest of smiles. "Yeah, I guess. Sort of."

"Woooo—oooooo!" I jerked around to see that Ben and Stephen had come through the gate from the pasture without us hearing them. They each had their back to us, their arms wrapped around themselves, miming people making out. "Woooooo—ooooooo!" They said again, falling to the ground, giggling.

Joshua stood up and said, "I'm glad you're okay, Ashley." He walked to the steps and watched Ben and Stephen, who'd managed to regain enough self-control to be able to walk toward us without collapsing again. "Your little brothers seem . . . nice."

"Ben's my brother. The other pain in the butt is my cousin Stephen." Stephen stuck out his tongue at me as he and Ben walked right between us and went inside. Within seconds, Zelda was blasting. I heard Bev yell, "Turn that *down*!" and the sound decreased slightly.

"Well, you met Cody, so I guess you know that I get what you're going through."

No you don't! I thought, then realized he was talking about annoying little brothers.

Joshua looked at his feet and said shyly, "Ash . . . I know last night was, you know, pretty much horrible, but . . . would you like to go out sometime? I promise I won't go off and leave you anywhere next time."

"Yeah," I said. "I'd like that."

"Really? That's great!" He held up three fingers in a scout salute and said, "Scout's honor, I will not take you anywhere scary." His smile was so huge, it looked like his face might crack.

"Could you promise me something else, Joshua? Could you promise not to tell anybody the stuff I told you about my stepdad?"

Joshua's smile faded into a straight line, and he looked into my eyes. "I'll never tell anybody, Ashley. I promise."

〰

Monday morning, Z.Z. met me at my locker. She shook her head and said, "Girl, you are a mess. What're you doin', goin' all *Man vs. Wild* when I'm not around?"

"Huh?" I handed her two of my textbooks to hold while I carefully worked my binder into my backpack.

"Dub called me yesterday and told me you got lost at the Tour of Terror." I held my backpack open, and she slid the books in for me.

"Oh. Yeah. Bear Grylls has nothing on me. Didn't resort to drinking my own pee or anything, though, so"—I slashed the air with my index finger—"score one for the home team."

"How was Pam?" Z.Z. made a face, as if just saying Pam's name made her queasy.

"She wasn't there, thank God. She was glorifying pumpkins and scarecrows at her church, as opposed to hanging out with us pagans."

Z.Z. pulled me close in a sideways hug. "So seriously, Ash. You okay?"

I sighed. "Yeah, yeah. Embarrassed, mortified, ashamed—my usual condition. Dunno what this does to me for the rest of the cross-country season, though. I've got a deep hole in my foot, and I can't run until the doctor says it's okay. Sorry, Z.Z."

She clucked her tongue and said, "No worries. I have complete confidence in my ability to maintain our back-of-the-pack tradition. You'll come to all the meets, though, right?"

"Absolutely."

❧

Coach Griffin leaned back in his chair with his feet on his desk and read from the PowerPoint graphic projected on the screen. "Japan began its expansion and power grab by occupying parts of China in the 1930s. Japan took this action because it was dependent on other countries for resources." He moved his feet off his desk, then sat up and put his hand over his heart. "Yet another reason America is a superior country: our commitment to being independent of other countries for what we need."

K.C. raised her hand and spoke up. "We're not completely independent. The United States gets a lot of its oil from the Middle East, and the war in Iraq was about oil, in spite of—"

"Miss Williamson, you are out of line. *Again.* Why you insist on debating every point I make is beyond me." Coach Griffin opened his desk drawer, withdrew a form, and began scribbling on it.

"Yeah—I mean—yes, uh, sir, but I just think it's important to—" K.C. stopped when Coach Griffin held the form up for her. When she didn't come forward to get it, he rose from his chair and placed the paper on her desk, picked up her pen, and placed it in her hand.

"Another detention for insubordination. Tomorrow, 3:45 to 4:30. I have, yet again, checked this box. See this box? It says, 'Teacher requests parent conference.' Just need your autograph on the line with the X."

"But I didn't mean to be—"

"Just sign it," he said tersely as he moved back to his chair. "And Miss Williamson, if your mom or dad—or whoever it is that buys you those Nerveener shirts—does not indicate that they are coming in for a conference, you may expect me to show up at your door."

"It's not *Nerveener*, sir, it's *Nirvana*," K.C. said through gritted teeth as she signed the form, tore off the top copy, and handed the bottom part to him.

Coach Griffin leaned back in his chair again and put his feet on top of his desk. "Want another one, Miss Williamson? I can bury you in detentions through the end of this semester if you want."

"No. Sir."

"Fine, then. The United States was unified by the attack on Pearl Harbor on December 7, 1941. Fortunately, the Japanese plan was imperfect and the United States mobilized for revenge."

❦

After history class, I dragged myself back from Coach Griffin's distant portable classroom, which is almost all the way to the stadium—or maybe I should call it the *shrine to*

191

football. That's why I'd barely slid into my seat in Human Ecology when the tardy bell rang.

Ms. Manos said, "Ashley, I'd like to see you in the hall, please." She followed me out and closed the door behind us. A conversational hum immediately started inside the classroom as she said, "I heard about your weekend. I'm glad you're safe and sound."

"Thanks," I said. "How'd you hear about it?"

"My sister's husband is a deputy. He was one of the people who was called out to search for you. You might remember him. He has red hair and—" She made a face. "He dips snuff."

"Oh. No, I don't remember seeing him."

She put her hand on my shoulder and said, "Ashley, I'm worried about you."

"I'm fine, really. I just have to take it easy for a while."

She shook her head. "It's not that. I mean your grades. But more than that, this isn't like you. I know it's only the second six weeks of the term, but this is *not* the Ashley I saw in the first six weeks—the one who turned in every assignment, usually before class even ended. What's going on?"

I looked at my feet but said nothing.

Ms. Manos leaned in and whispered, "Is everything all right at home? I think I know your mom pretty well, but—"

"Bev's not my mom, Ms. Manos. She's my stepmom," I mumbled.

"Oh! Okay. But I guess what I'm asking is, well, are things okay with your dad? He's nice to you guys and everything, right?"

I burst out laughing, and Ms. Manos looked confused. "You think that David—my dad—might be abusing me, and that's why I look like this?"

She turned red. "I'm not assuming anything, Ashley, I'm just trying to figure out what's up with you. And, well, I *have* noticed the marks on your body—the scratches—and the way you've been acting—"

"*I* did this"—I pointed at my neck—"to myself. My dad would never do anything like that. Not to me. Never."

We could hear the hum inside the classroom growing to a roar. Ms. Manos put her hand on the doorknob but then turned back to me. "I'd like to talk to you more about this, Ashley. I don't want you to fail my class. Progress reports come out a week from today, and if you don't turn in your missing work, there's no way you're going to be able to pass."

"Part of the study of literature is relating the text to ourselves, to our world," Bev said as class began. "Through our study of *Farewell to Manzanar*, I've been asking you to connect your own life and experiences to those of the author—to try to imagine what it must have been like for her, as a child, to have been imprisoned. I found a website that documents the firsthand accounts of people who were sent to places like Manzanar. The gentleman speaking is Dennis Bambauer, whose father was French-Irish and whose mom was Japanese. Dennis was just a six-year-old orphan and American-born, but because he had some percentage of Japanese ancestry and lived on the West Coast, he was interned along with 110,000 other people."

The video showed an older man with glasses relating his experiences as a child who was considered a threat to U.S. security. He told about learning the Pledge of Allegiance at the school at Manzanar. He didn't find out until he was older what the United States' motive was for imprisoning him so young.

After the video, Bev asked, "So what made up Dennis's identity? His eye color? Shoe size? The fact that he was orphaned?"

Marcus Merriweather raised his hand. "What religion was he?"

Bev shot me a warning look, but it was totally unnecessary; I'd decided that until I no longer resembled a scratching post, I'd try to be invisible unless I was with my close friends like Z.Z. or Roxanne.

Bev exhaled loudly and said with a frown, "That again, Marcus? Could you please try to expand your thinking beyond boxing people in because of their religious beliefs?"

"But that *is* my identity, Mrs. Asher. I'm a child of God, saved from eternal hell by the sacrifice of Jesus Christ my Lord."

"Amen! Preach it, boy!" some of Marcus's friends agreed.

Bev plunged ahead with her lesson, ignoring them. On the board, she wrote, "family size, choice of music, food you eat, hobbies, interests, friends, dream profession." She turned around and asked, "What about these? Do these concepts make up your identity?"

"What does this have to do with what the dude in the video said, Miss Asher?" Kevin asked.

"Glad you asked, Kev. In many ways, what you believe about yourself as a result of your childhood history will influence the choices you make as you grow into adulthood. Not only that, but the way you think the world works may be influenced by your experiences as a child."

"I still don't get it," he said.

Bev smiled and said, "Okay, let's try it this way." She went to her computer and pulled up a poem, then projected it onto the screen.

"This poem, called "In Response to Executive Order 9066," was written by Dwight Okita. Dwight's mom was fourteen when she was sent to live in an internment camp. Up until the United States became involved in World War II, his mom lived a typical Japanese American kid's life, with emphasis on the word *American*.

"He wrote this poem after talking to her about what it was like to leave her friends behind and be sent away because of who people assumed she was. He imagined the letter that she might have written after her family received the order to leave behind their everyday lives to report to the camp—which is what our government called a *relocation center*."

Bev read aloud:

In Response to Executive Order 9066
All Americans of Japanese Descent Must Report to
Relocation Centers

Dear Sirs:
Of course I'll come. I've packed my galoshes
and three packets of tomato seeds. Denise calls them
love apples. My father says where we're going
they won't grow.

I am a fourteen-year-old girl with bad spelling
and a messy room. If it helps any, I will tell you
I have always felt funny using chopsticks
and my favorite food is hot dogs.
My best friend is a white girl named Denise—
we look at boys together. She sat in front of me
all through grade school because of our names:
O'Connor, Ozawa. I know the back of Denise's head
     very well.

I tell her she's going bald. She tells me I copy on tests.
We're best friends.

I saw Denise today in Geography class.
She was sitting on the other side of the room.
"You're trying to start a war," she said, "giving secrets
away to the Enemy. Why can't you keep your big
mouth shut?"

I didn't know what to say.

I gave her a pack of tomato seeds
and asked her to plant them for me,
told her
when the first tomato ripened
she'd miss me.

"If I hadn't already told you that Dwight Okita's mom was of Japanese descent, what clues are there about her race in the poem?" Bev moved to the edge of her desk and leaned against it.

"The line 'All Americans of Japanese Descent Must Report to Relocation Centers,' " T.W. volunteered.

"Her last name, Ozawa. That could be Japanese," said Pam.

"When Denise accuses her of trying to start a war, giving away secrets, that's Denise making assumptions about her only because she's Japanese," K.C. said.

"Those are all good points," Bev observed. "Now I want to go ahead and give you your—"

Z.Z. interrupted her. "Why would she call Denise 'a *white girl*'? Why didn't she just call her a *girl*?" She turned to me. "Ashley, do you tell people you're best friends with a black girl?" She didn't wait for me to answer. Shaking her head, she wondered, "Why did it matter to Dwight's mom that Denise was white, if they were best friends?"

"Those are questions with no easy answers, Z.Z. For now, let's assume that until the war broke out, it probably was not important to Dwight's mom that Denise was white. But when Japanese Americans came to be openly viewed with suspicion, their race began to matter very much." She clicked her keyboard, and a poster appeared on the screen.

"This was published in the December 1941 issue of *Life* magazine. See the title? 'How to Tell Japs from Chinese.' How disgusting is that? And Marcus, if you ask what religion they were, I'm warning you now that you won't want to hear what I'm thinking."

Marcus frowned and began thumbing through the Bible he carries everywhere.

Bev clicked off the projector. "Here's your homework assignment: I want you to apply the sorts of questions that I asked about a person's identity to yourselves and to Jeanne, the narrator of *Farewell to Manzanar*. What is it that makes you who you are? Is it your place in your family? Are you the oldest, middle, or youngest? Is it the kind of movies you like? Is it"—she looked pointedly at Marcus—"based solely on your religious convictions? Or is there more to you than that? Identify at least five things about yourself that, in your opinion, make you who you are. Put your ideas into a paragraph, and bring it to class tomorrow."

Great, another assignment from hell. Let's see, I guess I could just list my disorders. . . .

Bev answered the usual questions about how many sentences the paragraph had to be, whether spelling counted or not, could it be printed from the computer, and so forth. Finally, she made the time-out sign with her hands and said, "Open your books, and let's start trying to figure out why this sort of thing happened to Jeanne and people like Dwight Okita's mom."

I hobbled to Bev's classroom at the end of the day. I told myself that I was too tired to even try being a team player by attending cross-country practice, but more than that, I regretted telling Joshua about my past. Being tired seemed as good an excuse as any to avoid seeing him, and I had my hand on the doorknob of the classroom when I heard Coach Griffin in Bev's room. He did not sound happy, and I cracked the door the tiniest bit so I could see inside.

"T.W. was reading this during my class, and I took it away from him." Coach Griffin slapped a copy of *Farewell to Manzanar* onto Bev's desk and crossed his arms.

Bev slid the book off the papers she was grading and carefully straightened them before looking up at him. "And?"

"And? *And?*" He stepped away from her desk, and I could see that for an old guy, he had really muscular arms. For a moment, I thought he might punch Bev, and I held my breath. He pulled a chair from a table and reversed it with a slam before sitting down hard on it. He put his head in his hands, and I reminded myself to breathe.

"Dayton, what's the problem with the book? It's on the approved list, and, my hand to God, there's not one swear word or homosexual in the whole book. Of course," Bev tilted her head from side to side as if weighing her words, "10 percent of the world's population *is* gay, so chances are that one or two homosexuals might have sneaked in. The good news is that back then, people were still too ashamed to be open about it. And it's not—whew, what a relief!—a Chris Crutcher book. So the children of Patience should be safe with this one." She got up and walked around to the front of her desk and leaned against it.

Coach Griffin shook his head slowly; when he finally spoke, it sounded like he was choking back tears. "Can't you . . . leave me with . . . anything, Bev?"

Bev looked stunned. She sputtered, "Wh-What?!"

He jumped to his feet and put his face close to hers. She quickly moved back behind her desk. "What are you talking about, Dayton?"

He slammed his fists on her desk and growled, "You took my son away from me. You managed to undo in one summer school session what I'd built with him over fourteen years!"

She shook her head, then held up her hand and started to speak, but he cut her off.

"No. No! You listen to me. *You* are gonna listen to *me*. The *only* things I care about in this world outside of my family are"—he held up two fingers and used them to count the items—"football and World War II. You stole my dreams for my son. But that wasn't enough, was it?" He snatched up the book and waved it in her face. "Am I supposed to think it's a coincidence that you chose *this* book, out of all of 'em on the list?"

Bev's tone was incredulous. "This isn't about *you*, Dayton. It's a great story and just as relevant in the twenty-first century as it was—"

"Save it, Beverly! I don't want to hear your liberal-progressive-socialist-hippie bullshit!"

Bev crossed her arms slowly and spoke in a tone I'd only heard once before: when she was nose to nose with my mom in the courtroom. "You may leave now."

Coach Griffin laughed at her. "Oh, yeah. You're real brave now that you've got this desk between us, aren't you?"

"Get. Out." Bev's mouth hung slightly open, and she looked like pictures I've seen of this actress from way back named Bette Davis. She was great at playing pissed-off people.

He threw the book at her and turned to leave. I hop-skipped as quickly as I could away from the door and came face to face with Ms. Manos.

"Ah! Just the girl I wanted to see," she said, wrapping an arm around my shoulder as she steered me back in the direction of Bev's room. Suddenly, Bev's door flew open so hard that it bounced off the lockers, and Coach Griffin barreled down the hall away from us, muttering to himself.

∞

"Bev? Is everything all right in here?" Ms. Manos stepped tentatively into Bev's classroom with me still in tow.

Bev was staring out the window; we moved to stand next to her and watched as Coach Griffin, still talking to himself, got into his truck, slammed the door, and tore out of the parking lot. Bev closed her eyes and took a deep breath. "What is it the Frank Costanza character used to say on *Seinfeld*? 'Serenity now'?"

"Yes, but I think it was more like a demand, as in 'SERENITY NOW!'" Ms. Manos said, laughing.

Bev waved her hands in the air. "Yeah. Serenity now!"

She sat down in her chair, then pulled a Diet Coke out of her mini-fridge and handed it to Ms. Manos. She took another two out and gave one to me, then popped the top on hers, sipped it, and said, "This is missing something. I think it's rum."

"I know what you mean," said Ms. Manos as she sat down in a student desk next to Bev's and gestured to me to do the same.

"Bev, do you have a minute? I have some concerns about Ashley."

Bev set her Diet Coke down. "Ash, do you have any idea what this is about?"

I rolled my eyes. "I . . . have a couple zeroes, because I . . . haven't done a couple assignments."

"Really? Gosh, that doesn't sound like you, Ash."

"I know! That's what I told her," Ms. Manos said.

I tried playing two against one. "Yeah, Bev. *Ms. Manos* thought the reason I wasn't doing my work was that David was, like, abusing me or something," I said, punctuating the statement with an incredulous laugh.

I thought Bev would join me in making Ms. Manos feel uncomfortable. She didn't, so I tried harder.

"See, that's, you know, funny, because, you know, he'd never do"—I gulped—"that."

"That isn't exactly what I said." Ms. Manos blushed, so that even her neck was covered in red blotches. "I've noticed the way Ashley's been carrying herself, as well as the scratches on her neck. That, coupled with the change in academic behavior, made me suspect something was wrong at home. I never seriously entertained the thought that—"

Bev held up a hand. "You don't have to explain, Mary Ann. I understand why you'd think that way, and I appreciate your concern. It's a sign of a good teacher that you watch for that kind of stuff."

Turning to me, Bev said, "Ash, tell me about these assignments you didn't turn in."

I sighed. "One was writing a statement of what family means to me. And the other was a genogram of my family on the front with a picture of what a family is on the back."

"Oh," Bev said softly. I looked down and fidgeted with the bandage on my hand.

"Do you mind if I ask what's going on?" Ms. Manos said.

Bev thought a few minutes before responding. "Ashley, is it okay with you if I let Ms. Manos know what you've been dealing with?"

I picked at the bandage where the tape was fraying and nodded slightly.

Bev noticed that her door was ajar, so she got up and closed it all the way. Then she pulled a student desk to face Ms. Manos and me, and sat in it.

"Ashley might be having a hard time with assignments that deal with family because this past May, she was removed from her mother's home after her stepfather behaved extremely inappropriately with her. Anything you want to add to that, Ash?"

I shook my head; I repeatedly peeled the tape away from the bandage on my palm, then smoothed it down again, pressing a little harder each time so that the puncture wound would hurt.

I focused on the pain and allowed *whoosh* . . . to over-take my mind, so I heard only a broken version of what Bev was telling Ms. Manos about my broken arm, the trial, and my therapy, ending with "There's always hope."

I noticed movement out of the corner of my eye and saw that Bev had her hand on Ms. Manos's forearm. I tuned back in as best I could, which isn't saying much. Bev was reassuring my teacher: "You didn't know, Mary Ann. . . . nothing at all wrong with the assignments. It's an opportunity for Ashley to do some more healing work."

I stole a glance at Ms. Manos, who dragged a finger under her eye. Bev reached back to her desk and handed her a tissue. Ms. Manos nodded and tried to smile a little.

"So we know what we need to do," Bev said, slapping my desk once. I jumped and clenched my fists, then re-flexively jerked back in the chair when I felt a sharp pain in my left hand. Bev patted my wrist and gave me a sideways glance.

Ms. Manos sighed and got up from the desk. Bev stood too, gave Ms. Manos a hug, then said, "Thank you for caring about your kids so much, Mary Ann."

Ms. Manos blinked back tears and looked down at me, patted my shoulder, and said, "Let me know if there's anything I can do, Bev. I hope Ashley can get those assignments to me by the end of the week." Then she left.

I waited until the door closed and blurted, "You mean I still have to do them? Can't I do something else, like write a report on, I don't know, something that doesn't suck to think about?"

Bev pulled her purse out of her desk drawer and took out her car keys. "You know, you *do* have a family. There's no reason you can't use your dad's side for the genogram. In fact, it'd be a great way for you to get to know your dad a little better."

The tape around my bandage was now dangling and useless. I stood up and pulled some transparent tape off the dispenser on Bev's desk and wrapped it around my hand. I winced, mentally kicking myself for hurting myself again.

"What about the feelings shit, Bev? Do I have to do the feelings shit, too?"

Bev pulled on her jacket and picked up her Diet Coke. "The feelings shit, my dear, is why Dr. Matt is such an awesome part of our lives."

CHAPTER 9

I couldn't believe my eyes when I walked into Dr. Matt's waiting room and saw K.C. slouched on the love seat's armrest, thumbing through a copy of *Popular Mechanics*. What is a person supposed to say in a situation like this? Fancy meeting you here? Wanna start a crazies club?

She glanced in my direction and dropped the magazine. "Oh." She grimaced. "Hi."

I waved halfheartedly. She picked up the magazine, flipped it open to the center, and lowered her head. The lady I had seen at the gas station on the day of Charlie's trial came out of the restroom and plopped down on the love seat. "Krystle, I told you not to sit on the arm of the couch," she said in an annoyed voice.

K.C. sighed and slid down the armrest onto the cushion. I took her place on the armrest and said to the lady, "Hi. I'm Ashley. I'm one of K.C.'s friends at school."

"You told me you hadn't made any friends yet," the lady said accusingly to K.C. Barely taking a breath, she said to me, "She told me she wanted to go back to Houston 'cause she hasn't made any friends here—"

"Mom, do you mind?" K.C. mumbled and lowered her head a little more.

"Well, it's true. You did say that!" Her mom shrugged at me, as if to say, *What did I say?*

K.C. didn't respond; instead, she just pulled the magazine close to her face and hid behind it.

Beverly came in a few minutes later and smiled widely when she saw K.C. "Hi! I'm Bev Asher, K.C.'s English teacher," she said, offering a hand to K.C.'s mother. "I think your daughter's a really cool person. Wonderful writer—so creative!"

Her mom grudgingly took Bev's hand. "You know, I really didn't think we'd run into anyone we knew here, coming all the way to Palestine for this, um, appointment."

"Oh. I understand. And I assure you, I won't tell anyone at school that we saw K.C. here."

"It's not that I'm ashamed, you understand. It's just, we wanted Krystle—we refuse to call her that ridiculous nickname she's given herself—we wanted her to have a fresh start in Patience, after all the ugliness in Houston—"

"*Mom!*" K.C. said from behind her magazine.

"What?" her mother held up her hands in surrender.

K.C. lowered the magazine and said through gritted teeth, "Shut. Up! Will you *please*?"

"Maybe it's best if we leave you alone right now," Bev said as she took my arm and pulled me up. I moved across the room to the bulletin board and tried to focus on the comic strips and newspaper articles haphazardly thumb-tacked all over it. As a "feelings sponge," I was soaking up the tension between K.C. and her mother.

K.C.'s mother kept babbling. "I guess you're ashamed about what happened in Houston, Krystle, but I'm not ashamed. Anyway, it was just a phase, just experimentation; that's what that lady at the counseling center said."

The *Popular Mechanics* sailed by me and landed behind the long reception counter. K.C. said loudly, *"Mom! Please! I'm walking out of here if you don't shut up!"*

"You're *not* a lesbian, Krystle; you just need to wear something besides T-shirts and jeans. Want to go shopping after this? I saw some cute skirts on sale at Penney's."

"And you wonder why I tried to kill myself!" K.C. roared. She stomped out the front door and slammed it shut.

Just then, the inner office door opened and Dr. Trevino, her ever-present smile in place, said, "Mrs. Williamson? Are you—where's your daughter?"

K.C.'s mom had stood up and started to pull on her coat. "I just don't understand it, Doctor, we were sitting here visiting with her English teacher and her friend—you know, she told me she hadn't made any friends, but here's one right here, so—"

"Where is she?"

"She left. Went right out the door, and I don't know why. I—"

"Would you like me to try to talk to her?" Dr. Trevino said.

"I don't see why she'll talk to you if she won't talk to me. But sure, if you want to try, go right ahead," Mrs. Williamson said. She shrugged off her coat and folded it over the armrest, then sighed loudly as she sat back down.

Dr. Trevino went after K.C. The front door had barely

closed behind her before Mrs. Williamson cleared her throat and said, "Tell me, Ashley, do *you* think Krystle's a lesbian? Because that's what people at her old school in Houston thought." She snorted. "She even supposedly had this—" Mrs. Williamson formed air quotes with her fingers. "*Girl-friend*. Well, we put a stop to that, you'd better believe me. We told her, 'Krystle, enough is enough. We are a Christian family, and what you are doing is an abomination, so you can just snap out of this right now.' "

I looked over at Bev, hoping she'd tell the lady to shut up, but she was pretending to read an *Oprah* magazine that I know she's already read at least twice.

Mrs. Williamson continued talking, and her voice faded until she was talking only to herself. "The damage was already done. We were the talk of our church. Her dad and I nearly split up over it; he was so willing to just look the other way, but I—it's why we moved here—for a fresh start. I was hoping that if we got Krystle away from all that—those—influences . . ."

I felt my shoulders relax a little when she stopped talking. But my relief was short-lived; Mrs. Williamson was just catching her second wind.

"You tell me, Ashley. Do *you* think Krystle's a lesbian? Because we just don't have those people in our family; I've never even known a lesbian in my life, much less given birth to one. I—"

Dr. Matt had opened the inner office door without us hearing him do so. I don't know how long he was there, but he'd heard enough to say politely, "Ma'am, this discussion is inappropriate. You may think your daughter isn't affected by it, but, trust me, she is. I advise you to stop talking immediately."

Mrs. Williamson's mouth hung open in mid-sentence. Dr. Matt smiled past her to us. "Bev, please come in. Ashley, I'll be with you shortly." He shot a warning glance in Mrs. Williamson's direction. She blushed, looked down, and began searching for something in her purse.

Less than thirty seconds after he had closed the door, she sputtered, "The very nerve! Did you hear him talk to me like that?"

I pretended to be engrossed in reading a yellowed article about school bullies that I'd read a few thousand times before.

"What's your name? Ashley? Did you hear me?"

I slowly turned from the bulletin board. "Huh?"

That's when the front door opened and Dr. Trevino came in, followed by K.C. "Mrs. Williamson, I'd like to talk to K.C. first, then I'll call you in."

"Dr. Trevino, her name is not K.C. It's Krystle. Krystle Clarity Williamson. I may not know much, but I do know what I named my daughter after eighteen hours of hard labor and it wasn't mere initials!"

Dr. Trevino smiled and nodded. "I'll let you know when I need to talk to you."

"But—"

"Right," Dr. Trevino smiled. "It'll be about forty minutes or so. You just wait right here and make yourself at home."

"I need a cigarette," K.C.'s mom said as she marched past her daughter and slammed the front door on her way out.

"Bev told me you had a helluva weekend," Dr. Matt said as he closed the door and moved to his chair.

"Did you see it on *Fox News* or was it on MSNBC?"

He gave me a puzzled look.

"You should hear the stories going around about me at school. Everything from alien abduction to being attacked by coyotes."

Dr. Matt nodded, took a sip of water, set the mug down, and seemed to be carefully choosing his words. "How much . . . of your getting lost in the woods . . . do you think was your fault?"

"Huh?"

"Do you think you could have done anything different when you found yourself scared and running into the woods?"

"You're making this my fault?"

"Let's not get sidetracked with blame—"

"But isn't that what you're doing? Trying to get me to take all the blame?" I started babbling a litany of excuses: the guy looked like Charlie; I always run when Charlie is after me; I know very bad things will happen if Charlie catches me, and on and on.

Dr. Matt held his hand above his desk in midair, palm down. He raised his eyebrows and smiled slightly.

I lunged forward and grabbed the edge of his desk. *"Don't slap the desk!* I'm thinking, not spinning!"

A few months ago, when Dr. Matt slapped his desk the first time to jar me out of my mental spin cycle, I just about had to be peeled off the ceiling. It's become sort of a running joke with us now. At first, I thought he did it because he was angry, but he explained that it's aversion therapy, meaning that he wants me to associate spinning thinking with having the shit shocked out of me, so that when I start doing it, I have the memory cue of being startled to help me stop running circles in my mind. If I had a "Top Ten List for Things I Hate to Happen to My Body," the obvious yucky ones would be there, but so would hitting my head, stubbing my toe, and being startled. Once, when Stephen snuck up on me and yelled, "Boo!" I became so enraged that I picked up the cordless phone and threw it at him. Pegged him right on the forehead, too.

After the first few times, Dr. Matt figured out that I was watching for his hand to come down for the slap, so he started abruptly kicking the desk instead. Sometimes I wonder whether, in his quiet moments working on his farm, he bursts out laughing at the memory of the faces I make when he shocks me out of spinning.

∾

"Looks like spinning to me," he warned, then smiled and lowered his hand.

I breathed a sigh of relief and relaxed back into my chair.

"Have you thought about how badly your weekend *could* have gone?" he asked, serious again.

"You mean, besides having wounds in my hand and foot, scratches and bruises all over my body—"

"Yes, but some of those scratches are self-inflicted, don't forget," he said, giving me The Look: that penetrating, blue-eyed stare that could peel paint.

"I know," I sighed, rolling my eyes. "Are you just going to bitch at me for an hour or what?"

He balked. "I don't think I'm bitching at you, Ashley. I'm trying to help you see that your poor impulse control is what got you lost. Did I ever tell you the story about my grandfather and the wasp?"

I shook my head.

"When I was a little boy, I was terrified of wasps. If I saw one, I'd freak out. I guess I'd been stung once, and that was enough to make me panic at the sight of one. One day, my grandpa and I were sitting on his front porch, and a wasp landed on my arm. I started to go into my usual response of screaming and crying and running around.

"My grandfather noticed I was kickin' it into high gear, so he put a hand on my shoulder and quietly said, 'Just wait.' " Then Dr. Matt sat back in his chair, put his feet up on a stool, and crossed his legs at the ankles.

"That's it?" I said. "So . . . what happened?"

"What d'ya mean?"

"Well, did you get stung or what?"

"No."

I sighed and shook my head at him. "So what did you do?"

Dr. Matt put his feet on the floor and pushed the stool away. He leaned toward me and said, "I. Waited."

I nodded as if he was making sense. "O-kayyy."

He rolled his chair closer to me and said, "You need to learn to wait. Did you pause even for a second and tell yourself, 'Hey, I know this guy's not Charlie'?"

I felt my cheeks getting red. I looked down and, in a small voice, said, "No."

"Ashley, we're going to have to work harder on getting you to separate facts from crap. You're going to have to work at staying in the present—and that requires just waiting—inserting even five seconds between your perception of what's happening and your reaction, checking to see whether that's what's really goin' on."

"But if I wait, he might get me," I blurted without thinking.

Dr. Matt rolled back his chair a little. "Who?"

"Char—" I started to say, heard myself saying it, and stopped cold. "Oh, my God, Dr. Matt, I'm crazier than I thought I was."

He shook his head at me. "Ashley, that's the kind of thinking that's going to get you nowhere. Don't go crawling back into yourself right now; we've got too much to do today."

"Okay."

Dr. Matt moved over to his computer and tapped the keys to wake it up. "I'm going to create something called an affirmation to help you pull out of your spins."

"Does it involve beating up furniture?" I asked.

He cut his eyes to me and smiled. He nodded in acknowledgment but said, "No."

A few minutes later, Dr. Matt printed out and handed me this:

*I can't change the past. It is over with. When I
spin, I am making a choice to try to change the past.
I am not going to be abused by anyone. I am safe. I
have everything I need to function well in the here and
now. There will still be times when I have unpleasant
thoughts, experiences, and feelings. The thoughts will
pass unless I do something impulsive to make my life
worse.*

I read over it. "I'm not trying to change the past, Dr.
Matt." I held it out for him to take back and correct.

"Yes, Ashley, you are," he said, folding his arms over
his chest.

"What, I mean—uh—how . . . am I doing that?" Without
out even really thinking about it, I began folding the corners
of the affirmation page down so that the words were covered
up. Dr. Matt leaned over and took it away from me,
then unfolded it and laid it next to his keyboard.

"Well, gee, Ashley, let's see: you're not doing your assignments
signments that have to do with family because you're so
afraid of what that's gonna feel like. You ran away from an
actor at a haunted house, as if by doing so you could actually
ally escape what your stepfather did to you. And Bev's worried
ried that the assignments that go with this book she's using
in her class will put you right over the edge. To me, it looks
like you're on this journey that's like a barefoot walk from
Texas to Alaska, and you're sittin' on a curb waitin' on your
mama to arrive so she can, oh, I don't know, lay some more
broken glass in your path. Or maybe direct you to a dead
end?"

"I don't want her to do that," I whispered. I found my standby "emotional disconnect" object to focus on—the green marker smudge on Dr. Matt's desk—and rubbed at it incessantly. I imagined being able to spread the smudge from one end of the desk to the other, like icing on a cake.

Dr. Matt didn't say anything as I kept rubbing at that smudge like my life depended on it. The silence between us expanded, and I finally stole a glance at him. He was looking through some CDs, then pulled one out and said, "I'm gonna play a song for you, Ash. It's by a Texas singer-songwriter named Tom Russell. Just listen to the words, okay?"

"What's it called?" I was intent on spreading my imaginary green icing all over the desk, even though my finger was still just running over that two-inch smudge.

"It Goes Away." He inserted the CD into his computer, and the first notes began to play. Before I knew it, I'd put my head in my hands and I was crying.

When it ended, Dr. Matt said quietly, "Why do you think I wanted you to hear that song?"

My reply was muffled by my hands and the river of snot that was running out of my face. "For the . . . chorus . . .mainly, I guess."

Dr. Matt silently pulled some tissues out of the box and nudged my hand with them. I sat up and wiped my face. Finally, softly, he said the lines that had made me weep:

> It might take years
> Or a hundred thousand tears
> But someday the skies will clear
> It goes away.

I took a deep, shuddery breath in and let it out slowly.

"I know you can't see it right now, Ashley, but the pain you're in will lessen eventually. It probably won't ever be completely gone; there will always be some sadness associated with your mom."

"But Dr. Matt, she—she has to ch-change. She has to—to w-want to be my mom. She has to—" I was crying so hard, I thought I was going to throw up. "She has to c-care th-that Ch-Charlie did that stuff to me."

He shook his head sadly and said, "That's what I'm talking about, Ash, when I say you're trying to change the past. But you can't, and no amount of refusing to move on with your life is going to make it happen, either. Your mom's handled this situation in a piss-poor way. There's just no other way to say it than 'What a bitch.'"

"Y-yeah," I said, the word sounding hollow in my chest. I ran my finger along the tape on my bandaged hand and picked at the fraying edges, then pressed down on my palm to make it hurt.

"Do I need to drop-kick the teddy bear, Ash?" Dr. Matt asked softly. I snapped my head up, shocked that he'd caught me hurting myself. I shook my head, put my hand in my lap, and tried to not think about it.

I took a breath and blew it out. "How . . . do I . . . stop?"

"Self-harm?" he asked.

I shrugged. "I guess."

"The same way you're going to stop trying to change the past."

"Hmm," I said noncommittally and stared at the Feelings poster on the wall. I narrowed my eyes and tried to figure out which of the pictures of kids depicting emotions was most like me at that moment. But there was no picture of *numb*; I dragged my eyes back to Dr. Matt.

"I want you to live in the present, Ashley. When you do the assignments that have to do with family, I want you to base them on the family you have now, not the family you used to have. When you do Bev's assignments that have to do with identity—which are the ones she's most worried about for you—I want you to base them on what you know about yourself today. And Ashley?"

"Yeah?"

"Anything you write about yourself, I want you to focus on what *you* are doing in the present to overcome your past, *not* what people in your past did *to* you. Got it?"

I scanned the Feelings poster again. *Clueless* wasn't on there, either. Damn.

❧

"Ashley? I'm ready to start the genogram when you are," David called from the kitchen.

"Okay, I'm finishing up the family statement." I reread what I had written: "Family means being safe and people loving you, even when you're having a bad day."

I compared it with my other attempts at defining family: "Nobody comes in your room at night to mess with you." "People can get mad, but it doesn't mean they hate you." "You have an annoying little brother, but it's kind of fun." "You get to keep the dog that wandered up one day." Hmm, which statement sucked the least? I'd have to think about it some more.

"Ash?"

"Coming."

I slid into the chair next to my dad and wrote, "Asher Family Genogram" across the top of the page.

David smiled and nodded. "Good start. Now what?"

"Well, this is what I *do* know," I said as I drew a boxy U and wrote his and Bev's names above it. Then I drew some vertical lines and wrote Ben's and my names below it. Above his name, I drew another boxy U and said, "What are your parents' names?"

He leaned back in his chair, stretched, and clasped his hands behind his head. "My mom's name is Francine Asher, and my dad's name is William . . . I *think* it's William. Just write William and a question mark."

"You don't know your dad's name?" I asked.

"I never knew him, and my mother referred to him as *that rat bastard.*"

I wrinkled my nose. "What about your grandparents?"

He shrugged. "Didn't know them much, either. I do know that my grandmother died right after I was born. I don't think my mom got along with her parents very well. Frank's house is the family homestead; when our grandfather died, he left the house and land to Frank and me. Blew our minds, but hey, we took it."

"Where's your mom now, David?"

"I have no idea. Last I heard, she was in Vegas. That was about, oh, five years ago. She only tries to pop back into my life when one of her marriages goes sour. She showed up one day, apologized for being a shitty mom, and said, 'I want us to have a fresh start. I want to know my grandsons!'

"I was dumb enough to let her into our lives. As soon as she met another guy, she was gone, just like that. She's almost sixty years old and just as immature as the day she had me. Knew the guy about a week and took off with him.

"It nearly killed Frank and me. Couldn't believe we'd been fooled again. None of us needs that kind of person around. The best thing she can do is just stay the hell away, 'cause I don't think she's ever gonna grow up."

"Doesn't it bother you that your mom doesn't act like she's supposed to?"

David sighed and leaned back in his chair. He looked down at his T-shirt, which depicted a farmer on a tractor and was captioned "Dirt Does a Body Good." He rubbed his chin as if he was considering his answer.

"Dad, can you help me with my math?" Ben called from his bedroom.

"In a little while, Ben," David said. He studied my face a moment. "There's a saying, Ashley—'You can't lose what you never had.' Even when my mom *was* around for Frank and me, which wasn't often, she sloughed us off on one relative after another. She was never able to overcome her own selfishness long enough to give us what we needed.

"That's what nearly ate me alive all those years I wasn't there for you: I knew in my heart that I was repeating the same cycle of abandoning my child, but I told myself it wasn't the same thing." His eyes were filled with tears now. "I've told you before, it's my greatest regret, Ash, and I'll spend the rest of my life making it up to you."

I studied the genogram. "What about your dad?"

David tapped the question mark with his index finger and smiled ruefully. "Ole Rat Bastard? Your guess is as good as mine. Francine's maiden name was Asher, and that's why Frank and I have the same last name even though we have different dads. He didn't know *his* father, either."

"Then how—why are you such a good dad?"

David blinked a few times. "I . . . hmm. That's nice of you to say. Well, I try really, really hard because I want so desperately for things to be different for you and Ben than they were for Frank and me. I want to break the cycle of shitty parenting. Got a late start with you," he smiled sadly, shaking his head. "Therapy—*professional co-parenting*, I guess you'd call it—helps a lot, too. And Beverly. I've learned a lot from her."

"David, where's Stephen's mom?"

"Sharla? She's a carbon copy of Francine, I'm afraid. By the time Stephen was a year old, Frank was getting a pretty clear picture that Sharla wasn't happy being a wife and mom. The breaking point was a hot summer day when she went to the Tyler Mall and left Stephen in the car with the windows rolled up. Thank God, somebody walking by noticed him inside and called the police. They broke the windows and got him out. He'd already passed out, and he nearly died. We're lucky his brain damage isn't worse. It shows up in his learning disabilities.

"Sharla couldn't even understand why she was arrested; she seemed more pissed about the damage to her car than the fact that her child nearly died. I think she lives in Oklahoma now. I know she's remarried, and I think she has kids, but she doesn't have any contact with Stephen any more."

"Does Frank ever, you know, go out with anybody?"

"Da-aaa-d, I don't understand decimals. Could you hurry up?" Ben whined from the hallway.

"Yes, Ben." David got up slowly and grimaced at his creaking bones. "Eh, Frank's gone out a few times. There's not a lot of single women dropping by the shop though, you know. And I guess you could say he's very careful with his heart now, too. So are we good with the genogram?"

I looked it over. "Kinda looks like we just have to start from where we are now. But yeah, we're good. Thanks."

CHAPTER 10

"What do we know about Jeanne Wakatsuki Houston and her family, so far?" Bev asked. We were three-quarters of the way through the book. Thanksgiving break was coming up, and Bev wanted us to finish discussing *Farewell to Manzanar* before the holiday week.

"Her mom kept bringing her dad the stuff to make apricot brandy, even though he was a stinkin' drunk," Dub said. "Kinda reminds me of the way my mom used to keep my stepdad stocked up on longnecks, even though he was an assho—I mean a jerk—when he drank."

"Good," Bev said, jotting on the whiteboard, "Jeanne's mom enabled her dad to drink." She cocked an eyebrow Dub's way and said, "Thank you for editing yourself, Mr. White."

Dub replied with a thumbs-up and a wide grin. Pam Littlejohn flipped to the back of her spiral notebook and made notes. Roxanne raised her hand. "The high school students at Manzanar had to put on a play about a typical American home—and the family was white. And the problems the family in the play had were nothing compared to what Jeanne was dealing with."

"Did they enjoy putting on the play?" Bev prompted.

Z.Z. volunteered, "See, even though they were stuck inside this unreal existence, they all wanted to be normal like everybody else, like they used to feel before they were interned. So yeah, I think maybe they liked doin' the play."

I read a quote: "The fact that America had accused us, or excluded us, or imprisoned us, or whatever it might be called, did not change the kind of world we wanted."

"What examples from present time can you think of in which people might feel excluded from society because of who or what they are?" Bev asked.

Travis Hager stood up and put his hand on his heart. "There is prejudice against people who wear coyote heads to school."

"Man, that was just gross," T.W. said. "I think that thing is rotting."

Travis shrugged. "It's still a little . . . moist. In places."

The class groaned. Bev rolled her eyes and sighed. "Travis, you're the only person I know who has done something like that, so I don't think it's widespread enough to consider it societal exclusion."

"But Mr. Walden made me put it in a bag by the Ag barn all day, and somebody could have stolen it!"

"Given that vultures were circling it, I don't think human theft should have been your main concern. If you're going to keep wearing coyote corpses, you need to perfect your method of preservation." Bev shuddered. "God, I can't believe I just said that. I've lived here too long. Anyway, I'm talking about a group of people who're excluded from the rights that other people have because of, for example, their gender—"

"That means sex!" Dub interrupted. The class exploded in laughter. Pam pursed her lips and scribbled some more in the back of her notebook.

Bev ignored the outburst, took a deep breath, and gathered her thoughts. "As recently as the 1960s, the civil rights movement sought to ensure equal rights for everyone."

"We skipped the Sixties in American History, Miss Asher," Kevin said.

"Yes, I know," Bev said flatly. "Those of you who did the independent study unit of the Sixties, can you tell me which two groups were loudest in terms of arguing for equal rights?"

"African Americans and women," Roxanne said.

"Okay, good. Now, which group of people nowadays is still fighting for the same rights that the rest of society has?"

"Gay people. They don't have the basic rights that the rest of society has," K.C. said. She shot me a look as if daring me to reveal what her mother had said that day in our therapists' waiting room. The class fell silent.

"What would *you* know about it?" Teresa Benedict asked her.

K.C. blushed and looked at her hands, then chanced another glance at me. I gave her a little smile as if to say, "Your secret's safe with me."

"Doesn't matter," Marcus Merriweather announced. "They're all going to hell anyway."

"Who died and made you God?" I spat, punctuating it with my go-to-hell look.

"Ashley," Bev warned. "Marcus, it's not okay with me for you to say stuff like that in my—"

He shook his head and held up his Bible. "Says it right here, Miss Asher. 'In a similar way, Sodom and Gomorrah and the surrounding towns gave themselves up to immorality and perversion. They serve as an example of those who suffer the punishment of eternal fire.' Jude 7."

"Yeah, well, the Bible also says that God made people in His likeness, so doesn't it freak you out a little that God could be playing for the Pink Team? I mean, King James himself was rumored to be, ya know . . ." K.C. said, winking and making a limp hand gesture.

"Which Bible have *you* been reading?" Marcus challenged.

"Here we go again! Marcus, I tol' you, there's just one Bible. Your church does not have the only one that's right," Z.Z. said, then sat back in her chair and shook her head.

"Which church do you go to, Z.Z.?" Marcus asked.

"African Methodist Episcopal. A.M.E. for short. Why?"

"See, that's the problem, right there. The church I go to, we use the Word of God." Marcus patted his Bible, sat back in his seat, and folded his hands on his belly.

"Boy, you are one thick-headed backwoods hillbilly," Z.Z. said.

"But Marcus, I'm Catholic, and my priest calls the Bible the Word of God, too," Teresa Benedict said.

Marcus held up his Bible and pointed at the title. "Does your Bible say, '*The* Bible'? or just 'Holy Bible'? Or '*The* Holy Bible'? As you can see, mine says, '*The* Holy Bible.' So there ya go," he said, as if that ended the debate.

"My dad says we go to the Church of the Holy Mattress," Travis Hager said, smiling. Dub gave him a thumbs-up and said, "Amen!"

"I'm with Z.Z.; it's all the same Bible. Can we move on now?" T.W. said in a monotone.

K.C. said, "From what I've read, people are born gay or straight, and that's that. There are even some animal species that have homosexuals. Marcus, since you believe that God created the entire world and everything in it, you're just going to have to accept that, number one, het-erosexuals *and* homosexuals are part of God's plan, and number two—"

Marcus stood up, reached for the ceiling with his palms up, closed his eyes, and prayed, "Heavenly Father, I come to you today to ask that you—"

Bam! Bam! Bam! Bev used her stapler as a gavel. "Time out! Separation of church and state! Read the Con-stitution of the United States, people!" The buzz of discus-sion only grew, and Bev gave the desk a few more whacks with the stapler. "Hellooooo, let's get back to *Farewell to Manzanar!*"

It was so unusual for Bev to lose her cool that we all stared at her like her hair was on fire. She blinked rapidly and said, "Thank you!" then gave a quick nod and said, "Moving on . . . "

She picked up a glass canister with slips of paper in it. "I am going to draw your names in groups of four. Each group will write a very brief skit, no longer than five min-utes. The big idea is to give an example of identity and show how a person's identity shapes his or her experience in America."

"You mean like when my mom got a Sarah Palin makeover and started referring to herself as 'Mavericky'?" T.W. asked with a frown.

"Um, not so much," Bev said. "Think of it like this: How was Jeanne's identity affected by being imprisoned at Manzanar because of her race?"

"So we need to write it as if we're at Manzanar?" Roxanne asked.

"Mmm, no, that's not what I'm looking for, either." Bev gazed out the window for a moment, then turned back to us. "Let's narrow it down a bit. Use this concept as your guide: How can a person get others to see him or her as an individual? You'll present your skit on the Friday before Thanksgiving break. That's about a week and a half away."

There was a collective groan. Bev's eyebrows snapped up. "Oh? You wanna go there with me? Okay, if you're going to have a bad attitude about this, I can dispense with this unit and we can go back to diagramming sentences."

"No, no!" we said. "Miss Asher, this is a great idea!" and "I love the theater!" And Travis added, "Can I wear my coyote hat? I'll soak it in Febreze!"

❦

Coach Morrison asked me to come to practice and make posters for the upcoming meet. He told me that I was still an important part of the team, even though I was out for the season. It was Thursday, a distance challenge day, so I had a good hour or so to work. I spread pencils, markers, and poster board on the floor in the gym foyer, and I was just getting started when Pam Littlejohn came out of the locker room and planted her neon pink Nikes on my first poster.

I focused on trying to get my lettering even. "Hey, could you move? The only shoes I want on here are the ones I draw."

She stayed put, so I looked up at her. She sneered at me, hands on her hips, and said, "Is it true?"

"Is what true? That I want you to move your freakin' feet? Yes." I pushed her foot, but she didn't move.

She shook her head slowly at me and narrowed her eyes. "You had an affair with your stepfather?"

I dropped my pencil. "Wh-what?"

"I heard all about it," she said, her eyes huge. "That's why you moved here. That's— that's just so . . . gross. Does Mrs. Asher know?"

I struggled to stand, tried to pull myself up the wall, but I slipped and fell down hard on my wounded left hand. I cried out in pain and fell to my elbows.

"I knew there was a reason I didn't like you. You're disgusting," Pam hissed, then turned on her heel and headed toward Old Blue. "Joshua!" she called. "Save a spot for me!" She looked back over her shoulder with a smirk.

I watched Old Blue drive away as my head buzzed with *whoosh*; the imaginary squirrel on speed was warming up, and my thoughts were spinning. Seconds later, I threw up all over my poster-making materials, then fell back and landed hard on my butt. I pushed back with my heels till I leaned against the wall. I don't even know where I went in my head; I just zoned out.

I was totally numb from head to toe until the smell of vomit snapped me back to reality. Alert once again, I was horrified by the mess I'd made. I found a trash bag in the custodian's closet and shoved my barf-covered markers and the ruined poster board into it, then slung my backpack over my shoulder and used the phone in Coach's office to call Bev. "I need you to pick me up, Bev. Now, please. Not at six. *Now*."

"Why, honey?"

My stomach clenched, and I didn't answer; I just hung up and started limping out of the gym as fast as I could. I threw the trash bag in the Dumpster and hid behind it until David pulled up in his old Ford truck. His eyes widened when he saw me scuttle like a rat from behind the Dumpster.

"Bev was at Walmart when you called. Said you sounded like you needed to come home right away. So what's up?"

I slid my backpack to the floor, clicked my seat belt on, and looked out the window.

"Ya in trouble or somethin'?"

I shook my head and focused on my handprint on the inside of the glass. Tears blurred the handprint into the scenery flying by outside. I gagged on bile and swallowed hard, surprised there was anything left in my stomach.

David turned on the radio. Jackson Browne was singing "Some Bridges," and I envisioned taking a nose-dive off a tall one, like one of the huge concrete structures in Dallas. No tall bridges in Patience, dammit.

Thinking about the Dallas area and why I came to Patience led to the bright idea to jump out of David's truck and dart into oncoming traffic—that is, until I realized that I'd be, like, limping along so slowly that the semi I envisioned smashing me to bits would have enough time to stop and avoid hitting me. I sighed and looked at the screwdriver on the dashboard, started to reach for it, and stopped myself. Stabbing myself in the neck would definitely be a drop-kick-the-teddy-bear moment. Then I remembered Dr. Matt's words and told myself, *Just wait.*

David and I rode in silence the rest of the way home as my mental squirrel spun one suicidal fantasy after another and I argued with myself that each one was a very bad idea.

Telling what was going on with me would have required talking, and I'd fallen into the same kind of silence I used to practice when hiding from Charlie.

"If you don't want to talk to us, will you please talk to Dr. Matt about it?" Bev asked.

I closed my eyes, shook my head, and crawled a little deeper inside myself. I still couldn't wrap my mind around what Pam said. Where had she heard something like that? Had my mom been on some trashy talk show about daughters who sleep with their mom's husband? Man, that squirrel in my head must have been chugging Red Bull; it just never slowed down.

The next morning, Bev was still trying to figure out what was wrong with me. She took my temperature, but of course I didn't have one. That was disappointing; I was hoping to have miraculously contracted some kind of fatal disease so I could die—or at least miss school.

I settled into my seat in Coach Griffin's room and went through the motions of pretending to take notes, but instead, I drew hexagons, flowerpots, and nooses. Hanging—now, there was a method I hadn't thought of. I drew an arrow next to the noose and wrote "Google" as a reminder to look up how to make a noose, then just as quickly scratched it out and wrote, "Just wait!"

Meanwhile, Coach Griffin looked like he was barely controlling himself. Two broken yardsticks already lay across his desk; the third one that he carried as he strode between the rows of desks was taking on a slightly curved appearance.

"About 40 percent of the American soldiers taken prisoner by the Japanese during World War II died in the hands of the enemy," he read from the PowerPoint graphic, his upper lip curled back in a sneer. "The Japanese military thought of surrender as contemptible, and they treated our men worse than dogs."

K.C. raised her hand, and Coach Griffin whirled on her. It looked for a moment as if he was going to swing the yardstick like a sword and behead her on the spot. "Question, Miss Williamson?"

She ducked. "Um, no. Sir."

He advanced the slide and read, "At least 5,200 Americans died on the Bataan Death March. Of the ones who were lucky enough to survive—if you call being spared the relief of death *lucky*—hundreds more died in prison camp, were beheaded, or were stabbed with bayonets."

"Coach Griffin, we've been talking about American prisoners of war for over a week now," Roxanne ventured.

"Have we, Miss Blake? I guess I've been so horrified by the atrocities committed on our soldiers by the Japanese, I hadn't noticed. It took more than a year for a slave force of Allied POWs to build railroad tracks from Bangkok to Rangoon, and over 12,000 Allied troops died while they worked on it. Do you think they noticed the passage of time?"

Roxanne's eyes widened, and she sank down in her seat.

"This is so weird!" Kevin said. "We're learnin' about Japanese people in English, too. But they must not be the same kind of Japanese as these were."

Coach Griffin watched Kevin a moment to see whether he was being facetious, and I guess he figured out pretty quickly that Kevin was just being Kevin.

Roxanne leaned over to Kevin and whispered, "Those were the Japanese Americans in internment camps. It was different!"

Coach Griffin caught her. "Miss Blake, would you like to share your thoughts? I'd love to hear them."

I caught a glimpse of the steely Roxanne that she rarely lets anyone see. She sat up straight, put her chin in the air, and said, "The Japanese people in *Farewell to Manzanar* were Japanese Americans, Coach Griffin. They were not soldiers; they were just everyday people. Our government even put orphaned children of Japanese ancestry into those prison camps, as if they were a threat to national security."

"Internment camps were *not* prisons! The United

States government did what it had to do to protect the sovereignty of our nation during a time of war! You sound just like those whiners who think those animals at Guantanamo should have trials!" Coach Griffin slammed the yardstick down on Roxanne's desk, and it splintered into two jagged pieces. Roxanne screamed.

Kevin bolted out of his chair, his hands balled into fists; Coach Griffin wheeled on him, stood on his tiptoes, and got right up in Kevin's beet red face. Kevin was breathing hard.

Dub jumped between them, and Coach Griffin shoved him aside. "Do you have a problem, Cooper?"

Kevin's eyes were burning into Coach Griffin's, but he said nothing.

"Kevin, sit down!" Roxanne pleaded. Kevin's eyes cut slightly to Roxanne, then went right back to Coach Griffin. "Please, Kevin. I'm okay," she insisted.

Kevin took a step back and eased down into his desk. Coach Griffin moved toward him with his fists raised—but stopped himself. Suddenly, he spun on his heel and walked out of the room. A few minutes later, his assistant coach came in and put on an old World War II movie called *Midway*, then sat down at the computer and played Solitaire until the bell rang.

❧

I skipped Biology and went to hide in Bev's classroom. I just walked in without saying a word to anyone, pulled a beanbag chair out of her classroom library area, carried it behind her desk, and shoved it between the file cabinet and the wall. I eased myself down onto it, leaned against the wall, crossed my arms, and pulled my legs up to my chest until I was in a tight ball.

"Please turn to page 106 in the book," Bev instructed the class, and then she peeked behind her desk at me and raised her eyebrows. "What are you doing back there?" she hissed.

I pulled my legs in tighter and whispered back, "Wishing I could fit in your storage closet."

Bev frowned and whispered, singsong, "This is not goooo-oood, Ashley."

I closed my eyes again and whispered, "No shi—iiii-iiiit."

Bev gave her class their assignment. "Using the information you gain about the antagonist from pages 106 through 110, create a character profile of at least five traits. Questions, comments, concerns, quandaries?"

"What's a quandary?" one kid asked.

"A quandary is a problem that you think has no solution, but it actually does," Bev said and hit her desk with her knee. I jumped.

∽

The bell rang, and I started to get up, but Bev said, "Stay right there. I'm on my conference period now, and if there's one thing you and I need to do, it's confer."

I shrugged and stayed where I was. Bev pulled a Diet Coke out of her mini-fridge and offered it to me. I shook my head. She plopped down in her chair, opened the drink, and put her feet up on her desk. "What's up, Ashley?"

I put my head in my hands, locked down, and clammed up.

"Uh—*no*. No more of this!" she said and imitated my curved spine and head in my hands.

At last, I closed my eyes and let all the ugliness out. I told her everything, from what Pam had said, to my Barf Fest, to throwing away all the posters and hiding behind the Dumpster.

"Oh, Ashley! I'm so sorry," Bev said.

My head snapped up. "Why? Did *you* tell Pam I had an affair with Charlie?" It's amazing how quickly I can think the worst of people.

"Of course not! I'm just so sorry Pam said shitty stuff to you. That's terrible." Bev rose from her chair and pushed the office call button on her wall.

"Office," Marvella said through the speaker in the ceiling.

"Yeah, Marvella, I need you to track down Pam Littlejohn and send her to my room immediately, please."

I gasped. "No, no, no, Bev! You can't! I can't see her!"

"Will do, Bev," Marvella said and then clicked off.

Bev turned back to me, and her eyes were dark coals. "This is not something I'm going to let you hide from, Ashley. I'm getting to the bottom of this right now."

"You wanted to see me, Mrs. Asher?" Pam said from the doorway.

236

"Yes, Pam, please have a seat," Bev said. She moved from her desk and pulled three student desks into a triangle.

"Is somebody else coming?" Pam asked.

"Join us," Bev commanded, and I rose from the bean-bag chair behind Bev's desk.

"Oh, uh, hi, Ashley," Pam said, trying to get her mouth to form a smile. It didn't work. "Wh-what's going on, Mrs. Asher?"

"That's what I'd like to know," Bev said.

"What do you mean?" Pam asked in her little-girl voice.

"Cut the crap, Pam," Bev said.

I slid into the desk opposite Pam. *School Sux* was carved into the desktop, and I ran my finger over and over the word *Sux*.

"What did you say to Ashley yesterday before the distance challenge?"

Pam's face lost all its color. "I . . . um . . . I—" She locked her eyes onto the desktop and kept them there. "I told her that I knew the reason she came to Patience."

"And that was?"

Pam pursed her lips and shook her head. "I don't think it's appropriate for me to say," she finally squeaked.

Bev sat back abruptly. "Oh, so all of a sudden, you're aware of what's appropriate to say and what's not?"

Pam blushed.

"What I want to know is, why do you think that Ashley had an affair with her stepfather?" Bev's voice shook. Her hands were clasped tightly on the desktop, as if she didn't trust what she would do with them if she didn't hold on to it.

Pam only sniffled in response. I glanced at her and noticed that although she was producing the sounds of crying, there were no tears in her eyes. In that moment, I saw Pam as a carbon copy of my mother.

In July, a few weeks before Charlie broke my arm, when my mother showed up out of the blue one Saturday to try and convince me to go home with her, she told me that Charlie abusing me was all my problem. She, too, had pretended to cry. The bubbles of rage that had spilled out of me that day were simmering near boiling again now.

"You're on the student council, right, Pam? Didn't you sign a morality pledge when you were elected? Maybe I should check with the sponsor, Ms. Daly, to see whether saying vicious things to other students—"

"No! Please, Mrs. Asher, don't do that." Now there were real tears in Pam's eyes.

"Then you'd better start talking or this will get very ugly very quickly. Trust me when I tell you that I'm not afraid of upsetting your parents, and the notes you take about what goes on in my class don't faze me in the least."

Pam gave her best wide-eyed look. "Notes?"

Bev's eyes were fiery; I'd never seen her so angry. She said, "Fine, I'll just have Ms. Daly paged to my room," and moved toward the call button on the wall.

Pam started talking very fast. "It was Joshua! He told me. He said that Ashley told him that the reason she moved here was because she had an affair with her stepfather."

Still in the desk, I stood up and walked it the two feet that separated us, then slammed the desk hard into Pam's desk. "Liar! I didn't tell him that!"

"Ashley, sit down," Bev said.

I did, but I kept my desk butted right up against Pam's. Now I was the one clasping my hands together tightly, knowing that if I let go, I'd punch Pam in the face.

"Whether it's true that Joshua told you that or not, Pam, what possessed you to say such a horrible thing?"

Pam looked down at her shaking hands. "I . . . uh, guess I wasn't thinking. I'm sorry, Ashley."

I felt like spitting on her. No way was I going to tell her, "It's okay." No way. Charlie taught me all about forgiveness long ago. He'd molest me, then say, "I'm sorry, kiddo. Slap my hands."

I'd hear this little voice in my head telling me, *You're a Christian, and Christians forgive*, so I'd say, "I forgive you. But don't do it again."

And guess what? He did it again and again and again. Anytime Dr. Matt brings up the idea of forgiveness and tells me that someday I may reach that point so that I can move on, I feel my lips curling into a snarl and I think, *No way; I'll just get hurt again*.

"Did Joshua really tell you I had an . . . affair with my stepfather?" I choked the words out past the knot in my throat.

"Yes, he came up to me and said, 'You're not going to believe what I just found out about Ashley." She turned to Bev. "Mrs. Asher, I've learned my lesson. I'll never do anything like this again." To me, she said, "I didn't know it would hurt your feelings, Ashley."

The words flew from my mouth: "What a crock of shit! What are you, stupid?"

Pam wept now—for real this time. "I'm sorry! I'm so sorry!" she cried, and I immediately felt guilty.

"You can go now, Pam," Bev said.

Right after Pam left, Bev closed her door and asked, "Ash, where would Joshua have gotten the impression that your coming to Patience had anything to do with Charlie?"

I blushed. Bev sat down next to me and took my hand. "Ashley, did you tell Joshua about your history?"

"Sort of. He asked why I ran from the guy at the haunted house, and I told him that Charlie did some stuff to me that messed me up."

"How well do you know Joshua?"

I shrugged. "I . . . know he's a nice person, or at least I thought he was." My lower lip quivered, and hurt took over where the anger had been. I looked at Bev. "Why would he talk about me like that? Should I have lied when he asked me why I ran?"

Bev squeezed my hand. "It's difficult to know how much to tell people, Ash. It's really best if you get to know someone very well before revealing stuff like past abuse. Did you tell him that your mom thought you were trying to steal Charlie from her?"

"No. We didn't even talk about my mom." I covered my face with my hands. "I'm such an idiot! I can't believe I trusted him not to tell anybody!"

Dr. Matt set a piece of paper and a tube of toothpaste on his desk next to me. I looked at him like he'd lost his mind. He said, "When I say something kind, I want you to squeeze out a line of toothpaste on the paper. When I say something that's not so nice, squeeze out a circle. Ready?"

"I guess," I said. "Why are we doing this?"

"Just do it, will you please?"

"'kay."

"You are a very intelligent young lady."

I made a line.

"That guy's an idiot!"

I formed a circle.

"Doesn't she look nice today?"

Line.

"I'm so proud of you!"

Line.

"Dumbass! Why would you tell somebody you barely know about your past?"

I gasped. It felt like Dr. Matt had just punched me in the stomach.

"What are you waiting for? Line or circle?" he said.

"Dr. Matt, you called me a dumbass!"

"Who said I was talking to you, Ashley? Line or circle?"

I sighed. "Circle."

"Okay," he said. "Now, put all that toothpaste back in the tube."

Once again, I looked at my shrink as if he were as crazy as I was. "Huh?"

"Put. The. Toothpaste. Back. In. The. Tube," Dr. Matt

said, then leaned back in his chair, laced his fingers behind his head, and smirked at me.

"I . . . can't!"

He sat up abruptly and feigned surprise. "You can't? Really?"

I frowned at him. "Your point, please?"

"Since you asked . . . " He took the paper from me, carefully wadded it up, then threw it away. "Once words are out of your mouth, you can't take them back. Whether what you say is kind, ugly, or just carelessly spoken, once words are out in the world, you can't take them back. That's why you need to be so cautious about what you say."

"But I thought I could trust Joshua," I whined.

"Based on what? Trust has a prepositional phrase, Ashley."

"You lost me. Again."

"*If* you prove to me that you can be trusted, then I can trust you. *Because* you have shown me that you are an X, Y, or Z type of person, I have decided it's okay to trust you. *When* we have known each other long enough, then—"

"I get it now," I said, nodding. "By the way, I'm pretty sure *when* is an adverb, not a preposition. Bev made us diagram sentences, and—"

"Whatever," he said. He held up a finger. "Furthermore, when someone asks you a question that you're not sure how to answer, you can always apply my favorite two-word solution to the situation.

"*Fuck* and *You*?" I asked, smiling at him.

Dr. Matt rolled his eyes and shook his head. "*Just. Wait.*"

242

"Is this some kind of joke, Bev?" I pulled the list off the bulletin board in Bev's classroom and read aloud the four names listed under "Group 2": "Ashley Asher, Marcus Merriweather, Z.Z. Freeman, and K.C. Williamson. You put Marcus with us? Do you *want* blood in your classroom?"

"It was totally random, Ashley. I just drew the names and made the list." Bev was distracted, checking her e-mail.

"Hey, I'm cool with it. I can't wait to see Marcus, the poster child for sheep-like thinking, try to write a skit about being an individual," K.C. said. She started to dip her stick of French toast in syrup, then held it up in a mock salute and said, "I do believe I'll wear my rainbow shirt on Monday." K.C. had started hanging out in Bev's room in the morning before school started. Usually Z.Z. was there, too, but she hadn't arrived yet.

Bev logged off of her computer and frowned at us. "Do you honestly believe that when you're out in the real world, you're always going to get to choose the people you work with? You're going to have to learn to work with people you don't like. Diplomacy—it's a valuable skill to have."

"Can Kurt be in our group, too?" K.C. asked.

Bev looked confused. "Kurt?"

"Yeah, Kurt. He's my electric guitar. I used to take him to school all the time when I lived in Houston."

"Your teachers let you do that?" I asked.

K.C. smiled at Bev. "Well, usually, I'd ask my coolest teacher if he could stay in her room during the school day, and I'd visit him at lunch, and we'd meet up after school and jam."

"You . . . and . . . Kurt. Your . . . guitar. You named your guitar. Hmmm," said Bev.

"What's his last name, Williamson?" I asked.

K.C. pointed proudly to the Nirvana logo on her T-shirt. "Cobain, of course! I named him after the greatest songwriter of all time!" She lowered her voice conspiratorially and said, "How cool is it that we share the same initials, huh?" She smiled and sighed happily. "It was fate, pure and simple. Almost makes up for my mother giving me an asinine middle name."

Bev and I exchanged wide-eyed looks.

"So, Miss Asher? Can Kurt come to school and stay in your room, pleeeeeeaaase?"

Bev smiled. "Bring 'im on, K.C. I know just the place he can hang out. But you have to promise me something in return."

K.C. arched an eyebrow. "Oka-a-a-a-y . . . ?"

"You have to play "All Apologies" for me. I love that song."

CHAPTER 11

I was too embarrassed to talk to Coach Morrison about my Barf Fest, so David and Bev met with him instead.

"He couldn't believe Joshua would say what Pam said he did, but he wasn't that shocked that Pam would be such a snot. He offered to intervene, but I told him not to rock the boat right now. He doesn't need the aggravation of getting in the middle of this," Bev said.

"As the saying goes, 'The truth will out.' I'd talk to Joshua myself, but I don't want to be within five feet of that boy right now." David took one of those long breaths in and out that's a sign he's controlling his anger.

"Good sigh, David," I said. He smiled at me and ruffled my hair.

I spent the night at Z.Z.'s house so we could work on making new posters for the meet the next morning. I still couldn't bring myself to tell her what Pam had said to me. Even though I knew I hadn't had an affair with Charlie, the reminder that *my own mother* saw me as competition for her husband instead of as her child who she'd give her own life to protect was just too much to take.

I had to keep it in an iron lockbox deep inside myself. If I didn't, I was afraid I wouldn't be able to come up with enough reasons not to do things like stab myself in the neck or try to become roadkill. And I was afraid that no amount of desk slapping or sneaky desk kicking or just waiting or holding onto teddy bears would stop me from trying real hard to die.

"How's it going with Joshua?" Z.Z. asked. She frowned and, for the tenth time, erased the line she'd been trying to draw straight. Her bedroom floor was practically carpeted in poster board and markers. I elbow-crawled on my tummy across the floor and grabbed a ruler from my backpack, then tossed it to her.

"Mmm, I don't really think he's my type," I said. "So what kind of pace you gonna try for tomorrow?" I walked on my knees back to my poster and flopped onto my stomach.

She ignored my attempt to change the subject. "Not your type? Unh," she clucked her tongue. "Girl, I don't know what type you're lookin' for, but he sure is interested in you. He's cute, too. Course, I like my men to have a little more meat on their bones, but—"

"Well, if you call talkin' shit about me the same as being interested," I blurted—then immediately wished I hadn't said it. Damned toothpaste.

Z.Z. started to reply, but her cousin Jasper knocked on her open door. "Y'all? Granny says supper's ready, and Auntie Jewel said she ain't eatin' it cold, so hurry on down."

"'Kay; thanks, Jasper," Z.Z. said dismissively, but Jasper stayed in her doorway. "We'll be right down, okay? You can go downstairs. I need to ask Ashley something."

He shook his head solemnly. "Uh-uh. Auntie Jewel said for me not to come down without you. Said y'all would say, 'Okay, Jasper,' and then keep right on jawin' like you girls do. I—I have to wait for you, or else Auntie Jewel's gonna get mad at me, and I don't like it when she's mad at me."

"Ain't nobody like it when Jewel's on a tear," Z.Z. muttered.

I stood. "We're coming right now. Get up, Z.Z."

❦

We ate dinner, then finished up the posters while listening to Jasper read "Knock, knock" jokes to us from his favorite book. He especially liked the one in which he kept answering "Banana" each time we'd say, "Who's there?" Then he'd end the joke by answering, "Orange. Orange you glad I didn't say banana?" Every time he said it, he could barely control his laughter. It's so easy to forget that he's a grown man. When Jasper was a baby, he was in a car accident that left him with a head injury. Z.Z. told me he thinks like a six-year-old. Around the fifteenth time he told the same joke, we yelled out, "Orange!" before he could.

"No, I'm 'asposed to say that." He frowned and stuck

his lower lip out. "We're gonna have to try again," he said. "Knock, knock!—now this time you say, 'Who's there?' and don't say 'Orange!' "

I felt a wave of relief when Aurelia told Jasper it was time for bed, but Z.Z. immediately brought up Joshua again.

I said, "Knock, knock."

"Who's there?" she groaned.

"No one who wants to talk about Joshua." I smiled in a way that bared all my teeth, then went upstairs to take a shower.

~

I thought Z.Z. had given up, but just as I was falling asleep, she nudged my shoulder and said, "What do you mean, Joshua talked shit about you?"

I groaned. "That again?"

We were laying on pallets in front of the fireplace in Z.Z.'s living room. I mumbled, "You've gotta run tomorrow," and squinted at the clock on the DVD player. "It's one a.m., and we have to be at school at seven. Go to sleep." I punched my pillows down and turned away from her.

Z.Z. clapped her hands. The light on top of the TV came on. "Ashley, I'm not lettin' you go to sleep until you talk to me!"

I opened one eye. "Aren't you worried about guarding your solid last-place finish? Go to sleep."

Z.Z. snorted and jumped to her feet. She went into the kitchen, and when she came back, she held a pitcher of water over my head.

"Don't you even—"

She arched an eyebrow at me, and a smile spread slowly across her face. She tilted the pitcher slightly, and ice-cold water splashed onto my forehead. "You gonna talk to me?"

I covered my face with the quilt and growled, "Dammit, Z.Z.!"

"So? You *are* gonna talk to me?"

I peeked at her and was immediately doused again. "Yessssssss! Now stop it, or I'm goin' home!"

"Stop it, or I'm goin' home," she mocked in a whiny voice.

"Ah, you made me need to pee." I shoved off the quilt, grabbed Z.Z.'s still-dry blanket and wrapped it around myself, then shoved my feet into her Cookie Monster slippers and shuffled off toward the bathroom.

"I'm gonna make us some popcorn. When you come back—" she called as she went into the kitchen.

"Yeah, yeah. I'll talk to you."

◈

"That bitch!" Z.Z. shoved a handful of popcorn in her mouth.

"I just can't figure out why Pam said I had an affair with Charlie. I don't believe that Joshua told her, because all I told Joshua was that I get scared easily because—" I didn't want to say the rest. I picked a piece of popcorn off the carpet, broke it into tiny pieces, and rubbed the bits in circles on my napkin.

"I know," Z.Z. said.

"I know you know what happened to me, it's just—" I took a deep breath and let it out slowly.

"No. Ashley. I mean, I know where Joshua heard something about your having an affair with your stepdad."

"The only person who has ever thought that is my mom." I wrinkled my nose and looked at Z.Z. "Do you think Joshua met my mom, somehow?"

When Z.Z. stared at her hands, I started to get a clue. I sat up abruptly. "You're the only person I've ever trusted enough to tell everything about my life in Northside, and *you* told him?" I got to my feet. My heart was racing. "You *told* him?"

"It wasn't like that, Ash, honest—"

"I have to go. I have to go now. I—I can't be here." I started for the stairs. Z.Z. leapt up and grabbed my arm, but I yanked it away from her. "Don't touch me! Leave me alone!"

My hands were shaking and rage was doing my thinking as I tried to gather my stuff. I ripped our carefully created posters into pieces and threw them all over her bed.

"Joshua knows that we're best friends, Ashley. He was trying to understand you better, that's all. I guess he can tell you have problems trusting people."

"Well, gee, I wonder why?" I snapped from her bathroom. When I wig out, I can't remember even basic things. I snatched both of our toothbrushes off her counter and held them out to her. "Which one is mine?"

"The purple one," Z.Z. said quietly.

"Thanks." I threw it into my backpack and fumbled with the zipper. When it stuck, I started to cry.

Z.Z. sat on the edge of her bed and said, "Ashley, please come here and at least let me try to explain. Then if you still want to leave, that's fine."

I muttered bitterly, "Well, it'll be a long walk home, 'cause I can't even remember my phone number right now." I sat next to her and put my head in my hands.

"I'll dial the number for you if you need me to," Z.Z. said softly. She rubbed my back and said, "I told Joshua how messed up your mom is—how, when you told her what Charlie was doing to you, she accused you of having an affair with him. Josh thought that was some sad-ass shit, and he said you must be a really strong person."

"Then why would he say that to Pam?" I bent at the waist and bawled. I'm surprised I didn't wake up the rest of Z.Z.'s household.

Z.Z. bent her body like mine and put her arm across my back. "I'm so sorry, Ashley. I never would have told him anything about you if I'd had any idea this would happen. I didn't think he was the type of person to do something like this. You know I'd never hurt you on purpose, don't you?"

I was struck with an idea and sat up suddenly. "Z.Z., where were you when you talked to him? Was anybody else around?"

"Last Tuesday after practice, he asked if he could talk to me. We went up in the bleachers. I thought we were alone; we didn't see anybody else. "

The hope I'd felt that Joshua wasn't a jerk evaporated, and I sank again. "So it has to be true. He must have told Pam some version of what you told him."

"I'll find out tomorrow," Z.Z. said.

I said into my lap, "It won't do any good."

"Ashley, no matter what anybody else says, you didn't have an affair with Charlie. You were a kid. My granny always says, 'Just 'cause somebody says somethin' doesn't make it so.' "

"Kinda like separating facts from crap?" I sat up and wiped my face with the hem of my nightshirt.

"Yeah. And if that boy don't want parts of his body separated from the rest of him, he's gonna—"

I smiled at the image of Z.Z. trying to catch Joshua. "Z.Z., you've seen how fast he runs. You'd never catch him."

She stood up and worked her neck. "Unh. Girl, this whole time, I've been givin' ever'body false hope, lettin' 'em get overconfident. I'm gonna break out of the pack tomorrow! And you're gonna be there to see it!"

"I'm thinking this is one of those times when your granny's saying applies," I said dryly.

She offered me her hand and pulled me up. "Still wanna leave?"

"And miss your come-from-the-very-back-of-the-pack victory tomorrow? Never."

❧

"Hi, Ashley!" Pam smiled and waved when she saw me. Then, with a sneer, she said, "Hello, Z.Z."

Z.Z. narrowed her eyes, leaned into Pam, and tilted her head, seeming to study her face. "Ew! Pam, you got a brown spot right on the end of your nose."

Pam gasped. "I do?" She covered her nose with her hand.

"Yeah, you'd better run into the locker room and get it off," Z.Z. said.

"Thanks, Z.Z.!" Pam said, running back into the gym with her hand still over her nose.

"She doesn't have anything on her nose," I said.

"Well, I figured she must, seein' how she's brown-nosin' you like she is," Z.Z. said as she high-fived me. "If it looks like shit and smells like shit . . . that's all I'm sayin'."

"What are you laughing at?" Junior said from behind us. I turned to see Joshua coming up right behind him. My knees buckled.

"Oh, nothing," Z.Z. said. She put her arm around my shoulders and kept me from falling over. "How's Three, Junior?"

"He's good, he's good. Moreyma's bringin' 'im to the meet. You won't believe how big he's gettin'."

I gritted my teeth against the churning in my stomach. *Don't throw up. Don't throw up.* Junior narrowed his eyes at me. "Are you okay? You look the way you do after a distance challenge."

"She's fine!" Z.Z. said and gave my shoulders a squeeze. "Aren't you, Ashley?"

"Mm-hmm," I nodded, trying to smile.

"The bus will be here in ten minutes, so make sure

you're ready to go," Coach Morrison called from the gym doorway. Pam squeezed by him and marched toward us with her fists balled up.

Junior said, "*Ay dios mio*, the witch is on her broom. I suddenly remember something I forgot in my car." He sauntered off toward his blue Geo Prism.

"I did *not* have anything on my nose! Is that your idea of a joke?" Pam spat.

"Hmm. I guess it just looked to me like you did—you know, like you got some of that bullshit you're spreadin' around on your face or somethin'."

"Arrrrgh! Ugh! I can't stand you!"

"Oh, no!" Z.Z. said, giving Pam a wide-eyed look. "Did I—did I say something inappropriate to you? Gee, Pam, I didn't know it would upset you."

I felt a smile coming on and looked at my feet.

Sounding more like a five-year-old than a fifteen-year-old, Pam yelled, "I'm telling!" She ran over to Coach Morrison and gesticulated wildly, pointing at Z.Z. and then at her nose. Coach Morrison shrugged indifferently and walked away from her. Pam, slack-jawed, watched him, then pulled her cell phone out of her duffle bag.

"She's probably calling her mommy to tattle on me, which means Granny'll get a phone call later," Z.Z. said. "Oh, well. Granny sees them for who they are. I'm not worried about it."

"What's going on?" Joshua said. My stomach hit the ground, and I tried to escape, but Z.Z. kept me firmly in place.

"We need to talk to you, Mr. Man," Z.Z. said.

"Mr. . . . Man?" Joshua said.

"Mm-hmmmm." Z.Z. worked her neck at him. *Uh-oh.* She hooked one arm through his elbow and held me tightly with her other one.

"Do you remember what we talked about the last time we were here, Joshua?" Z.Z. asked as she stepped up to a row of bleachers. She sat, pulling Joshua and me down with her. I lowered my head and closed my eyes. My heart was pounding so hard, I bet they could see it through my shirt.

"Y-yeah," Joshua said.

Z.Z. released my shoulders, and I felt my spine curve over a little. *Please don't throw up. Please don't throw up.*

"Are you okay, Ashley?" Joshua asked.

"She's fine. Talk to *me*, guy. I'm the one you gotta be worryin' 'bout right now."

"Worry—why?"

Z.Z. clucked her tongue. "Well, ya see, your frien' Pam, over there—"

"Pam's not what I'd call a friend—"

"I'm talkin'. You're listenin'. You got that?"

"Yeah, sure; I just—"

She clucked her tongue again. "Now, see? There you go talkin' again."

"Oh."

"Here's the thing, Joshua. . . . " Z.Z. said and then went on, recounting the events leading up to the Barf Fest, as well as what Pam said in the meeting with Bev and me in

Bev's classroom. She ended her speech: "And that's why I am gonna have to hurt ya, boy, and I mean, P-A-I-N."

At that point, the rumble of the bus and the whine of its air brakes sounded. *Sweet timing!* "We've gotta go," I said and started to get up. Z.Z. pulled me back down.

"What you got to say for yourself, Joshua?" she said, sounding just like her granny. I looked at her, and she was wagging her finger at Josh just like her granny would.

"I—I—" He stood and looked down at me. "I *didn't* tell Pam that. I'd never . . . ! You've got to believe me."

Coach Morrison blew his whistle. "Asher! Brandt! Freeman!"

I forced myself to meet Joshua's gaze. God, how I wanted what he was saying to be true. I mumbled, "Then where did she hear that?"

He shook his head, and his eyes seemed red. "I don't know, but I'm gonna find out."

"Scared me for a minute. I thought our star runner wasn't coming." Coach Morrison tapped his clipboard as Joshua, Z.Z., and I boarded the bus.

"Aw, Coach, you can always count on me!" Z.Z. said with just a touch of sarcasm. Coach Morrison playfully swung his clipboard at her.

"Josh, come sit next to me," Pam called from the very back of the bus.

"No, thanks," he said without even glancing at her. "Coach, I need to talk to you in private, okay?"

256

"Sure, Joshua," Coach Morrison said. He gestured to the first seat on the bus. "Is this gonna be private enough?"

"Yeah, that's fine."

I followed Z.Z. to the middle section. I started to sit down next to her, but she said, "I need to get some sleep on the way there, so could you sit across from me? Somebody kept me up late last night, talkin' my ear off." She made her duffle bag into a pillow, lay back on it as best she could, and closed her eyes.

"Really? I guess I remember it differently," I said dryly.

"How long's it gonna take to get to Crockett, Coach?" Dub called from behind us.

"'Bout an hour or so," Coach Morrison yelled, then bent his head back to Joshua's.

The bus pulled to a stop, and Pam raced up the aisle. "I have to be the first one off! It's part of my ritual!"

The driver opened the door, and Pam made a big show of exiting the bus, swinging her ponytail—*Look at me!*—and beginning her stretches before the rest of us had even unloaded. It was the last meet before the district championship, as Pam had reminded us all the way to Deep East Texas. I had not for one second regretted missing out on hearing "I'm going to state, so I'm going for eight" in the last few weeks.

Coach Morrison went to check us in and came back with the bibs for the team. Pam practically tackled him. "I hope my number has an eight in it! Come on, eight!"

"Let's see; Junior? Step on up here," Coach said.

"Where's mine? Where's mine?" Pam said.

"I'm gettin' to it; just calm down," he said.

"She looks like a hyper Chihuahua," Z.Z. whispered. I nodded.

"Z.Z.? Well, now, Z.Z., *your* number is 282. Maybe some of Pam's luck will rub off on you." He handed Z.Z. her bib and safety pins.

"Ha!" Pam snorted. Coach shot her a sharp look; she took a sip of water, spritzed a little on her forehead, and jogged in place.

I started pinning Z.Z.'s bib on her.

"I'm ready! I'm ready!" Pam breathed deeply and did a hamstring stretch.

"Dub," Coach said and handed Dub his number. Dub passed Pam in an exaggerated slow-motion jog and swung his head back and forth as if he was swinging a ponytail.

Junior cough-laughed and said in a high-pitched voice, "It's part of my ritual!" But Pam didn't notice; she was watching Coach Morrison like a dog watches somebody's dinner.

"Z.Z., Dub, and Junior, could you excuse us, please?" Coach asked.

I started to follow Z.Z., but Coach said, "Ashley, I need you to stay here with Joshua and Pam." I grimaced, but I did a U-turn and joined them in front of Coach Morrison.

He nodded at Joshua, who'd been standing stoically with his arms folded across his chest during check-in. I could see that his jaw was clenched and his eyes burned into the side of Pam's face. "Look at me, Pam," Josh said.

She slowly turned her head toward him.

"Are we friends, Pam?" Josh's voice shook.

"Um, yeah. Sure," she said in her little-girl voice, then ran her finger over his bicep.

I glanced at Coach Morrison, and he nodded at me reassuringly. I wondered what was going on.

"This race . . . it's really important to you, isn't it?" Josh said.

"Of course, silly! Isn't it important to you?" she asked. Joshua looked at her coldly. She glanced at Coach Morrison. "What's this about?"

"You . . . said some horrible things to Ashley." Joshua snorted and shook his head. "I mean, Pam, I knew you were a spoiled brat, but—"

Pam gasped. "Are you gonna let him talk to me like that?" Coach Morrison put his hands behind his back, pursed his lips, and shifted his feet a little.

"But I didn't know you were capable of such . . . evil." Josh gazed at her as if seeing her true nature for the first time.

"Evil?" Pam whirled on me. "What did you do, Ashley, go crying to Joshua? Wasn't your stepmom threatening to get me kicked off student council enough for you?"

"No. I, I—" I fumbled, choking on my own spit.

Josh said, "No, Pam, we're *not* friends. No friend of mine would ever act the way you do." He held out his hand, and Coach placed the last two racing bibs in it. "These are our bibs, Pam." Josh showed her their names printed on the tear strips. He handed his bib back to Coach Morrison, then held Pam's up and ripped it right down the middle.

Pam grabbed for it, but Joshua held it out of her reach. "Are you just going to stand there?" she shrieked at Coach Morrison. He just shrugged.

"Pam, you're a liar. You said I told you that Ashley moved to Patience because . . . Jesus, I don't even want to say it. You make me sick—you hear me?" Joshua's eyes filled with tears, and his voice shook with anger. He tore Pam's bib a little more.

She laughed at him. "Go ahead and tear it. I'll just get another one." She turned her back on Joshua, folded her arms, and stuck her chin in the air.

Coach Morrison cleared his throat. "You'd, uh . . . you'd need me to help you with that."

Pam's eyes widened in realization, and she whipped back around. "No, Joshua! Please! You—you know I can't race without it! Why are you doing this to me?"

Joshua's face was bright red by now. "Tell the truth, Pam! Tell Ashley and me the truth—right now—or I'm ripping this thing to pieces and you're done."

"You'd let him do that?" Pam yelled at Coach Morrison. He turned his back on her, as if she wasn't even there.

"But without me, our team can't advance!" She pointed at me. "It's not like she or Z.Z. ever did anything to help our standings! You need me!"

"And you need to tell the truth!" Josh screamed. "Do it now, or I swear to God—" He ripped the bib a bit further.

"Okay, okay!" Pam sat down on the ground and put her fists over her eyes. She mumbled something, but Joshua said, "You'd better speak up," and tore the bib even further.

She rose to her knees. "I just wanted a ride home, Joshua!"

"What?!" he said.

"I just wanted a ride home, and you told me you couldn't give me one because you had to talk to Z.Z. So when I saw you two heading for the bleachers, I went around the field house the other way and . . . I was under the bleachers when you two were talking."

She looked up angrily and said, "Z.Z. told *you* that Ashley moved here because she had an affair with her step-father. *I heard her.*"

"*No!*" I screamed. Pam fell back on her hands and looked up at me, shocked. "She said that my *mother* accused me of having an affair with her husband, *after* I told my mother that he was *molesting me!*"

Pam looked confused. "Oh. Well, that's different. Um, sorry," she said. But she didn't sound sorry at all.

" 'Oh, sorry'? That's all you can *say*?" I wanted to kick that smirk right off her face, but I forced myself to turn around and walk toward the fence, where Z.Z. was waiting for me.

"Ashley, wait up!" Joshua called. It didn't take long for him to catch up—probably two long strides. "I'm sorry about all this," he said.

I stopped and looked up at him. "Why are *you* sorry?"

He blushed. "If I hadn't asked Z.Z. about you, none of this would have happened. I just wanted to—"

"Know some of the dirt?" I cut him off and narrowed my eyes at him.

His eyes widened. "No, I just . . . wanted to . . . God, I can't believe your mom treated you like that." He put his hand on my shoulder, but I grabbed his wrist and threw it back at him.

"Look, I don't want to talk about this with you. I should never have told you as much as I did about myself in the first place, because that's what opened up this—tube of toothpaste."

Joshua cocked his head. "Toothpaste?"

"Never mind. I appreciate what you did back there. So hey, thanks. I'm glad you didn't really tell Pam that stuff."

"I'd never do that—"

"Yeah, I get it. You're a saint. Now . . . go run your race, do your thing, whatever." I made an abrupt left turn and walked purposefully toward a crowd of kids just getting off their buses, with the sole intent of losing myself in them.

※

I can think of a lot of nasty words to call Pam Little-john, but here's one that would never apply: *quitter*. Pam's no quitter. She may have been rattled to the core by nearly missing her chance to run, but she beat her own best time and came in second in the girls' 2A division. She was headed to district, just as she'd hoped.

Joshua didn't fare as well; he ran as hard as ever, but finished only eighteenth. He didn't join the rest of us right away in our team's area. I guess he needed to be by himself for a little while. I wondered whether he'd been unable to focus, given the brouhaha with Pam, and I kicked myself for being such a jerk when he tried to talk to me. I wanted to tell him I was sorry, but I couldn't. Sometimes I'm such a weenie.

Z.Z. was elated. She'd finished long before the last runner. "I think I need to get really, really angry just before a race," she told me. "I kept thinkin' 'bout all this mess with Pam, and the madder I got, the faster I ran."

I pretended to write on an imaginary notepad and said aloud, "Note to self: piss off Z.Z. before every race." I mimed tearing off the page, folding it, and putting it in my pocket. "Got it."

"Woo! Did you see me fly over that ditch, man?" Dub took off his singlet and whipped it above his head like a lasso. "I'm part deer!"

Junior took Three from Moreyma and put him on his shoulders, then galloped around with him. Three's laugh was bubbly and full.

Coach Morrison grinned and said, "Good season, everybody. Let's head for Pizza Hut."

CHAPTER 12

The last full week of school before Thanksgiving, Bev put us into our groups to write our skits on individuality. As promised, K.C. wore her rainbow T-shirt. Beneath the emblem, it read, "Will God judge me for loving or you for hating?"

Marcus took one look at her shirt and blasted at Bev, "I object to being in a group with K.C.!"

Bev looked up from speaking with another group of students. "Okay," she said.

Marcus stood up with his books. "Which group do you want me to join?"

"Oh, you're not moving from the one you're in," Bev said, turning back to what she was doing.

"But you said, 'Okay,' Miss Asher." Marcus walked to the front of the room and looked at her expectantly.

"Yes, I said, 'Okay,' because you're free to express your objection, Marcus, but that doesn't mean I'm moving you. I would think that you, of all people, would have experience in dealing with people who don't see eye to eye with you. Don't you recognize what an opportunity this is?" Bev said.

264

"Opportunity?"

"Yes, this assignment is an opportunity to express how you set yourself apart from others in the world, how you get people to see you as an individual. I'd say that a difference of opinion is a great way to start figuring that out."

Marcus's eyes bulged, and he looked like a toad when it puffs up its neck.

"Aw, don't get all huffy, Marcus," K.C. said. "I promise, you're not one of the people I love. Does that make you feel any better?"

Marcus ignored her and insisted, "It's about taking a stand, Miss Asher."

"I agree; it is. And isn't it cool that you have the freedom to be who and what you are without being put into some sort of prison because of it? Just think, you have the Constitution of the United States protecting your freedom to believe as you do. Just like K.C. does."

Marcus looked confused. "No. I mean, well, yeah, but . . . "

"Sit down, Marcus. Your project is due Friday, and I'm not accepting blustery behavior as an excuse for not having it completed."

~

The next morning, Marcus came into Bev's room before school and paraded in front of K.C., who was playing an unplugged version of "Smells Like Teen Spirit" on Kurt.

Not that Marcus needed any help stretching out the logo, but he made a point of holding the material away from his body so that K.C. could read, "Marriage = 1 Man + 1 Woman."

K.C. said, "Nice shirt. Now you have a billboard showing the world how closed-minded you are." She set Kurt aside. "You really didn't need the shirt. You radiate homophobia."

"All right, that's it," Bev said. She turned from writing notes on the board, pointed to the chair next to K.C., and issued an order to Marcus: "You. Sit." Then she joined them.

"This debate you two are engaging in is not going to be resolved through T-shirts or snide comments. While I believe in free speech, I also have the right to set limits within my classroom so that we can accomplish what needs to be done. I am hereby imposing a moratorium on the gay marriage debate for at least the remainder of this week."

"But this is my way of being an individual!" Marcus said, pointing at the emblem on his T-shirt.

"Yeah, that's what my T-shirts are, too," K.C. said. A look of horror crossed her face. "Oh, my God. We actually agree on something."

"You probably agree on a lot more than you disagree on," Bev said. "I'm going to propose something to you, and it may blow your minds, but hear me out anyway. Even though this project is about expressing yourselves as individuals, I want your group to find something you all have in common. Then figure out how you approach it as individuals."

"I don't get it," Marcus and K.C. said at the same time.

Bev slapped the desktop happily and said, "Woo-hoo! Another thing you have in common! See? I knew you could do this!" She got up and did a little hip-shake dance all the way to her door, and we could hear her singing as she went down the hall.

Coming up with an idea we could all agree on seemed impossible. "I propose that we write a musical," K.C. said. "Kurt can be the lead."

"Since it's due Friday, we only have three days plus the rest of this class period to write it," I said. "That's not enough time for a musical. Besides, it's supposed to be five minutes or less."

K.C. leaned down and pretended to be listening to Kurt. She strummed his strings and nodded. "He says he understands. Maybe next time."

Marcus rolled his eyes heavenward and mouthed the words, "Why me?"

"Okay, y'all, here we go. Best idea ever." We looked expectantly at Z.Z. "Dancing! We could each do an individual dance move." She stood and moved to a beat that only she could hear.

"Dancing is a sin," Marcus stated flatly, looking up at the ceiling to avoid watching Z.Z. Her eyes took on a look of delight, and she backed her rear up to Marcus, then rocked back and forth, bumping his shoulders rhythmically.

"Get down with yo bad self, Marcus! You gotta learn to live, boy! Unh!"

Marcus moved his hands up to either side of his eyes like horse blinders and stared at the ceiling.

K.C. and I exchanged smirks as Z.Z. continued to dance in a circle all around Marcus.

"Miss Asher!" Marcus whined.

"Z.Z.," Bev said in a warning tone. Z.Z. said nothing but shimmied down into her seat and wiggled her fingers Marcus's way. He glanced at her quickly, then back at the ceiling.

"She's still doing it!" he said.

"My fingers? My fingers are dancing, and you got a problem with that? Boy, what are you afraid of?"

"That's it! That's it! Everybody's afraid of something! That's what we have in common! But how we handle fear is what can be individual!" I started writing my idea immediately, as if it would vanish as quickly as it had appeared.

"Yeah," K.C. nodded. "Yeah!"

"Fear?" Marcus said flatly. He shook his head. "This is just more proof that you aren't living a righteous life."

Z.Z. worked her neck and wiggled her fingers at him, but he didn't react. She dropped her hands. "Say what?"

"I can't wait to hear this one," K.C. sighed. She picked up Kurt and strummed a few chords, all the while studying Marcus with narrowed eyes.

I made the time-out sign. "Let's take a vote. How many of us want our scene to be about how we handle fear?" I nodded at Z.Z. and K.C.'s raised hands. "Majority rules. Let's write!"

"But—" Marcus said.

K.C. put her hand on Marcus's wrist and said sweetly, "Your part can be about how you're so afraid of what you don't understand; you hide behind your Bible and pick on people who are different from you. 'Kay?"

Marcus jerked his hand back and wiped it on his pants leg. K.C. pretended to be filming his actions and said, "Hold it right there, Marcus! Ashley, did you see what he did? Write that down! I think we've found the perfect role for Marcus!"

His mouth curled into a sneer. "You're not really . . . ya know"—he made his wrist limp—"gay . . . are you?" The buzz of conversation around us suddenly stopped, and it seemed that everyone was leaning toward our group, listening. K.C. sat up in her chair and started to reply.

"Toothpaste!" I blurted.

Marcus's eyebrows came up to his hairline. "Wh-what?" he gasped and shook his head at me.

"Tooth . . . paste." I nodded at K.C., my eyes huge.

She stared at me a moment, stood Kurt against Z.Z.'s desk, then leaned over to me and placed the back of her hand on my forehead. "Doesn't *feel* like you have a fever." She leaned back in her chair, nodded at me, and said, "Toilet . . . paper." She cut her eyes to Z.Z. and said, "Your turn. I think the theme is 'Things Found in the Bathroom.' "

❦

"Did you guys make any progress on your skit today, Ashley?" Bev said, sliding a pan of enchiladas into the oven.

"Well, we agreed on our topic, sort of." I looked up from my Human Ecology homework. "Bev, we're studying grandparents and what rights they have, and it's got me thinking."

"Yeah, I noticed smoke from over there. Wondered what was causing it."

"Very funny. Your mom lives in Colorado, right?"

"Yep."

"Don't you . . . I mean, do you ever see her? Like, does she ever come for the holidays?"

Bev rinsed a head of lettuce under the tap and didn't answer.

"Did you hear me?"

She shook the excess water from the lettuce and began tearing the leaves into pieces. She seemed to be trying to choose the right words. "Yeah, I heard you. No, she doesn't ever come here. Not really."

"Why not?"

"Uh, it's kinda like we were in a war together. The whole time I was growing up, my parents fought a lot. They were in the middle of a real knock-down-drag-out when my dad dropped dead of a heart attack. I think Mom blamed herself for it—and for a while, I did, too. Then she remarried, and her new husband has a lot of family in Fort Collins." Bev brought the salad bowl and cutting board to the kitchen table and sat down next to me. She picked up a tomato and began slicing it slowly as she spoke. "I think it's just easier for her to lose herself in being part of her new family instead of being reminded of her old life here." She frowned and blinked a few times.

I touched her shoulder. "I'm sorry."

She leaned her head against my hand in a sort of hug

and scraped the tomato slices into the salad bowl. "Thanks, Ashley." Then she picked up a cucumber and began peeling it. She took a deep breath and blew it out. "I know, I know," she laughed. "Good sigh, Bev."

"Yeah," I gave her a sideways hug. "Good sigh, Bev." I slid my homework papers into my textbook and reached for my backpack.

"I don't know about you, Ash, but I sure am ready for our break next week!" Bev placed the salad bowl in the center of the table.

"What's Thanksgiving like here?" I shoved my stuff into my backpack and went to hang it on the hook by the front door.

Bev rinsed her hands and dried them with a dish towel. "We get up early and go to downtown Dallas, and I run the eight-mile Turkey Trot. Frank, your dad, Ben, and Stephen walk the shorter course. If you think you're up to it, you could bring Emma and do it with them. Lots of people bring their dogs. We get home and play cards while the turkey's roasting, then we eat and watch the Cowboys game. What did your family in Northside do?"

"Let's see, we'd go to Papaw and Nanny's country club for lunch, then head back to their house and watch the Cowboys game. When it was over, Mom and Charlie'd fight over the car keys because Charlie was always so drunk. Mom always gave in, so the ride home was like playing Russian roulette; our Toyota was the bullet, and everybody else on the road . . . well, you get the idea."

Bev looked horrified. "It's bad enough that he drives drunk, but with you and your mom in the car too?"

I said in mock seriousness, "Aw, come on, Bev! He had the windows down! The cold air sobered him right up!"

She opened her arms, and I moved into them. She hugged me tight and murmured, "I know one thing I'm especially thankful for this year, Ash."

I closed my eyes and breathed in her scent. "Me too, Bev."

"I'm telling you, if you asked the Lord Jesus Christ into your hearts, you wouldn't be afraid of anything!" Marcus slapped his Bible onto Z.Z.'s desk for emphasis.

Z.Z. sighed loudly and rolled her eyes toward the ceiling. "And I'm tellin' you, quit assumin' that I don't have religion just 'cause I don't go to your church!"

"For the zillionth time, you two, we don't have time for this! The skit's due tomorrow!" I gripped the edge of my desk and pulled myself toward Marcus. "Please, focus. In *Farewell to Manzanar*, just because Jeanne's family was Japanese, people assumed they were a danger to the United States. We've narrowed the idea to 'Just because I . . . people assume I'm . . . ' and where we differ is how we try to get people to see us as individuals, okay?"

"Well, that's different. You said before it was about fear," Marcus said.

"It *is* about fear, because it's fear that makes people assume things about other people and decide to lock them out of society. Got it?" Z.Z. wiggled her fingers at him as if casting a spell.

"Whatever." Marcus sat back and folded his hands over his belly.

"That's the first thing you've said all day that wasn't a closed-minded judgment on someone else," K.C. said. "Good job!"

He picked up his Bible and started thumbing through it.

K.C. held up her fingers in a cross. "Please! No more quoting Scripture!"

Marcus jabbed an index finger at her. "Aha! A cross! I *am* having an impact on you!" He sent his palms skyward. "Thank you, Jesus!"

"Arrrrrrgh!" I put my head in my hands. "Okay, every-body. Just write your own lines tonight. At least we have a basic structure. Dub said he'd help us out. But I give up. This is going to be a disaster."

❧

The closing credits of *Pearl Harbor* began to roll. Coach Griffin flipped on the lights and stood before us with his arms folded over his chest. "I hope you enjoyed our World War II unit. I, for one, did not. When we return from our break, we'll be moving on to the Depression era."

"Isn't that where we've been the past three weeks?" Kevin asked. "Man, this has been really depressing, Coach!"

"I love Ben Affleck!" Pam cooed. "I learned a lot about World War II from him!" The other girls giggled and said things like "He's hot!" "Josh Hartnett's my man!" "Kate Beckinsale's one lucky *chica*."

"Did you notice how stereotyped the Japanese characters were, compared with the Americans?" I asked.

"I'm not surprised to hear you say that, Miss Asher," Coach Griffin said dismissively.

"It's true; didn't you see—"

"Enough!" Coach Griffin slammed his yardstick down on my desk. I sprang out of my chair and ran to the back wall.

He laughed and waved his hands at me. "Ooooo, I guess I should have said, 'Boo!' That'll make you hit the road too, won't it, Asher?"

I blushed and looked at my feet. He turned from my desk and moved to the front of the room. I sheepishly sat back down at my desk and hated myself for being such a coward.

"Wow, what a big man," K.C. muttered.

"Did you say something, Miss Williamson?"

She looked up at him. "Yeah, I just think it's pathetic the way you use scare tactics and your position of authority to intimidate people."

Coach Griffin pulled her out of her desk by her arm and shoved her toward the door. "Go to the office, dyke."

I stood up. "Hey!"

"You too, Asher. Get out!"

I bolted out the door and caught up with K.C., who was sobbing as she trudged toward the office. I put my arm around her, and she stepped away.

"Oooh—careful now, Ashley! People are gonna think you're a dyke, too!"

I steered her into the girls' bathroom, checked the stalls

for occupants, then closed the door behind us and locked it. Not knowing what else to say, I took a breath and said, "Just . . . wait. Just wait, K.C., okay? Let's calm down first."

K.C. stood before the mirror, crying as she looked at herself. "God! I—I just want to die soooo bad." She grabbed the sides of the sink and bent over the basin. Her sobs echoed off the walls.

I moved to her and rubbed her back until her breathing slowed. "That's not the answer. Trust me."

She abruptly stood up and looked me in the eye. "Yeah, well, I tried it before. Didn't work. I couldn't even do that right; I just ended up getting my stomach pumped." She slid down the bathroom wall, and I joined her on the floor.

"I've never actually tried to kill myself. Just thought of different ways to do it."

"Why would *you* want to die, Ashley? You've got a cool stepmom, and, hey, you're straight! So that's one thing you've got going for ya." She thought a moment and said, "Actually, I guess that's two."

I took her hand. "It's not important right now, K.C. Look, I . . . your mom told me some stuff that day at our therapists' office. Said you moved here because things were bad in Houston?"

K.C. snorted. "My parents freaked out because I fell in love with my best friend—who was a girl. Her name was Kathleen, and her brother caught us kissing in her room. All hell broke loose after that. Kathleen's parents pulled her out of school and put her in a private academy, and her brother told everybody that I'm a dyke."

"Do you and Kathleen still keep in touch?" I asked.

K.C. shook her head and sighed. "Nah. She . . ." K.C. made air quotes. "*Decided* that she's not gay. Last I heard, she was dating some jock—a guy, I assume."

"So is that why you tried to kill yourself? That had to hurt—"

"Not as much as the way my parents look at me now, like they're disgusted by me. Can you imagine what it's like to have your own mother hate you?"

I closed my eyes and lowered my head. "Believe it or not, yeah, I can."

K.C. stood up and brushed off her butt, then offered me a hand and pulled me up. She turned to the mirror and smoothed her unruly long curls behind her ears, then splashed cold water on her face. She looked back at me in the reflection. "You know, Ashley, my parents dragged me from one counselor to another in Houston, trying to find somebody to fix me. There was this one Christian counselor—and I mean, Marcus the windbag has nothin' on this guy—who told me that *Satan* was causing me to have feelings for girls. That's when I went home and swallowed every pill in the house."

"Damn!"

"Yeah. The thing is, some of the therapists they took me to tried to tell my parents, 'Hey, your daughter's a lesbian; that's who she is, and you need to learn to accept her or lose her.' But my parents didn't want to hear that. So then they decided the problem was the big city, I guess." She smiled ruefully.

"What about Dr. Trevino? What does she say?"

K.C. washed her hands and cranked the handle on the paper towel dispenser. Finding it empty, she wiped her hands on her jeans and turned toward me. "That's what's so awesome about her, Ashley. She totally understands me, and she's helping me learn to accept who I am. She's the first therapist I've met who seems to know how to handle my mom. And I gotta tell you, it's freakin' fantastic!"

I smiled. "That's great! So . . . you okay now?"

K.C. shrugged. "I'm not thrilled about being sent to the office, if that's what you mean."

"I've got an idea, K.C." I told her how nervous Mr. Walden is about Kevin's mom being a reporter. "When we tell Mr. Walden about Coach Griffin pulling you out of your seat, I don't think you're the one he's going to be upset with."

"We? You mean you're going with me?"

"He kicked *me* out of the room, too. Hell, yeah, I'm going with you! You're not alone, K.C. Not any more. Don't forget that."

❧

"Again, Ashley?" Marvella called after me as K.C. and I walked past her desk to the bench outside Mr. Walden's office. She gestured to me, and I tiptoed back to her. K.C. followed. Marvella's eyes widened when we explained what had happened.

"He called you a *dyke*, sweetheart? I'm so sorry," she said to K.C. "Some of the people 'round here are stuck in a cotton-pickin' time warp or somethin'."

"Yeah, but what about Mr. Walden?" K.C. said.

"Oh, honey, he's not even here today. He's seein' a dermatologist in Dallas, tryin' to find out why he keeps breakin' out in some sorta stress rash."

Marvella's eyes lit up, and she started digging through papers on her desk. "You know what?" she said, dragging the word *what* into three syllables. "We just got a notice from the state education agency, sayin' that each campus in our district needs to send a representative for a week of diversity awareness training, week after next. . . . Found it!" She grinned from ear to ear and held up the form for us to see.

"So?" K.C. and I said.

She began filling out the form in her large, loopy handwriting. "Well, I'm just gonna sign up Mr. Dayton Griffin to be our campus representative. Sounds like he could use a week of workshops—might help him calm down a little. Anyway, after I tell Mr. Walden what Coach Griffin did to you and what he called you, I'm sure he'll thank me for forging—I mean *signing*—his name and faxing the form to Austin. I'll just do that right now.

"Prevention of bad publicity's worth a pound of school board meetings, I always say! Think about it, girls: it would be *such a shame* if Trini Cooper heard about another case of a female student being manhandled by a male staff member. I *sure* hope she doesn't get a call from, oh, I don't know, a student who was in that class."

"You really are cool!" K.C. said, clearly shocked by the sudden improvement in her day.

Marvella blushed. "Aw, thank you, sweetheart. I may be country, but I know right from wrong. Y'all run along now. I need to make a phone call."

We were almost to the door when we heard Marvella say, "Hey, Trini? It's Marvella. How are ya, honey?"

⌒

"You want me to wear this *dress*?" Dub held up the black T-shirt with the word "Fear" written on it in white fabric paint. We stood in the hallway, waiting for the go-ahead to enter the room for our skit. Dub slipped the shirt on, and it swallowed his small frame. "Damn, this thing is huge!"

"It was my Auntie Jewel's shirt, and she's a big girl," Z.Z. said. "You just gotta do like we talked about, okay?"

"I could use the extra material to strangle Marcus," Dub offered hopefully.

"Get in line," K.C. said flatly.

"Not funny," Marcus said. He shifted from one foot to the other and wiped beads of perspiration from his upper lip.

"You're not nervous, are you?" I asked him.

"No, no. Warriors for Christ don't get nervous."

"Well, it's only natural if you are—" Z.Z. said.

"I'm *not* nervous, okay?" Marcus snapped.

Z.Z. grabbed my arm. "Ash, Roxanne's ready with the CD, right?"

"Yeah, she's got it."

Teresa Benedict opened the door and said, "You're on."

Z.Z. walked in first, then pulled a chair to the front of the room and sat in it. I was next, followed by Marcus and K.C., who carried Kurt. She closed her eyes and began to play very softly.

Dub entered the room and stood in front of us. "I am Fear," he said and moved to stand behind each of us as he spoke. "I color perception. I give birth to assumption. I create tragedy. I disguise myself as anger and sometimes as self-righteousness. I am Fear."

Z.Z. stood. "I am afraid when people think they know who I am just by looking at me. It scares me when people do evil things to my family, like beat up my cousin Jasper or poison our dog. I don't know what to do with the feelings. So sometimes I dance them away."

Roxanne started the CD, and Beyoncé's "Single Ladies" began playing. The class began clapping, and Z.Z. danced around the perimeter of the room. She shimmied back toward us, making sure to shake it especially hard in Marcus's direction. He locked his eyes on the ceiling and shook his head. Then she sat down.

Marcus stood and nodded her way. "Now, *that's* scary stuff," he said dryly. She smiled and wiggled her fingers at him. He closed his eyes and held up his Bible. Finally, he sighed, "I . . . talk. A lot."

"Yeah, you do!" someone said. Then another called out, "Amen!"

Marcus shook his head and looked down for what felt like a long time. K.C. played the first few notes of Green

Day's "Time of Your Life," then began strumming it. Marcus looked back at her, surprised. She paused, and he said, "No, no. Keep going. I like it." K.C. shrugged and played on.

"I . . . haven't been an easy person to work with on this project, because I just insisted that there's nothing I'm afraid of . . . but I couldn't sleep last night, trying to think of what I'd say today. And I realized that I *am* afraid of something. I'm afraid of . . . not having all the answers."

He looked down at his Bible and flipped through the pages. "What if . . . what if all the answers *aren't* in here? Where does that leave me and my family? What if our way isn't the only way? Like, there are people in the world who've never heard of Jesus. What if they all go to heaven, too?"

Marcus turned back and looked at the three of us, and his eyes were full of tears. "It's all I've got," he whispered. "This certainty in being right—it's all I've got."

He sat down and put his head in his hands. I put my hand on his shoulder, and when he turned to me and I looked into his eyes, for the first time I saw him for who he is: just another scared person, trying to do the best he can with the answers he thinks he has.

K.C. nodded at me, and I stood. "Until I moved to Patience last May, I lived in a constant state of fear. It was so bad that even though I'm no longer in that situation, there are times when the memories make me act on that incredible sense of fear. If I let it, fear controls every aspect of my life. Giving in to fear is what knocked me out of cross-country for the season, 'cause I got hurt when I let the fear

281

control me. Fear is what used to drive me into small spaces to hide. Fear is what kept me silent and alone for years. Z.Z. dances through her fear. Marcus relies on his faith. And me? I'm learning to . . . wait." Waiting seemed like such a simple thing to do; I felt silly when I sat down after saying it.

K.C. stood and riffed on Stevie Ray Vaughan's "Life by the Drop." She walked toward our classmates, clearly enjoying the way they were clapping along. Then she abruptly stopped.

"Hey, that was really good! Why'd you stop? Keep goin', girl!" they called out.

K.C. leaned Kurt against Bev's desk and walked back to where we sat. She turned, her fingers steepled under her chin, and surveyed the classroom. "I wonder whether you'll still be seeing me as K.C. the musician after I tell you what I'm afraid of." She took a big breath in and let it out. There wasn't a sound in the room now.

"Toothpaste!" I hissed from my seat.

K.C. turned and regarded me with raised eyebrows. She smiled and whispered back, "We'll play Password later, 'kay, Ash?" I made a zipping gesture along my lips. She shook her head at me and turned back to face our classmates.

"I'm afraid to be myself because so many people in the world, including my parents, don't like the way I turned out. Look at me," she said as she turned in place. "Two arms, two legs—"

She wiggled her fingers and lifted one foot at a time. "Five fingers on each hand, five toes on each foot. Do you ever hear people say, 'I just want a healthy baby; I don't care if it's a boy or a girl'?"

K.C. stopped turning around, put her hands on her hips and said bitterly, "The thing is, when parents say that, it's not always true. I think if they were really honest, they'd add, 'And the baby has to be heterosexual. No fags. No dykes.' "

The walls of the room seemed to contract with the collective gasp of our audience. I glanced at Pam to see if she was scribbling in the back of her spiral notebook; she wasn't. Bev's eyes were soft, and her face held sympathy.

"So . . ." K.C. blew out a big breath. "How do I deal with my fear?" She gestured toward Kurt. "I play my guitar. I make wise-ass comments. I *try* not to let the fact that my own parents are ashamed of me bug me too much. And I just keep going." She turned and walked out the open door, and the rest of us followed.

T.W. Griffin and his group had been watching the entire thing from the hallway. "That was awesome." He hugged K.C. "I wish my dad could've been there to see it. I'm sorry he's such a closed-minded prick."

K.C. was shaking from head to toe. "I'm so proud of you," I said.

She hugged me and said, "Thanks, Ashley—for everything." Then she turned to Marcus and offered him her hand. "Friends, Marcus?"

He slowly shook his head and said, "I'm sorry, K.C. I just can't."

CHAPTER 13

The phone rang, and I startled awake. I squinted at the clock on my nightstand: 1:47 a.m. I was just falling back asleep when there was a tap at my door. "Ashley?"

"Huh?"

"I need to come in." David jiggled the doorknob. "Door's locked."

"Oh. Sorry." Some nights, I feel secure enough to leave my door unlocked. Maybe it was the holiday coming up, but my mom and Charlie had been on my mind a lot, so I slept better with the door locked. I climbed over Emma, who was still stretched out on her side with her head on my pillow, and unlocked the door. "Sorry," I said again.

"No need to apologize," he said. He hugged himself and said, "It's cold in here! If you're okay with leaving your door open, the heat'll circulate better."

"I don't know," I mumbled as I crawled over Emma and burrowed back under my covers. I pulled them up to my chin and watched David.

"That's fine. Okay with you if I sit down?" He gestured to the end of my bed.

I nodded. "Is something wrong, David?"

He bit his lip, then leaned over and scratched Emma's ears. "Hey, Em." She cracked one eye open, moaned, stretched, and crawled off my bed.

"David, who was on the phone? Is something wrong?" My spinning squirrel was trading bunny slippers for racing flats.

David scooted a little closer to me, took my hand, and said, "That was your mom, Ashley. She was calling from the hospital in Northside. There's been an accident."

I gasped. "Is she okay?"

"She's alive, Ash. She's in the emergency room right now. But . . . Charlie's dead."

I jumped out of bed and started pulling clothes out of my drawers, throwing them all over the place. "I've got to go to her, David. You—you've got to take me to her—"

"Wait a minute, Ashley, we need to—"

"You can't keep me from seeing her, David! I have to be there for her, I have to."

He rose from the bed and came toward me, motioning with his hands like a conductor telling the musicians to take it down a notch. "Calm down. No problem, Ashley; I can do that, but—"

"Get out, David! I've got to get dressed!"

He threw up his hands and backed out of my room, pulling the door closed behind him.

∾

A few minutes later, I emerged from my room, fully dressed. David and Bev were at the kitchen table. "I'm ready," I announced.

Bev gestured to the chair next to her. "Ash, sit down, sweetie. We're supposed to wait until somebody calls us back to let us know whether the hospital is keeping your mom or sending her home, okay?"

I shook my head vehemently. "No, I've gotta go to her now. She needs me. She's alone. She's afraid of being alone."

David narrowed his eyes at me. "Are you okay, Ashley?"

"My mom needs me. I've got to go."

"I didn't ask about Cheryl, Ashley. I asked if *you're* okay. I don't think you've had time to—"

"Don't worry about me, David. I know my mom needs me. Please take me to her."

He nodded slowly. "I will, just—"

I threw myself onto a chair so hard that the table moved. "What happened? Why is she hurt?" Suddenly, I was crying like a little kid and digging my fingernails into my face. I pulled my hands back and stared at them like they belonged to someone else, then looked at my dad. I was scaring *myself*.

David and Bev exchanged glances. Bev took a breath and said, "Remember how you and I were talking a few days ago, and you told me that Charlie drives drunk? Well . . . " She tilted her head from side to side and grimaced. "He had been drinking, and he took a corner too fast. He lost control of his truck and crashed into a tree. Your mom was with him, but she was wearing a seat belt, and the air bag—"

"Charlie's dead?" It was as if I was hearing it for the first time.

"Yes, sweetheart. Charlie was thrown from the truck. Your mom said he died instantly."

"Oh." I started sobbing, "Charlie's dead." I repeated again and again to myself, "My mom's alone. Charlie's dead." I rocked back and forth, giving in to the rhythm.

❧

The sun was just beginning to rise when David, Bev, and I pulled into the hospital parking garage. David cut the engine and turned to me. "I know you're probably all mixed up right now, Ash. I just . . . Honey, this may not turn out the way you're thinkin' it will."

"What do you mean?"

He frowned. "I know you believe your mom needs you, Ash; I just—" He shook his head at Bev.

She patted his shoulder and said, "I understand you want to protect her, David, but Ashley needs to see that her mom's okay. We can't control how other people feel, one way or another. We'll have to take this one step at a time. It's all anyone can do."

❧

My grandfather was smoking a cigarette just outside the hospital entrance. "What are *you* doing here?" He dropped the cigarette and ground it to a powder with his heel, all the while looking at me.

"Cheryl called us, Joe. Ashley just wants to make sure she's all right," David said.

"Ha! That's hilarious. After everything you did to them, *now* you—" Papaw shook his head and muttered to himself as he reached into his jacket for another cigarette and lit up. He took a long drag and blew smoke out through his nostrils.

"Please, we're not here to cause any trouble," Bev said. She took me by the elbow and moved me to her right, away from Papaw. Seeing how much Papaw hates me brought back Charlie's trial, and I suddenly wished I hadn't come. I felt as if I was choking on the lump in my throat, and I looked away from Papaw so he wouldn't see my tears.

He waved a hand in my direction. "Nah, Ashley'd never try to cause trouble. Obviously, she's sold you two a bill of goods, too. You'll learn about her lying ways soon enough." He took another drag on his cigarette and turned away from us.

David steered Bev and me through the doors. Papaw called after us, "You'll learn!"

❧

"It's not too late to change your mind, Ashley. You hear me?" David said once the elevator doors had closed behind us. We began our ascent to the third floor.

I nodded. I stared at my shoes and observed, "I got dressed in such a hurry, I'm wearing two different types of shoes." Bev put her arm around me and held me tight. The elevator doors opened, and my feet were frozen in place. "This might be a really bad idea," I exhaled.

"Still not too late," David said and held his finger on the "Close Door" button.

I bit my lip and closed my eyes. The image I had conjured of my mom lying in a hospital bed, frightened and alone, had been driving my actions since the moment David had told me about the accident. I took a deep breath and blew it out. "No. I—I need to do this. I need to see her; I need to let her know she's not all alone." I started to cry and said, "She hates being alone, do you understand?"

David's eyes filled with tears, and he whispered, "Yes, sweetie, I get that; I'm just worried you're walkin' into gettin' your heart broken again."

I swallowed hard, pulled David's hand away from the elevator button, and held it tightly in my own. I took Bev's hand in my other one, and the three of us left the safety of the elevator together.

∽

I nearly fell over when we walked into the room. My mother looked tiny and frail in the center of her bed. Her head was bandaged, and she was very pale.

Bev stopped just inside the doorway, but David followed me into the room and stood by the window. Just then, Nanny came out of the bathroom, wiping the side of a water pitcher with a white washcloth. A little cry escaped her lips when she saw us, and she dropped the cloth on the floor. She almost dropped the pitcher, but she caught herself and shakily placed it on the side table. "What are *you* doing here?"

"I—just—" I began.

"Cheryl called us," David said.

"Ashley Nicole?" my mom murmured and fluttered open her eyes.

"Mama!" I rushed to her and buried my face on her chest. I breathed in her scent like it was life itself. My mother laid her hand on my head.

"Careful, now," Nanny cautioned. "Her ribs are cracked."

I pulled away, but I held my mom's hand against my face and sobbed. "Oh, Mama, Mama, you're alive, you're alive."

"Yes, I'm . . . I'm okay, Ashley." She pulled her hand away so that I released it, then stroked my hair. We looked deeply into each other's eyes. Then her face crumpled, and she cried, "Charlie's dead, Ashley—"

"I know, Mama, I know," I sobbed.

Nanny put her arm behind Mom and gently lifted her, pulling her back toward the pillows, then placed a pillow gently atop her midsection. Mom moaned in pain.

"I'm sorry, baby," Nanny said.

I started to stand up, but my mother grabbed my arm. "Ashley—" she whispered and tilted her head for me to come closer. She closed her eyes, and I leaned down, mindful of not crushing her again. She whispered again, "Ashley."

I softly said, "I'm here, Mama."

"Ashley. You know. You *know* . . ." Her eyes were pleading with me.

"I know what, Mama?"

Her eyes half closed, she murmured, "You know . . . Charlie was a good man." She opened her eyes fully and nodded at me. "Say it."

A feeling of repulsion filled me, and I started to pull away from her. She grasped my upper arm with surprising strength, and it almost hurt. Bile reached the back of my throat, and I shook, inside and out. I held my breath, and *whoosh* . . . echoed through my mind.

My mother struggled to sit up, to get her face even closer to mine. Her eyebrows knit together, and she gritted her teeth against the pain. "Say it, Ashley—because you know it's true," she whispered as tears ran down her cheeks. "He was a good man."

I closed my eyes tightly and forced myself to take a breath. "I—can't say that, Mama. *Please* understand. I—I just can't."

Memories of Charlie tackling me, grabbing my breasts, his face like a madman's, blacking out and then coming to in our guest bedroom and finding the lower half of my body covered in blood—it all sped through my mind.

I shook my head hard against the images and barely recognized the little-girl voice that was coming from me. "Noooooo, Mama, please, please don't ask me to say it." I lowered my head to her shoulder and whined, much like a puppy does when it's lonely.

Then, in a voice so low, it almost sounded like a growl, she said, "Then, get out!" I opened my eyes to find that hers were fixed on me in an icy stare. "Get out. Get out. GET OUT!" She viciously twisted the skin of my upper arm, then abruptly released it and turned her face away from me.

I gasp-sobbed; I was falling into a spiraling black hole. I felt David's hands on my waist, pulling me away from her. He took me into his arms and half carried me from the room as my mother wept, "He was all I had. He was all I had."

I lay in the back seat of Bev's car and covered my head with my jacket. It wasn't a closet, but it was the best small, dark space I could get, for now. But I was already mapping out a strategy for the day:

1. Get home.
2. Lock bedroom door.
3. Crawl into pine wardrobe.
4. Stay there.

About halfway home, David pulled to a stop outside the Cotton Gin restaurant off Highway 175.

I popped up in the back seat. "Why are we stopping here?" I demanded.

"I'm hungry; Bev's hungry. . . . You hungry?" David asked me in the rearview mirror.

I grunted indignantly. "No! Why can't you just eat at home?"

His eyebrows high, he said, "Because . . . it's been a helluva night. I need some coffee, and we want to eat now. You don't have to come in if you don't want to—"

"I want to go home!" I said and kicked Bev's seat like a five-year-old.

"Hey!" Bev said. "Cut that out!"

I threw myself against the back seat and crossed my arms, feeling as much like a little kid as I was acting. David rolled his eyes and sighed. "Come on, Bev."

"Goddammit!" I kicked Bev's seat again and again as I watched them walk into the restaurant, furious with them for not knowing I had plans. Big plans.

When I heard the car doors open, I sat up, the jacket still over my head.

"You feeling better, Ashley?" David asked.

"No!" I spat from under my jacket.

"It's okay for you to be angry, Ashley." Bev closed her door, and I heard her seat belt click. "I'd like you to think about who you're angry with, though. That really had to be—"

"Grrrrr!" I flopped face-down in the back seat, covered my ears against Bev's calm words; I allowed the hate surging through my body to hammer me like a tsunami. I felt tears burning my eyes, and I pressed my fingers against them until I couldn't stand the pain.

I could hear Dr. Matt's voice in my mind: *Do I need to drop-kick the teddy bear, Ashley?* I moved my clawing hands to the sides of my head and raked my scalp until I felt warm liquid on my fingertips. The sobs in my chest that I'd been holding in crawled steadily to the back of my throat. And with every sob that finally escaped, I could hear Dr. Matt softly saying, *What a bitch. What a bitch. What a bitch.*

I could hear Dr. Matt softly saying, *What a bitch. What a bitch. What a bitch.*

"Ashley? We're home," Bev called.

I must have dozed off; I sat up, wiped the drool off my cheek, and squinted at the sunlight. "What time is it?" I sleepily said.

"Almost nine a.m.," Bev said.

"Why are we—? Ooooooh," I said, remembering the events of a few hours before. I sighed heavily and undid my seat belt.

The three of us shuffled to the front porch like zombies. Ben opened the door for us, and Emma came out. She sniffed my legs curiously.

"I probably smell like antiseptic and bitch, Emma," I mumbled, bending to scratch her ears. *Ah, yes. To the Ash-Cave!*

I murmured, "Hey, Ben," as I passed him on the way to my room.

Bev called after me, "Try to get some sleep for a few hours, Ash. Your buds will be here around one o'clock."

I whipped around. "What? Who?"

"Bev called Z.Z., Roxanne, and—what's the other girl's name?" David asked.

"K.C." Bev smiled at the shocked expression on my face.

"Wh-why'd you call them, Bev?"

"We're going to have a girls' day out, Ash. We're heading to Tyler for lunch out, a movie, and whatever other trouble we can get into."

I shook my head rapidly. "I don't want to go anywhere. I just want to be alo—"

Bev shrugged. "Sorry, Ashley, we're going. But for now," she sighed, "I'm going to lie down for a little while."

I watched her walk out of the room, let go a grunt of exasperation, and petulantly threw myself onto the sofa. Emma crawled up next to me, and I traced the freckles on her nose.

Tears filled my eyes, and I wiped them away roughly with the back of my hand. My chest ached, and it felt like sadness was swallowing me whole. I just wanted to be alone with it. What was the big problem with letting me wallow for a while?

Ben paused his video game and looked at me like I was crazy. "*You* don't wanna go to the movies?" He turned back to the TV and yelled to Bev, "If she doesn't wanna go, will you take me and Stephen, Mom?" But all we heard was the sound of her closing her bedroom door.

"After I snooze a little while, I thought you guys could help out in the shop today, Ben." David sat down heavily on a bar stool and pulled off his boots.

"Aaawww, Da—aaa—aad—"

"Yeah, Frank and I saw a corn snake in there the other day. We think it might have even had some babies back there behind the air filters. We wanted you two to help us root 'em out, but if you don't want to . . ."

Ben was out of there like a shot, screaming his jubilation all the way down the hall. "I'll get my BB gun! Can we use paintball guns, too?"

"No guns, Ben!" David called after him, then leaned over the back of the sofa and kissed me on the top of my head. He came around to the front of the sofa and sat down on the edge of the coffee table. "Ashley, I don't know what to say about what happened with your mom at the hospital. I—don't even have words to offer you. That was so rotten of her. Makes me wonder why she even called us."

I shook my head numbly and whispered, "Dr. Matt says . . . she's a bitch."

Beth Fehlbaum

David's eyebrows raised, and he shrugged. "Y-yeah, I guess that pretty much sums it up."

The tears I'd been holding back escaped, and my father held me while I cried and cried. I don't know how long we sat together, but by the time I pulled back from him, his shirt was soaked. I wiped the snot from my mouth and chin with his handkerchief.

David smoothed my hair and put his forehead against mine. "I love you so much, Ashley. I wish the love I have for you could make up for what your mom can't give you."

I nodded slightly and closed my eyes. "I wish I wasn't so . . . empty inside. It's like . . . no matter what anybody else does, the fact that she's the way she is just—I wish she didn't matter to me so much."

David sat back a little and let out a sigh. "Can I ask you somethin', Ash?"

I shrugged and nodded.

"What would you rather be doin' today instead of goin' with Bev and your friends to Tyler?"

I blushed, embarrassed to tell him. I spied a cardinal through the window and focused on it, but I said nothing.

David waved his hand before my face and said, "Hel-looooo. . . . Stay with me now, okay?"

I forced my eyes back to his and bit my lip.

"I'm gonna guess that you were plannin' on hidin' out in your room all day." He nodded and narrowed his eyes at me, a small smile on his lips. "Maybe in a certain dark place, starin' at your hands or somethin'?"

I rolled my eyes and lowered my head. *God, I'm so transparent.* David lifted my chin so that I had to look at him.

"That's the kinda stuff you did when you first came here, at the very start of your journey, isn't it?"

I pulled my face away from him and averted my eyes. I could feel my shoulders creeping up to my ears. If my head lowered any more, it was going to be sitting in my lap.

"Haven't you come any further than that, Ashley?"

My only response was sniffling.

"I think you have. And the reason Bev called your friends when we were at the restaurant is because we kinda want to force you to stay with us in the life you have now—instead of sliding back into that dark place."

"But . . . how am I supposed to go have a good time today when all I can think about is what happened with Mom? It hurts SOOOOO bad, David."

He hugged me hard and said into my hair, "I know it does, sweetie. But you're surrounded by people who love you and who'd *never* ask you to say that Charlie was a good man. We're asking you to choose to acknowledge that by *living* your life instead of longing for someone who's never going to be who you need her to be. Ash, are you breathing right now? 'Cause I haven't felt you take a breath since—"

"You're . . . squeezing . . . me . . . too . . . tight—" I managed.

David laughed and let me go. He patted and rubbed my back, then kissed me on the forehead. I smiled up at him and said, "I love you. Thank you for being my dad."

"I love you, too, Ashley. Thanks for letting me."

CHAPTER 14

"Now, what movie are you going to see?" K.C.'s mom had been interrogating Bev for a good ten minutes while Roxanne, Z.Z., and I were sitting on the porch swing and K.C. was in the rocking chair next to us.

"I'm not sure yet; it depends on what's playing by the time we finish eating." Bev turned the key in the front door lock and shifted her purse on her shoulder; she glanced at her watch and attempted a patient smile. She was giving every kind of hint that we were ready to leave, but Mrs. Williamson was either ignoring them or totally dense.

"I only ask because we're a Christian family, and we do not permit Krystle to see movies that portray excessive violence, sex, or alternative lifestyles."

Bev cut her eyes to us and nodded toward the car. "I see. Would you like K.C. to call you and let you know—"

"No, no, *Krystle's* therapist says I need to give her more freedom. Not sure I agree with that, but I also don't like the initials she substitutes for such a beautiful name. Dr. Trevino says I should just go along with it, but—"

K.C. rose from the rocker, put her arm around her

mother, and steered her down the steps to the driveway. "Mom, is it just possible that you could have a conversation with someone without bringing up Dr. Trevino? I'm almost positive that the cashier at Walmart doesn't give a shit about me being in therapy."

"Language, Krystle! Well—I—I'm not *ashamed* that you're in therapy!" She looked back over her shoulder at Bev. "She thinks I'm embarrassed that she has all these problems, but I'm not. Well, you know all about these things, I'm sure, since we saw you and Ashley in Dr. Trevino's waiting room. I'm not sure I like her partner, Dr. Matthews. He seems a little abrupt—"

K.C. opened the driver's door of her mom's car and maneuvered her into the seat. "Of course you're not ashamed of me being in counseling, Mom. After all, there's so much *more* about me that bothers you." K.C. closed the door, leaned back against it, and crossed her arms with a big grin on her face. Her mother was still talking to herself as she started the car and drove away.

"Whew! That was enlightening, wasn't it?" Bev said. "If y'all are ready, let's go!"

"Okay if we play a mix CD I made?" Z.Z. asked Bev. "Sure, put it in," Bev said.

Z.Z. handed the CD to K.C., who was sitting up front next to Bev. Roxanne, Z.Z., and I were like sardines in the back seat, and Bev's little Ford Focus rocked all the way to Tyler; I mean, it was literally bouncing from side to side with all the shimmying and shaking we were doing. We sang at the top of our lungs and laughed at Bev's reaction to some of the lyrics.

"Shake your what-thang? Oh, my, K.C., I don't think your mom would be too happy with the suggestions in that song!"

"Eh, that song's about a guy. Might be the first time in her life my mom would be happy I'm not interested in them."

"I brought a CD, too. Kevin made it for me," Roxanne said. "It's so sweet! The first track is our song." She dug the CD out of her purse.

"What's the song called?" I asked.

"That's it: 'Our Song.' It's by Taylor Swift."

"Speaking of romantic stuff," Z.Z. said, "How's it going with Joshua, Ashley?"

"It's *not*," I said. "I was a bitch to him at the cross-country meet." Calling myself a bitch made me think about my mom, and my stomach clenched. *What a bitch. What a bitch.* I felt my throat tightening up and turned to stare out the window.

"Well, I want to hear your song, Roxanne," Bev said. She held up her hand, and Roxanne handed her the CD from the back seat. We listened to it twice.

"Play it again!" Z.Z. yelled. She hooked one arm around my neck and the other around Roxanne's, then pulled us back and forth to the beat, until I found that I was laughing and singing right along with everyone else. We made silly faces at each other and tapped on K.C.'s shoulder to get her to turn around and look at us. She rolled her eyes, but she smiled and sang along.

Our voices were hoarse by the time we reached the restaurant. We decided to be real goofs and told Bev we wanted to go to Chuck E. Cheese, a pizza place and arcade for little kids. Bev took pictures of us in the ball pit, then she tilted her head and listened to an announcement over the PA system. "Hey, I just heard our number called. I'm gonna go pick up our food; you guys come on out now."

Roxanne, Z.Z., and K.C. had already crawled out over the other little kids, but I was still trying to find my balance and walk to the doorway of the ball pit. I'd just made it out when a little boy bumped into me; somebody caught me by the arm and steadied me, and I looked up to see that the somebody was Joshua.

"Hey, aren't you kind of big for the ball pit?" he smiled.

"Uh—hi. Wh-what are you doing here?"

"It's my cousin's birthday. See that little girl over there? The one with the pink crown on her head and chocolate ice cream all over her face?" He pointed to a chubby, dark-haired toddler in the dining area.

"Aw, she's so cute," I said.

"Yeah, she is." He shrugged. "I didn't have anything better to do today, since the season's over, so . . . "

I sat on a bench and started putting on my shoes. Joshua joined me.

"So how are you?" he asked.

"I'm okay. What about you? Still pretty disappointed with the way the season ended?"

He looked at the floor and said, "Yeah, maybe a little. But there's always next year. Gotta have hope."

I considered what he'd said. "Yeah. I guess you do. Hey, Joshua, I—I'm sorry, if, you know, anything I said or did made you slower that day."

His head snapped up, and he looked at me oddly. "You? You didn't have anything to do with that. Other people were faster that day. It just wasn't my day. No big deal."

"Yeah, tell that to Pam," I said. "To her . . . "

"Oh, she can go to hell," he said.

"Joshua, I'm shocked! You're supposed to be Mr. Nice Guy!" I feigned shock.

He smiled wryly. "You don't know me like you think you do, Ashley. I'm more than . . . " He worked his eyebrows up and down. "Mr. Nice Guy."

"Oh, really? Hmm." I rose and started walking toward our table. He followed.

"Ashley." He put his hand on my shoulder.

I stopped and looked up at him.

"I'd really like to start over with you. Do you think we could do that?"

"Joshua, I—" I shook my head. "I don't know if I can do that—if I can—you know." I sighed. "I don't know if you can expect very much from me. I've still got a long way to go."

"I'm okay with that, Ashley."

"We'd have to go really, really slow."

"I just want to get to know you better. No pressure. Nada. Zero, zip, zilch—"

"I get the point," I said. I thought about it for a moment. "Okay," I nodded. "Yeah. I'm willing to try if you are."

He gave me a huge smile. "Cool. Since we have this coming week off, maybe we could hang out?"

"Sure," I said.

"I'll call you."

❦

It was getting dark by the time we dropped off Z.Z., K.C., and Roxanne.

"Bye, Mrs. Asher. Thanks for inviting me! I had a great time," Roxanne said. We watched her head up the walk to her aunt and uncle's house. She flicked the porch light twice to let us know she was inside, then we drove away.

"So Ashley," Bev said, sounding as tired as I felt, "are you glad that I forced you to participate in your life today, or are you mad that I didn't let you crawl inside yourself?"

"This way was much better," I said. "Thanks, Bev."

"You're welcome, sweetheart. This is the thing that's going to get you through the tough stuff, Ash. Remembering that you have a choice about whether to keep going or give in to the sadness. I'm glad you chose not to give in to it today."

"Me, too."

❦

We could hear gunfire and explosions as we walked up to the front door. "Your dad's watching *Die Hard*," Bev said as she peeked in the window. Then she opened the door and shouted, "Do you think you've got it turned up loud enough?"

"It was either that or turn off the phone and answering machine, Mom!" Ben yelled.

David paused the movie.

"Why would you do that?" Bev asked.

"Ashley's mom's been calling all day, leaving messages on the machine," Ben said. "We didn't want to turn off the phone in case you guys called, but we got tired of listening to her cry."

"She's been calling?" Suddenly, I felt queasy. As if on cue, the phone rang.

Bev picked it up and looked at the caller ID. "Northside Memorial Hospital," she said and shook her head, frowning. "Hello? Cheryl . . . it's Bev. "

Bev looked at me, and I shook my head, backing away, then turned and went to my room. I closed the door, locked it, and, as if on autopilot, walked toward the wardrobe. I mean, this is what I *do* when I'm freaked out, right? I hide. I crawl as far into myself as I can go and surrender to the darkness, right?

Just wait. I took a few steps back from the wardrobe and stopped. I looked back at my bedroom door. Outside that door, my mom was on the phone. Why? What could she possibly have to say to me now? The idea of talking to her made my knees weak.

I turned back to the wardrobe. I could get inside and go back to the hurt I'd felt when my mom told me to get out of her hospital room, and, hell, while I was in there, I could even mentally send myself back in time to the nights when I hid from Charlie. Were those really my only choices?

"Know what? Fuck *you*," I gave my door and my mom the finger. "And, fuck *you*, too," I said to the wardrobe and to Charlie. Then I kicked off my shoes, got undressed, and went to take a shower.

Dr. Matt nodded at me. "So you flipped off your door and your wardrobe. Tell me again why this is progress?"

"Oh, come *on*, Dr. Matt, don't you get it? I *just waited*, even though I was freaked out. I made a choice not to do anything right then except shower! I didn't put myself through trying to fix my mom—who, it turns out, just wanted me to make her feel better about herself. *And* I also didn't go back down memory lane and think about Charlie!"

"*I* get it. I was just seeing if *you* really got it. Good job, Ashley!"

I worked my arms left and right, doing a little dance move à la Z.Z. "Better look out, Dr. Matt! Before you know it, I'm going to be mentally healthy, and then who will you drop-kick teddy bears with?"

But he said nothing, just smiled and winked at me. "Speaking of that, how are you doing with the self-injury impulse?"

I deflated like a leaky balloon and gingerly touched the long lines I'd carved into my scalp on the drive home from the hospital just a few days before. I winced. "Um, I didn't do very well right after we left my mom in the hospital."

"Talk a little about that. David told me what happened—what your mom said."

"Yeah. Charlie's dead, Dr. Matt. Can you believe that?"

"Can you?"

I shrugged. "Well, yeah. It's just—it doesn't feel real. Do you know how much I used to lie awake at night, praying something would happen to him so that he wouldn't do that stuff to me any more?"

"I'll bet."

I nodded. "He always said that if I told my mom what he was doing, he'd leave her. And then she'd be all alone. He said . . . *I'd* have to tell her why he left her."

"That's a bad man."

"And then when I told her, he—he didn't leave. Just— nothing happened—"

"I disagree. Something did happen. Something very significant." Dr. Matt was giving me The Look. His pale blue eyes seemed to see right through me. "Can you tell me what it was?"

"Nothing. Nothing happened. He didn't leave, and—"

"Your mom didn't protect you from him. She chose him over you."

"Yeah, but—"

"No *buts*. No *ifs* or *ands*, either." Dr. Matt leaned forward in his chair. "You really, really need to get this, Ashley. It's very important."

"Okay," I said.

"What was your mom saying as you and David were leaving her hospital room?" he asked softly.

I felt like I'd been punched in the chest and swallowed hard. I closed my eyes and could hear the *whoosh* . . . in my head. I shook my head slowly and shuddered.

"Tell me, Ash. I know you remember, and I guarantee you, you're never going to forget it. Tell me what she said."

" 'He was all I had,' " I whispered and felt my body curling up. "She said that Charlie was all she had. God, I can't believe she said that. Doesn't she—" I started to cry and went on spin cycle.

SLAM! Dr. Matt hit his desk and yelled, "That's bull-shit!" He stood up and said, "Do you understand me, Ashley? He was *not* all she had. But it's all she *believes* she had. And you know what, darlin'?"

I shook my head slowly. I was sitting ramrod straight in my chair, and my eyes were huge. I'll bet my mental squirrel was plastered to the ceiling of my brain, scared shitless by Dr. Matt.

"Breathe!" Dr. Matt commanded. So I did.

He sat down and rolled his chair close to me. Very softly, he said, "It's a shame that your mom's so messed up that she thinks she's got nothing in her life without him, but it's *her* shame, not yours. And I think it's high time that you recognize that as FACT."

I inhaled a shuddery breath and slowly blew it out. "What do I do now?"

Dr. Matt rolled his chair back, took a sip of water, and set his mug down. "About what?"

"Her."

"There's nothin' you *can* do, Ashley, but let her find her own way. You have everything you need to function well in the here and now. Hitchin' yourself to the hope that one day she's gonna wake up and realize what a fool she is . . . well, that's a slap in the face to everyone around you who's tryin' so hard to make you see how loved you are."

"So it's okay to just . . . live?"

"Honey, you've earned the right. Just live."

A cold front and heavy showers moved in on Wednesday, and it began sleeting on Thanksgiving morning. So we didn't make the two-hour drive into Dallas for the Turkey Trot. Instead, we stayed home and drank hot cocoa, ate pancakes, and watched the Macy's parade on TV.

Bev stood at the window, watching the downpour. She was still in her road race shirt, leggings, and running shoes. "Oh, well. Maybe next year."

The phone rang, and David answered it. "Bev? It's your friend Mary Ann from school."

"Hey, Mary Ann. . . . Great! No, no. Don't bring anything. Yes, I'm sure! Well, I'm glad your plans fell apart, since it means you can join us! Yep. See you around four."

"Ms. Manos is coming for Thanksgiving?" I asked.

"Mm-hmm," Bev said with a twinkle in her eye.

"Bev, are you trying to play matchmaker for Frank again?" David asked from behind the newspaper.

"M-maybe just a little," she said.

"He'll be thrilled, I'm sure," David said flatly.

"No, David. Ms. Manos is cool!" I said.

"Is she scared of snakes?" Ben asked.

I made a face. "I don't know, why?"

He tried to sound casual. "No reason. No reason at all."

"And Ash, you said Joshua might join us too, since his family eats around noon?" Bev asked.

David peeked over the newspaper at me; his eyes were smiling.

"Yeah, he's planning on it." I blushed. "I think he wants to watch the Cowboys game here."

"Man, he's been over here every day this week!" Ben said.

"I like him," Bev said.

"Me, too," David said from behind the paper.

"Yeah," I said softly, smiling to myself. "I think . . . he's a good man."

Acknowledgments

Daniel, Mandy, Alissa, Kristen, and Matt: I love you all. You nourish my soul, and I am who I am today because of having you in my life.

My agent and friend, Gina Panettieri: Thank you for your support, advice, and advocacy.

My publisher and friend, Evelyn Fazio: I am supremely grateful for your insight and your dedication to your craft. You took *Hope in Patience* to new heights! Thank you!

Thank you to Dr. Mary Ann Manos, who was Heather Brookshire Llewellyn's *very* cool eighth-grade theater teacher. Dr. Manos gave me her blessing to use her name.

Thank you to my teaching partner, Alejandro Guzman, for granting me permission to use his name, as long as I made him a good guy. Alejandro, I love being your partner.

Thank you to my school family for their enthusiastic support!

Much gratitude to Krystle "K.C." Whittington, who was *my* very cool eighth-grade English student, and she's an incredible adult, too! K.C. shared her insights as well as her initials, and I will always think of her with fondness.

My Facebook friends, Kerry Gans and Kevin Gans, and my MySpace friend, Robert Watson, Jr.: Thank you for responding to my online plea for information about cross-country running. I appreciate your willingness to answer my newbie questions.

Finally, to the Eustace, Texas, varsity cross-country team, all of whom graciously volunteered their time and expertise to advise me about the intricacies of what it's like to be on a cross-country team: thank you to Kimberly Austin, Jaqlynn Bless, Greg Haynes, Amanda Herrera, Johnny Lee (and his dad), Brett Miner, Nancy Murff, and Coach Gene Myers. What a dedicated group of people. No wonder Eustace is known far and wide for its cross-country team!

A Note to the Reader

Sexual abuse is *never* okay. Nobody asks for it or deserves it. If you are a victim of sexual abuse, you are not alone. Help is available.

Tell a trusted teacher, school counselor, school resource officer, youth group leader, pastor, police officer, or friend's parent. If the first person you tell does not listen, keep telling people until someone does. **Don't give up.**

You can also get help from RAINN: the Rape, Abuse & Incest National Network. Get help online at http://www.rainn.org, or call 1-800-656-HOPE (1-800-656-4673). RAINN can refer you to people in your area who will listen and help.